RUN

RUN

B TILTON

Matador
5 Weir Road
Kibworth Beauchamp
Leicester LE8 0lQ, UK
Tel: (+44) 116 279 2299
Email: books@troubador.co.uk
Web: www.troubador.co.uk/matador

ISBN 9781848763630

A Cataloguing-in-Publication (CIP) catalogue record for this book
is available from the British Library.

This is a work of fiction. Any resemblance between characters in the book
and persons living or dead is purely coincidental.

b.tiltonwritings@gmail.com

Printed and bound in Great Britain by TJ International Ltd, Padstow, Cornwall

Matador is an imprint of Troubador Publishing Ltd

Dedicated to
All Those Who Helped
– You Know Who You Are

~

For The Children

CONTENTS

ONE

The Day That Changed Their Lives Forever

S hay Sullivan drove his black Mercedes car on a traffic free M25 with a smile on his tanned face. It was a Thursday evening in July, the sun was still shining. He had just had an Italian meal in St. Albans with Ruby Ward, the true love of his life. They had discreetly been seeing each other for three months.

Shay had recently formed a business partnership with Billy Gower. Billy was Ruby's mother's boyfriend and Shay knew that Billy would be unhappy regarding the relationship. The fifteen year age gap between Shay and Ruby would not be the real issue, Billy had his own hidden thoughts. It was common knowledge that Billy's feelings towards Ruby were not of the parental type.

As Shay drove, singing along to an Oasis CD, his in-car phone rang. Billy's name appeared as an incoming call on the screen, the C.D. muted automatically.

Shay answered the call, "Alright Billy?"

"Where you at?" said Billy in his usual abrupt tone.

"Driving home on the motorway," replied Shay.

"What, at this time!" Billy barked.

Shay laughed and said, "What's up? It's only 8pm." Shay knew instantly that Billy was onto them.

With that, Billy snapped, "Gotta go, I've got the old bill behind me," and hung up.

Shay immediately called Ruby who by now was driving home on the M25, Pinner bound. "Ruby, be careful, I just had Billy on and I think he knows."

"Oh no, he's calling me now! I'll call you back." With that Ruby hung up to take Billy's call.

Ruby and Shay had decided to meet for a meal as they had not seen each other for two weeks. Shay had been on holiday and they had missed each other madly. They had only been out for a couple of hours, yet for the entire time, Billy was constantly calling Ruby's mobile. Ruby purposely ignored his calls but he was relentless.

Ruby nervously answered the call, "Where are you?" Barked Billy.

"I'm on my way home from Keely's," Ruby replied, as she exited the M25.

"No Ruby, where exactly are you now?" he boomed.

"I'm on the roundabout by the supermarket."

Ruby exited the roundabout, she saw Billy in his Audi 4X4 driving at high speed on the other side of the road. Minutes later, she glanced into her rear view mirror and saw that Billy was now in pursuit of her. Ruby was still on the phone with Billy but she didn't let on that she was aware of his pursuit.

Billy's volume had increased significantly by now as he ordered, "Right, pull over now, into that lay-by!"

Ruby's mind was filled with fear as she recalled what had happened the last time she was forced to pull over into a lay-by by the pursuing Billy.

Twelve months prior to this evening's car chase, Billy had given Ruby no choice but to pull into a lay-by. Billy attacked Ruby through her open car window by grabbing her by the throat. He'd then removed her keys from the ignition and bent them. Another motorist, seeing Billy's six foot two, twenty stone frame attacking

Ruby who was slender and eight stone; pulled into the lay-by to assist Ruby.

The kind motorist was no hard man but was clearly a gentleman and his presence led to Billy's immediate departure. He then left having ensured Ruby was safe.

A very shaken Ruby called her mother, Janice, who arrived promptly and drove Ruby home.

On this particular evening Ruby decided that she would not pull into a lay-by, she knew better.

Ruby asked, "Why do you want me to stop?"

"I want to talk to you before you get home!" snapped Billy.

"I'm not pulling into a lay-by, if you want to talk to me, you can talk to me at home!"

Billy hung up, though still hot on Ruby's heels.

Ruby called Shay as she said she would. Her voice quivered "He knows! He's following me home now! I can tell by his face he's about to explode. It's gonna kick off, I know it."

Shay assured Ruby that everything would be ok, "If you want me to come and get you later, I will."

"Would you really do that?" She asked.

"Yeah, of course I will, you've only gotta ring me and I'll be there."

Shay was not intimidated by Billy and had no fear of him whatsoever. He had always regarded him as nothing but a big bully. Shay and Billy had met through football and both were involved with the Chelsea Firm. Shay had been very active for many years and was well respected by many firms in the football underworld. Whilst in total opposition, Billy was a barker and not a biter.

Despite this, Shay did have a concern with regard to his own personal money that he had invested into the partnership with Billy. Billy had full control over the finances, which Shay now realised was a stupid mistake that would prove to have a damning knock on effect. He knew he had unquestionably made the biggest mistake of his life by allowing Billy a partnership in his company.

The jetlag was starting to kick in as Shay drove heavy-eyed. He'd just returned from Mauritius that morning on a Virgin first class flight. Life could not be better for him; he was truly in love for the first time in his life, with Ruby. He loved everything about her, her good humour, maturity and intelligence, not to mention her incredible beauty; her tanned skin, blonde hair and amazing green eyes. In fact, his nickname for Ruby was 'Eyes'and he rarely called her by her actual name. Ruby too had a pet name for Shay, she affectionately referred to him as 'London' as he had a very strong London accent.

Shay was getting extremely tired by now and his eyes were like ten-tonne weights. He was struggling to drive, his mild jet lag had become a major tiredness. The fact that Shay knew in his heart that trouble was brewing was the only stimulant keeping him awake.

As Shay exited the M25 his car phone rang with Billy's name showing on the display.

Fully alert, he answered, "Hello."

An angry Billy barked, "Where the fuck have you been with my daughter?" Shay went to speak and was stopped as Billy continued his outburst, "I'm telling you now, you've crossed the wrong man this time! You're a dead man walking Sullivan! You think I'm fuck all, well, I tell you this for nothing Sullivan you're gonna be sliced up you prick!"

This time, Shay made sure he was heard. "What's the problem? We went out for something to eat! This isn't a seedy fling, we have feelings for each other."

Billy, infuriated boomed down the phone, "Feelings! She's my world, you can't have her! I'm telling you now, you're a dead man walking!" And hung up.

Shay continued his drive, he needed to sort this out. Maybe a toe to toe with Billy would do it? He had no doubt that in a one on one he could do Billy damage. His years of boxing and many street encounters had gifted him with the tools and skills required.

Shay's concern would normally be that he had just been verbally abused and threatened; however, his concern at this moment in time was his money. Shay had put everything he had, both financially and mentally into the new business.

Maybe a diplomatic approach with Billy would be best, Billy would calm down over night and see sense, Shay thought. A profitable air conditioning business was at stake, which he ran very efficiently. No Shay would mean no business, as Billy's role was that of a sleeping partner and air conditioning was not his field.

The phone rang again, it was Billy, "You slag! Three months! Three fucking months behind my back! I tell you this Shay, you or anyone belonging to you won't get a penny out of the firm and that's a fact! You phone your son up now and tell him his dad is a dead man! In fact, tell him he ain't got a dad. I'm gonna open you up!"

This was not impressing Shay one bit. Shay had a nineteen year old son, Connor, who he adored. As father and sons go, they were and always had been very close.

"You couldn't open up a tins of beans, Billy. I don't know what your problem is. It's nothing to do with you, we'll talk about this tomorrow."

Whilst Billy continued to shout, Janice was crying and screaming in the background. Shay had only met Janice twice but got on well with her. He felt sorry for her as he knew she was terrified of Billy who managed his personal life by ruling with an iron fist.

Shay wondered how Ruby was, although he was sure she was safe.

As Shay parked his car he answered another incoming call

from Billy, "Tick tock Sullivan, we're gonna kill you! Word on you is out already!" Billy abruptly ended his call.

We're gonna kill you, thought Shay. Had Billy intentions of involving a firm? It was common knowledge that he was very close to a few well known organised criminal families. This could be a problem, maybe diplomacy or a right hook would not be enough in this instance.

Now inside his house, Shay's tiredness was back with a vengeance and was overpowering. Strange as it may seem, all he wanted to do was sleep. He turned off his phone, showered and climbed into bed; falling asleep as soon as his head hit the pillow.

Ruby approached the florists at the top of her road feeling reassured by Shay's words yet was filled with anxiety about what was to happen when she got home. She parked her black Audi TT on the driveway of her home and noticed that the front door was already open. Her mum had obviously been told by Billy that they were due home any minute. She turned off the ignition and grabbed her handbag. Still in the car, Ruby saw Billy approaching the cul-de-sac with a face that she recognised all too well.

In previous situations when either Ruby, her mum, brother or even work colleagues were due to experience Billy's venom, he would always have the same appearance. He would always walk a certain way, walking as fast as his large heavy frame would allow him with both arms swinging just as quickly. His face would be bright red, his bottom jaw would protrude slightly and his eyes would bulge.

Most people would be petrified when seeing him like this; whether they were his target or purely just an onlooker. Billy's mentality was that he deserved respect and that everyone who knew him should give him respect by the bucket load, although his way of gaining respect was to bully and frighten them; it was not respect that he was gaining, it was fear.

Ruby had been in so many situations where she was the target and the receiver of his verbal, mental and physical abuse, yet for some reason was not feeling her usual petrified-self, as she normally would. Maybe it was because she knew that Shay would be there for her no matter what or maybe because she had simply had enough of Billy's barbaric behaviour and wanted out anyway?

Ruby quickly got out of her car and ran into the house where she was met by her mum who already looked somewhat distressed.

"Ruby, where have you really been?" Janice asked.

"I told you, out with Keely," she protested.

Before the interrogation could continue any further, Billy had thundered into the house like a man possessed. Here we go, thought Ruby. She could see that he was gearing up for one almighty explosion.

"Where have you been Ruby and don't fucking lie to me! I know you haven't been with Keely so where have you been?"

Ruby knew that this was not a situation that could be diffused with a couple of convincing lies but was not yet prepared to tell them both the truth as she was still not quite sure just how much they actually knew.

In response to be being spoken to like something Billy had just stepped in, Ruby yelled, "Okay, okay! I wasn't with Keely, I was with a bloke that I've been seeing and I didn't want you two knowing about him yet. It's my business and nothing to do with you. I haven't got to tell you everything that happens in my life. Anyway, what gives you the right to be checking up on me? I'm an adult, not a child! I'm sick of you always interfering, you don't treat Charlie like it so why treat me like it!"

Billy's eyes were now on the verge of popping out of his head and his tone of voice changed a little. The volume was just as loud but instead of just barking at Ruby, he added an element of smugness. "Where's your phone then Ruby? Give me your fucking phone! If you're telling the truth you'll give me your phone!"

Ruby now felt sheer panic. She knew that if Billy did not know for sure about Shay, seeing her mobile phone would confirm any suspicions he may have had. Ruby held onto her handbag tightly as Billy went to grab it. She tried to get some distance from him by moving away into the lounge. This tactic proved ineffective as Billy was quickly behind her as he grabbed Ruby in another attempt to snatch her bag. She held her bag close to her chest, curled over and turned her back to him. This made it difficult for Billy to get to her bag but in turn made him more forceful.

At this point, Janice, who had so far not even uttered a word, tried to intervene, "Billy, stop it! Leave her alone, it's not right!"

Words had no effect in this situation; like having a raging bear trying to rip your head off and you asking it nicely to sit and behave – it just doesn't work. Janice then resorted to physically try and get in-between Billy and Ruby. Not surprisingly, this did not help either. Many times before, Ruby and her mum had tried to restrain Billy from whichever one of them he was attacking to no avail.

After a while of struggling, Ruby and her mum could no longer hold him off. He had Ruby's bag. As Ruby watched him rummage for her mobile phone she knew that it was game over. In a state of utter panic, she grabbed her bunch of keys. She ran out to her car, got in and fumbled trying to get the key into the ignition, hastily reversed off of the driveway but with her legs shaking could not control the clutch properly and accidentally hit a neighbours garden wall. She put the car into first gear and looked up, only to see Billy standing in front of her car in an attempt to stop her from driving off. Standing there holding her mobile phone at arms length, he made it blatantly obvious that he was going through it.

"Get back in your house! No she hasn't!" Billy shouted.

Who was he shouting at? She looked behind to see the couple whose garden wall she'd damaged were now outside complaining.

Billy repeated, "Go on, fuck off, get back in your house!"

Ruby revved the car. Billy goaded her to accelerate forward

whilst he remained standing in front of the car. She accelerated forward and forced Billy to jump out of the way. She wheel-spun out of the cul-de-sac and reached for her packet of cigarettes that she had left on the passenger seat. Taking long hard drags on her cigarette, Ruby's shaking eased and she started to think. She was heading in the direction of the next town yet had no destination or plan in mind. With no money, no phone, nothing but a packet of cigarettes and a car that was running on fumes, she knew she had to go back and face the music. When able, Ruby pulled over, turned around and reluctantly headed back to the war zone.

Again, Ruby arrived to find the front door was open. She quickly removed her car key from the big bunch of key rings and shoved it down the front of her jeans, hoping that if Billy snatched her keys that he would not notice the car key was missing.

Before even getting inside the house, Ruby could hear Billy screaming and shouting at Shay on the phone, "Shay you prick! You're fucking dead, do you hear me, a dead man walking! I don't give a shit, I'm telling you that you're fucking dead!"

Ruby's arrival at the house caused Billy to end his call, his venom now immediately aimed at Ruby. Billy's appearance was now at his well known second stage of rage. He was starting to foam at the mouth, causing him to spit in his victim's face as he screamed at them. His lips turned very pale as the abuse started to flow. Billy shoved Ruby towards the stairs. With a slap of the back of his hand to her head, he knocked her off of her feet and she fell onto the stairs.

"Right, get up them stairs and pack your bags you stupid little whore, this time you ain't coming back!" shouted Billy.

Ruby ran up the stairs and burst into her bedroom. It had always been her haven, her own little Graceland where she could shut the door and be by herself. She was an Elvis fanatic and her bedroom definitely depicted this from floor to ceiling. Knowing that she may never see her Elvis Presley sanctuary again, she despondently grabbed her Elvis Presley holdall and threw it onto the bed. It was quite a small bag so Ruby grabbed her gym bag as well. She turned her gym bag upside down and shook it so that the contents fell out onto the cream carpet. Ruby stood and scanned the room. Numb and unable to think straight, she hesitated about what to pack first.

Ruby's mum entered her room with tears streaming down her face. She was obviously very upset and begged Ruby for answers,

"Why have you done this Ruby, why him?"

Ruby felt sorry for her mum who looked so child-like and devastated. She was sorry that she had hurt her mum who she loved very much but was not sorry for her relationship with Shay. As her mum weakly continued to ask more questions, Ruby started to pack. Trying to block out her mum's guilt trip, she concentrated on making sure that she had the necessities. In her head, she ran through her daily routine to help her remember what she needed. She went to the bathroom and got her toothbrush, toothpaste, mouthwash, shampoo, conditioner and hurriedly went back to her bedroom to throw everything into one of the bags. Ruby turned to her dressing table; hurriedly grabbed what she needed and stuffed it into a bag, as if carrying out a robbery.

Whilst doing so, Billy burst into her bedroom. He screamed and shouted, now with questions of his own along with the odd insult thrown in for good measure. "How long's it been going on? Have you slept with him? You dirty little slag! Do you really think that he thinks that much of you? I tell you what, you don't know the half of what he gets up to! He's banging silly little tarts like you all over the place!"

Janice had now ran next door to the bathroom and Ruby could clearly hear her wrenching into the toilet.

Billy saw Janice's departure as an opportunity. Like a bull with horns, he forcefully pressed his hot, red forehead into Ruby's. As she watched the whites of his eyes become bigger and bigger, Billy continued to rant through his gritted teeth, "I tell you what, I give it three months and then he'll drop you! You've fucked yourself now! And I tell you this for nothing, as God is my witness I promise that I'll do time for the pair of you! That shooter in the safe at work will put an end to that piece of shit. Pack your bags and get out of my house you little slag, but you go to him and I'll shoot the fucking pair of you. Where's your car key?"

Ruby took a step back and then gave him the bunch of key rings silently praying that he would not notice that the car key was missing.

"And where's the Log Book?" screamed Billy.

Ruby blinked as spit flew in her face and muttered in response that it was at the club, in the office. With that, Billy slammed the bedroom door back into the wall as he left the room and went down the stairs. Within minutes, he was back in her bedroom, breathless and demanding the car key.

Shit, thought Ruby. Now she wouldn't have a car, despite the fact that it was hers, in her name and wasn't his to confiscate.

Strangely, she was still calm and fixed on packing her bags, not even shedding a tear despite the fact that she is being kicked out of her house where she had lived since birth, on the order of her mum's boyfriend who had been there only six years.

Ruby started to pack a couple of tops and a pair of jeans into a bag when she heard Billy again downstairs. "You've ruined this family, Shay, and I'm gonna make sure you fucking suffer. We're gonna find you and cut you into pieces! If you think you're getting any money out of the firm you can think again!"

This abuse filled phone call was a bit shorter than the first one she had heard but just as venomous.

Ruby bustled down the stairs with her two bags, handbag and one of her leather jackets. She went straight to the kitchen to get a couple of items of washed clothes that were still wet and jammed them into her bag. Ruby walked towards the front door and was stopped by the tyrant who ordered her to stay put. Within seconds, he was on the phone again but this time to one of Shay's employees.

"Alright Simon, listen I need to get hold of Shay, do you know where he lives?"

Simon obviously didn't know where Shay lived as Billy did not hang about in calling another employee to ask the same question. Nobody could tell Billy where Shay lived. Unable to get the information he wanted, Billy pushed Ruby out of the front door and kicked her in the back as she went causing her to fall out onto the driveway.

Unbeknown to Ruby, she had literally just been kicked out of her home and her family's lives forever.

It was nine thirty pm and still reasonably light outdoors. Luckily, the weather was good as Ruby was on foot heading god knows where and struggling with her bags. Her hands were full so she was unable to use her phone. Ruby power walked out of the cul-de-sac and through the town to some garages that were set out of sight, hid there and dropped her bags. Her feet were throbbing from having had her heeled boots on since seven am that morning so she sat down on one of her bags to rest her feet and lit a cigarette. Ruby fumbled for her phone to call Shay as he was all she could think of. The call connected and went straight to answer phone. She called again and again and again and still only got his answer phone machine. She felt a rush of horror. Why was he not answering? Had he washed his hands of her? Had Billy got to him and hurt him? Whilst smoking another cigarette, Ruby decided to text Shay. She told him that she had been kicked out, that she was sorry for what had happened and that she loved him.

Now she needed to get out of the area and quick.

She rang Keely, her alibi for that night and many occasions before. Keely's phone was also going straight to answer phone. Ruby started to panic a little. She urgently sent Keely a text briefly explaining her dilemma and asked Keely to call back ASAP.

Ruby had a couple of close friends at work, close enough for her to feel she could trust them with the knowledge of her and Shay's relationship. She rang Bungle, one of her friends from work. Bungle worked in the office with Ruby and was pleased for Ruby and Shay when Ruby had told him a few weeks ago that they were together. Bungle was a nickname, based on the character from *Rainbow*, a children's television show; he had been known as Bungle since he was a teenager. Ruby wanted to call him to tell him what had happened before the jungle drums started and hoped that he may be able to help her.

He was shocked at what had happened and suggested that Ruby stay in a hotel for the night under a false name. He offered to arrange this for her but she said that she would sort it out herself. She thanked him and said she would be in touch.

Ruby now had a plan and some sort of direction. She called a local taxi firm and booked a cab under the name of Louise; she was told it would be about twenty minutes.

Ruby sat and chain-smoked, waiting for *"Hellooooo Baby…"*, The Big Bopper's Chantilly Lace to blast out of her phone. Ruby had set this song as Shay's caller I.D. for when he rang her. Ruby waited and waited for The Big Bopper to burst into song but it never happened.

Sitting idle, waiting for the taxi, Ruby tried to stop herself from thinking the worst. The very thought that Shay would now finish with her hurt her far more deeply than the fact that her life was fitted into two bags and that her own mum did nothing to help her.

Ruby loved Shay more than life itself, an emotion that she had never felt before. She'd always had a pessimistic outlook on love and relationships due to the fact that the relationships she had been brought up around had all been very sour. Her dad left bitterly years ago and Billy had turned out to be evil personified. Despite a very difficult childhood and love seeming to be just a word that is used a lot in films, Ruby knew that what she felt for Shay really was love and she loved everything about him.

Shay's voice had been the first thing that gained Ruby's attention. It was deep, gravelly and he had a strong London accent. They had spent a lot of time on the phone through work before they had even met. She knew that Shay could look the complete opposite to the way his voice made him sound but this didn't bother her. The day she met him, she was quietly very pleased with what she saw. The first thing that stood out was his extremely well styled dark hair, complemented with narrow, modish sideburns. In contrast to his dark hair were his piercing blue, smiling eyes. He had the type of build that she found attractive in a man; around six foot tall with very broad shoulders. Not only did he have the face and the stature, he knew how to dress too. All this matched a personality and a sense of humour that Ruby could not help falling in love with. To top it all off, Shay made Ruby feel loved. To love someone is one thing, but for that love to be reciprocated is an entirely different thing. For this reason, the fact that she was in her late twenties and Shay was in his early forties was not an issue for her.

All Ruby wanted was a phone call just so she knew that the man she loved still loved her.

Ruby's phone rang but it was not *The Big Bopper*, it was *The Jam*, the ring tone for all other incoming calls. It was Keely calling. Ruby answered and explained what had happened. Keely also knew about Ruby's secret relationship and also knew her family very well, including Billy's erratic and barbaric behaviour. Keely told Ruby to stay put and that she would come and collect her. She knew exactly where Ruby was as she had lived in the same Middlesex town since a child up to around five years ago.

Ruby peered over a hedge waiting for Keely to arrive, but as Ruby tried to keep the twigs from scratching her face she saw the taxi she ordered pull up.

Shit, thought Ruby, as the taxi parked at the entrance of the garages. How would Keely pull in to get her?

Seconds later Keely arrived indicating to get to the garages. The taxi moved enough to let her through. Keely jumped out and threw Ruby's bags into the boot and told her to get in the back of the car as Keely's friend, Natalie, was in the front. Ruby told both of them in more detail about what had happened.

Keely was far from impressed to say the least. Natalie also expressed her disgust as she too knew Ruby's family and had even been a victim of Billy's abuse some years ago.

Natalie was dropped off home and Ruby got into the front seat next to Keely. Ruby needed to stop and buy some cigarettes and asked if Keely could stop at a petrol station before going to the hotel. Whilst driving to the hotel, Keely became more and more wound up by Billy's actions. She was rather fiery and ranted about how she wouldn't be frightened if Billy was to turn up on her doorstep and that she would have a go at doing him some damage if she found out he laid a finger on Ruby again. Keely didn't say these things to amuse Ruby but Ruby couldn't help but grin at little Keely and her big threats.

At the hotel, Keely helped to get Ruby's bags and gave her a tight, reassuring hug; making Ruby promise to keep in touch. Keely sat in her car and made sure that Ruby got safely into the hotel's reception before she left.

Ruby approached the lady sitting at the reception. She was still a bit shaken and on a different planet, planet Shay. She asked if she could get a room for the night and luckily enough, there was a vacancy. The receptionist started to go through the formal booking-in process. Ruby stuttered whilst trying to explain that she didn't want to book in under her real name. Once it was very apparent to the receptionist that Ruby was distressed and frightened, she suggested a false name for her to book-in under. Once the payment details had been sorted out, the sympathetic receptionist gave Ruby the card to her room.

She didn't have to go far to get to the room and was relieved that it was on the ground floor. It was a new building, and the room was basic but clean. She dumped her bags on the floor and put the kettle on; her mouth felt like an ashtray and she was thirsty. Whilst she waited for the kettle to boil, she got out her damp clothes and hung them over the radiators to dry. Ruby glared at her phone willing it to ring as she made herself a coffee. She went outside where she sat in the car park so she could have two or three more cigarettes.

Ruby, with her box of cigarettes, was in and out of the hotel like a yoyo over the next couple of hours.

At two o'clock the next morning there was a new receptionist on shift. She stopped Ruby on her way back in and told her that she didn't like the thought of her sitting outside in the car park at that time of the morning. She told her that if she opened the window in her room and smoked by it, the smoke alarms wouldn't go off. Ruby was thankful and appreciated her kindness and concern.

Instead of getting some rest and going to bed, Ruby sat by that window for the next five hours going back over what had happened and tormenting herself with the idea that Shay had changed his mind about their relationship.

TWO

The Morning After

S hay awoke at seven am. Still tired, he staggered to the shower.
Today was a big day, he thought as he stood beneath the hot water. He had a deal to close with a major London Hotel Chain for the air conditioning maintenance of three hotels with a total of three thousand two hundred rooms. As he lathered, reality struck like lightening and Shay recalled Billy's threats.

He dried himself, picked up his mobile phone and turned it on. The message counter did overtime as the phone registered messages and missed calls.

He read a text message from Billy requesting that he return the car that was jointly owned, although it was registered in Billy's name. In the text, Billy also wished Shay and Ruby all the best in life.

As Shay scoffed to himself at Billy's text, his phone rang. It was Jack, who was a friend of Shay's and was well connected in the underworld. He also subcontracted jobs from Shay and Billy's company. Jack had no time for Billy and had him summed up from day one. He had advised Shay not to go into business with Billy in the prior months.

Jack sounded concerned, "Shay, I've had Billy on the phone all morning, you're in big trouble mate. He's been asking where you live."

Shay always kept his private life just that and thankfully, that trait proved to be a god send.

Jack went onto say, "He's well connected, he knows some proper naughty people, mate, you gotta be careful Shay."

"I'm gonna go and see him now and sort this shit out," replied Shay.

"If you're gonna to do that, take something that makes a bang, 'cos he means business!"

Shay exclaimed, "What's up with him? Bit of an over reaction!"

Jack laughed and said, "I told you not to mess about with Ruby, he's off his head when it comes to her. You knew you were running the gauntlet, you nutter! If I were you, mate, I'd get something noisy or if not, just lie low for a few days. You can stay at mine for a while if you want, we'll sort it out."

Shay told Jack that he would get back to him and ended the call.

Deep in thought Shay weighed up his options, he had three: get tooled up with a shooter? Lie low at Jacks? Or run? Running was not an option for Shay, he had done no wrong. Furthermore, all of his finances were tied up in the business.

Shay thought about calling his uncle Danny but felt no need to worry him. Danny was connected but Shay had his own contacts.

Shay decided to call Ted, better known as Spooner, "Alright Spooner?"

A laughing Spooner replied, "Fuck me! I've been waiting for you to call. It's all kicking off Shay, you got all kinds of enquiries being made about you, mate. Come and meet me now, we'll go and see this muppet and sort this out!"

Shay asked if Spooner had his tools.

"Yeah," replied Spooner, "Untraceable as well, probably no need to use it, we'll just scare him, but if he don't listen up then we'll pop him!"

"Ok," Shay said, "Let me make a call and I'll get back to you in a minute."

Shay gathered his thoughts. This was all out of hand, guns and shooting people was not his thing, never had been. He had had more fights than he could recall but all this gun business was not his scene.

He thought about how he and Ruby were in love and had done nothing wrong. As it was Friday, maybe a weekend away together would be better than being killed or becoming a killer.

He called Ruby, "Morning Eyes, are you alright? Where are you?"

"I am now you've rang," said an upset, relieved Ruby. "I'm in a hotel in Uxbridge."

"What happened last night babe? Sorry I fell asleep."

"I thought you'd never call me again, I thought you'd washed your hands of me," said Ruby and then told Shay of the previous night's events.

"Look Eyes, I love you, do you love me?"

"More than anything," Ruby replied.

"Ok, we have a couple of options, Eyes," Shay then suggested, "We can stay and I can go and sort this out; I've been offered something that makes a loud noise but it's not my way really. Or, we can have a weekend away to lay low and sort ourselves out?"

"Yeah, let's do that, we'll lay low 'till he calms down," said Ruby.

"How long will it take you to get ready?"

"I've not even been to bed, but I've showered and changed my clothes."

"Where do you want to meet?" Shay asked Ruby. "Can you get a train to Highgate and I will pick you up there? I've got a bloke who owes me a few thousand. I'll go and collect it and then wait for you in the station car park."

Ruby told Shay that she would meet him there in an hour and a half as she had to check out and cancel the room that she had booked for that evening.

Shay finished by saying, "Make sure no one follows you, be very aware of everyone at the train station and on the train."

Ruby had made several calls of her own that morning before speaking to Shay. She waited until seven am and called her elder brother, Charlie. She had no doubt that Charlie would have heard of last night's events and she was desperate to speak with him.

Ruby and Charlie were extremely close despite there being a couple of years age gap between them. Ruby could not have loved him more if she tried. They were both very protective of each other. Charlie had moved out of their home six weeks ago. Charlie was full of hate for Billy and couldn't control the guilt he felt for letting Billy do what he had done to Ruby and their mum over the years. This hate was enforced even more when Billy berated Charlie at work in front of everyone at the club to hear. For Charlie, this was the final straw; he left his job as a barman in the nightclub and moved out into his girlfriend's flat that same day. Ruby regularly saw Charlie after she had finished work, gave him money and made sure he was okay.

Ruby was anxious to tell Charlie about her and Shay. She waited until Charlie got back from holiday with his girlfriend and her two children and arranged to meet him. She paid his phone bill for him, gave him some money and told him that she had something to tell him. Charlie jumped to the conclusion that Ruby was pregnant. She laughed and nervously continued to go around the houses before telling him that she had been seeing someone for a while and that she loved him.

Ruby's voice quivered as she told him, "I've been seeing Shay."

Charlie laughed at first and then replied firmly, "Look Ruby, you're my sister and I love you. I don't care what you do so long as you're happy and I know that Shay will look after you, but you do know that Billy the bully ain't gonna be happy about this."

Ruby agreed that Billy wouldn't be happy but to her it was irrelevant. She was just so relieved that Charlie was happy for her and knew that he was already really fond of Shay anyway. Now Ruby had someone to share her secret with.

Charlie answered the phone straight away and told Ruby that their mum had called him last night, that she was hysterical and begged him to go over to the house. He told Ruby how all she did was cry and begged him not to go. Ruby told Charlie that she was going to make a few calls and would phone him back.

Ruby's next port of call was Bungle, who undoubtedly would have heard from Billy by now. Bungle told Ruby that her mum had called him last night and told him how Billy was uncontrollable and heading to the nightclub to get his gun. With that, Bungle phoned Richard and Trevor. Richard was also a fellow employee and friend, Trevor was Billy's business partner of many years in the nightclub business separate to that of Shay and Billy's.

At an unearthly hour, Bungle, Richard and Trevor raced to Shay's industrial unit, unsure of what they would find. They arrived to find that Billy had smashed Shay's office to pieces, including the entrance glass door. They tried to calm him down but he was too far gone to be pacified. Bungle added that his mood this morning had not improved, if anything it had got worse. He had already given Bungle orders to ring every hotel in the area to find out where Ruby was.

Ruby was not shocked to hear of Billy's behaviour but was alarmed that he had gone to get his gun from the safe at the nightclub and asked Bungle to keep her informed.

Ruby now knew that to stay at the hotel any longer was dangerous. Ruby rang Charlie and asked if he could take her to the train station so she could meet Shay. He agreed and told her to meet him at the front of the hotel. She waited in reception with her bags and watched the rain falling heavily. Charlie was soon there to meet Ruby and took her bags and put them in the car.

The train station was not too far away so the siblings did not have much time to talk. Ruby promised Charlie that she would be in touch and he promised in return that he would not tell anybody that he had seen her. They gave each other a kiss and an emotional hug, not knowing when they would see each other again.

Ruby awkwardly ran into the station with her bags and bought a single ticket to Highgate.

THREE

On the Move

Shay waited for ten minutes at Highgate train station, with an unaccustomed three thousand pounds in his front pocket. Ruby stepped off of the train and ran towards the car; he got out of the car to greet her. "Alright Eyes?"

"Yeah, I'm alright. You?" said Ruby.

A quick kiss and cuddle was all there was time for before both jumped into the car.

"Eyes, we'll just meet a mate of mine in this pub," said Shay.

Near the train station was The Queens Head where Steve waited inside for them. Steve was a good friend of Shay's and they had been close for twenty two years; he was a man who lived for his wife and children but not one to upset. He was a big lump who provided security at several London nightclubs, but had never had business with Billy although he certainly wanted Billy's doors to add to his portfolio.

Shay beckoned to Steve from the door of the pub.

Steve followed Shay back to the car. He greeted them both,

"Alright Shay, hello darling. Right Shay, I've made some enquiries. Best thing to do is hit the road for a couple of days. I'll look out for your boy, Connor will be safe, don't worry about that. Let me find out who Billy has got on you and then we'll move forward. At the end of the day, you've both done nothing wrong but fall in love. If necessary I'll put some of my boys on Billy, we'll set the dogs on him, but I'm sure this will all blow over. Fuck me! Love hurts!" laughed Steve as he gave them both a hug. "Dump your mobiles, get a new pay as you go phone and stay in touch with me," was his parting comment.

With that, Shay and Ruby sped off and headed to junction 23 of the M25.

Now, again without any direction or location in mind, Shay said to Ruby, "Right Eyes, pick a motorway, M1, M4 or M3?"

Ruby knew that the M1 would take them north but had no idea where the M3 or M4 would take them. "Erm, M4 I suppose! Wherever that goes?" she giggled.

"Right," Shay said, "We'll have a night in Bath or Bristol, they're both good cities and no one would think that we'd head there."

As they sat in traffic, a usual occurrence for Shay on the M25, Shay dismantled both phones and disposed of them in various spots of the motorway grass verge.

Shay tried to think as Billy would think. Shay's entire family now lived in Ireland, Billy would therefore think that Shay would head for Ireland.

Shay was born in London to Irish parents. They were good parents, kind hearted and loving. They were both lyrical people who loved to sing and dance; as the stereotypical Irish do. In fact, Shay's father was well known on the Irish music scene in London many years ago, just as he was well known for it in his native home. His father, Mick, was from Waterford and his mother, Josie, was a proud Kerry woman. Shay's long-married parents had returned from London to live in County Waterford many years ago.

Shay's sister, Bridget, to whom Shay was very close; had

returned to Ireland six years ago with her husband, Peter, and their two children. Peter, who was born and bred in Tipperary, shared a very successful catering business with Bridget.

Shay had a thought and shared his idea with Ruby, "Hey Eyes, forget Bristol and Bath, let's head to Fishguard in Wales. We can stay there tonight, leave the car at Fishguard dock, then take a train from Fishguard via Cardiff to London. We'll be back in London but Billy and his mob will think we're in Ireland."

"Sounds good to me, how far is Fishguard then?" Asked Ruby, who had never been to Wales.

"Four or five hours," said Shay.

The drive was mundane but they would hold each other's hands every now and then to say 'I Love You' without having to speak, letting each other's minds continue to race and envisage different scenarios of what lay ahead of them.

They crossed the Severn Bridge and entered Wales. They stopped at Port Talbot and purchased a cheap pay-as-you-go phone from a supermarket. They sat in the car making sure that the phone worked before continuing their journey. The short walk and little bit of fresh air did them both good and they perked up a little for the remainder of the journey in the drizzle and grey skies.

Ruby turned to Shay, "Oi, I'm a bit worried, London. Billy knows a bloke from Mile End called Ronnie, I met him at the house once. He's not the full ticket and he'd shoot someone for a pound. He's a proper nut-nut! I hope he ain't got him involved."

An alarmed Shay replied, "So how well does he know him?"

"Not that well, he's a mate of Billy's gangster mate, Dave. Dave's the one that's good mates with Ronnie."

"That don't sound good," said Shay who then hastily called Spooner to make enquires.

"Spooner, it's Shay. You ever heard of a shooter in Mile End called Ronnie?"

"Bloody hell Shay!" said Spooner, "Mile End is full of shooters!" He laughed, "What's his surname?"

"Ruby don't know it," said Shay.

"Ask Ruby to describe him. I know a couple of Ronnie's who are naughty in Mile End."

"What's he look like, Eyes?" asked Shay.

"He's short, quite skinny and scruffy looking," said Ruby. "He don't stand out in a crowd if you know what I mean. He definitely don't look like the sort to do the stuff he does!"

"Yeah, I know of him. Jesus Christ, Shay, you should have done what I said this morning! I waited to hear back from you but you never called till now. Shay, word round the camp fire is that he's got quite a few out looking for you. Where are you mate?" asked Spooner with concern.

"In Manchester." Shay felt no need to divulge his correct location, and because of Shay's football connections up that way, Manchester would be a feasible place for him to be.

"OK mate, you two be careful up there," said Spooner.

"See you soon mate." Shay ended the call.

Shay made another call, this time to his son, Connor.

"Alright son, how's it going?"

"Not good, Dad," Connor continued and added, "Billy keeps calling me, he said that a firm are after you and Ruby and that he will do time for you both."

"You ignore his calls, Con, the bloke's just a bully and he's trying to intimidate me by going through you. Just turn your phone off and blank him."

"Don't tell me or anyone where you are Dad, please, don't trust anyone!" said Connor.

Shay was thankful for his son's maturity, "Yeah, it's best you don't know where we are, Con, you're safe there at your mum's though. I love you and we'll speak in the morning and don't worry!" Shay said.

"Night Dad, love you too," Connor ended the conversation.

Connor had lived with Shay for three years up until two years previously. Both Shay and Connor's mum loved Connor dearly and Shay knew that he was safe at her house.

Shay had split up with Connor's mum when Connor was just two years old, no real drama, they just had no love for each other; however, they did still have one thing in common and that was a deep love for Connor.

Shay and Ruby drove as fast as they could through the winding roads of South Wales approaching Fishguard. Shay decided to make his final call of the night to Jack. He refrained from contacting his family in Ireland as he did not want to alarm them about something that he thought could be resolved somehow. Little did he know, his family were already aware.

Shay called Jack, "Alright Jack?"

"Shay! I've been waiting for you to call me! You got the girl with you?"

"Yeah, why?" asked Shay.

Jack was a bit flustered in his response, "Ooh Shay, that's wrong mate. You shouldn't have taken her with you. He's onto you, mate, he's got your laptop, passport and all kinds of information about you and your family in Ireland. Where are you?"

Shay told Jack that they were in Manchester. Again, this would make perfect sense to Jack who had also been a very active member of the Chelsea Firm.

"I noticed you withheld your number Shay, why'd you do that then?" asked Jack.

Shay now detected an amount of cynicism in Jack's voice.

"You know the score Jack, as we always said back in the day, the enemy always comes smiling!"

They both laughed and Shay told Jack he would be in touch.

Finally, they arrived at the hotel in Fishguard already feeling anxious about the night ahead. The unknown was scary. Had they been followed? Was Ronnie from Mile End or another firm employed by Billy to carry out a disposal job on them both?

FOUR

Woes in Wales

Shay pulled up the handbrake and turned off the ignition. "Right baby, let's book in under a false name to be on the safe side. How's about Mr and Mrs Jones as we're in Wales?"

Ruby grinned and began to sing Billy Paul's hit *Me & Mrs Jones*. They both laughed and after much deliberation finally agreed that they would go by the name, Richards.

Ruby started to gather up the empty drink bottles and chocolate bar wrappers whilst Shay got out of the car and went around to the boot to get out their small amount of luggage.

Both were very conscious dressers and loved to wear designer clothing. Due to there speedy departure, they only had enough clothes to last them for a couple of days. Vanity was soon to go out the window for the both of them.

They checked into the hotel under the name of Mr and Mrs Richards. Both noticed that there seemed to be a lot of people milling around the hotel, which is not a good thing when you're having to look over your shoulder and not know who you're looking for.

They were given directions to their room, which seemed miles away. Eventually, they got to their room. Shay put the card key into the door, the door would not open. Not really being in the mood for a temperamental card key, he viciously tried it again. Still the door would not open.

"For fuck's sake!" Shay snapped, "Why don't these places just stick to normal keys? I ain't gonna be too happy if I've gotta walk all the way back to reception!"

Taking the card from Shay, Ruby said, "Oi, give it here, let me do it instead of you getting your knickers in a twist!" She inserted the card and the door opened. She gave Shay a smug but cheeky grin.

"Yeah, well done Eyes. Go on, get your arse in there!" Shay laughed.

They went into the room and dropped their bags. As first appearances go, the room was really nice. Ruby went straight to the bathroom to carry out a quick inspection. This was a trait that she had picked up from her nan as a child. She had spent a lot of time with her nan and grandad as a child and used to accompany her nan to inspect the toilets whenever they visited a new place, like a restaurant or a pub. This inspection would then be followed by a lesson on how to layer the toilet seat with toilet roll before sitting on it.

Ruby skipped out of the bathroom to report, "Well, the bathroom's alright. It's actually quite nice in here ay!"

Shay agreed that the room was nice but was more concerned with moving the car out of sight. "Right, c'mon Eyes, let's go and find somewhere nearby to hide the car. Billy has probably reported it as stolen by now."

"Yeah, you're right. Have you got the room key?" Ruby asked before the heavy door swung shut.

They left the hotel and drove a short distance before discovering an estate of council flats. There were already a good number cars parked around the area and it was set far enough away from the main road. Shay parked the car and they got out. Holding hands and reassuring each other that the car would be safe there, they walked back to the hotel.

Having reached the hotel and walked the marathon back to their room; Ruby plonked down on the end of the bed whilst Shay went to the toilet. As Shay strolled out doing up his belt, he asked Ruby if she fancied a drink downstairs. It had been a stressful yet surreal day for them both, so some time to sit down and go over the days events was an appealing idea.

"Shall we have a shower first before we go? Travelling always makes me feel dirty," Ruby suggested.

"Alright Eyes, you jump in first. I'll see what channels we've got on the television while you're in there," Shay said.

The bar had a handful of guests. The furnishings were very modern with dark brown leather settees and chunky dark wooden tables. Adjacent to this bar they were in was another, smaller bar. There was a lot of noise coming from the next bar, some kind of rugby function was in full swing with lots of people and loud music. They had one quick drink and then decided to leave and order their dinner from the room.

Shay rang for room service and caught them just in time. He was told that they were not twenty four hours and that all they could offer was a roast chicken dinner. Shay loved his food and at that time would have eaten anything; hunger made Shay very grouchy.

The two dinners were brought up on a trolley about half an hour later. They did not hesitate to dig in and sat eating contently on the bed, dinners on their laps.

After a long, exhausting day and now with full bellies; Shay and Ruby inevitably began to feel a tired and decided to get ready for bed.

Prior to tonight, they had only once spent an entire night together, and that night did not really live up to their expectations as a result of all of the ducking and diving and lies that were needed to allow that one night together. This night was not much better. They wanted to be close and intimate but neither could really switch off from the fact that their lives had been turned upside down overnight.

"I'm sorry Eyes, I just can't get all of this madness out of my head," said Shay as he lay looking at the ceiling.

"I know, I'm the same. Let's just lay here and watch the telly for a bit, yeah?"

"Hold on, I'll be back in a minute," said Shay as he swung his legs out of the bed.

Slightly bemused, Ruby watched him get out of the bed and go over to the trolley that had been used to bring up the meals. She watched him barricade the door with it and re-arrange the glasses, plates and metal plate covers. As he came back to the bed with two knives he explained to Ruby that if anyone should try to come in or even try moving the door handle, the glass would fall onto the plates and the plates would then fall onto the metal covers and they would fall onto the floor; like a domino effect. The knives were to be kept on Shay's bedside, just in case. Impressed with Shay's idea and cautiousness, it made Ruby feel safe. She knew that Shay would do all he could to protect her. She thought to herself, Shay's protecting me, but who's protecting him? All she felt she could do was comfort him, remind him that they were in it together and that she loved him.

Ruby snuggled onto Shay's chest. After ten minutes spent fidgeting from his tickly chest hairs, she fell asleep in Shay's arms, for after all, she had not slept since Wednesday night. Shay was in deep thought and far too concerned to sleep. Shay and Ruby both suffered with IBS and tonight, he was in agony. He lay, looking at the television but not watching it. He assessed the situation, had they done the right thing fleeing the scene to avoid a bully? Should he have stayed and sorted Billy out?

He'd been involved in violence for more years than he could remember but in recent years he was focussed on business and leading a happy, peaceful life.

He thought long and hard. He had thousands of questions but not one answer. This situation could simmer down given a bit of time, he thought. But the theory of this Ronnie character being involved worried him immensely. Hit men, guns and talk of killing was a different world, and one he didn't want to know about. Shay concluded that the best thing to do was to try and sleep on it and figure it out in the morning with a clearer head. He was sure that the situation would be a lot calmer come Saturday morning.

Thoughts would negate Shay's intentions to sleep and he painfully clock watched through the night. Whilst he lay in bed thinking, he cast his mind back to the previous eighteen months he had known Billy. He found Billy to be a gentle giant; over Chelsea Billy talked it up and nothing more. Conversely, after just two weeks of joining in business with Billy, Shay had realised that he was a tyrant who loved to bully anyone who was weaker than him. Billy was tame when in Shay's company but treated all the staff awfully in Shay's absence. Why oh why had he allowed Billy to join his successful operation? Shay thought.

Ruby slept through till seven thirty am when Shay's phone rang. "Morning, Dad," Connor was on the phone.

"Cor you're up early Son! What's up? Everything ok?"

"Nah, not really Dad, I've got a text message from Fred telling me that Billy's paid some people to kill you. Fred wants you to call him. He said to tell you to ring him urgently and says there is a solution."

"Right, I'll call him. Best turn your phone off for a while, they know they can get to me through you. I will call you later today, so leave it off for a couple of hours. Speak to you later, Son," Shay woefully ended Connor's call.

Fred was better known over the Chelsea as Fred The Spiv. Fred had known Billy for five years, Shay had known Spiv for only three years but got on well with him. He was a witty bloke, loved a drink and always had an answer for any question or situation. Spiv was also on the Chelsea Firm and although he didn't look much, he was as game as they come. Shay actually met Billy through Spiv. Spiv never had a good word to say about Billy and in recent years he had disliked Billy. He was always remarking to Shay how he thought that the way Billy was with Ruby was not right and that it really grated him how he kept referring to Charlie and Ruby as his son and daughter.

He would often joke with Shay that Ruby probably fancied him. Spiv said to him many months ago, "Oi Shay, I think Ruby fancies you mate. You've got a bit of an Elvis thing going on and you know she's mad about him!"

Shay laughed and replied, "I don't look like Elvis... do I?"

Spiv was quick to reply, "Yeah you do, when he had rigor mortis, you plum!"

Now wide awake, Ruby asked, "Was that Connor? What's happened?"

"That fucking nut-nut is still at it! Billy's got Fred to text Connor. Fred wants me to call him. He reckons there's a solution," said Shay.

"Do you trust Fred though?" Ruby asked.

Shay pondered Ruby's question and said, "Not sure to be honest, Spiv's had a bad opinion of Billy since I've known him. I've known him for a while but him and Billy do go back a long way.... I think I'll give that call a miss as it happens.... The thing is though, Fred told Connor there's a hit on me. He wouldn't just make that up and he's not the type to involve Connor unnecessarily. Look, Eyes, I've never gone to the Police in my life but maybe we should." Shay paused and thought before continuing, "I'm not sure about dumping the car at Fishguard dock now, it might bring trouble to my family in Ireland. Let's just move about in the car for a day or two but we do need to tell the Police what's happened just in case Billy reports it as stolen. If he does that, we could get a tug and get arrested."

Ruby agreed with Shay, "Yeah, you're right, it will be safer than travelling by train anyway."

They rushed around the room getting washed, dressed and packed as quickly as they could, checked out of the hotel and walked back up to the estate each smoking their first cigarette of the day. They were relieved to find that the car was safe and sound.

They drove to Fishguard Police Station and parked outside. Before getting out of the car, Shay questioned again whether he was doing the right thing by involving the Police. Ruby reminded him of the threats that had been made and who was now involved.

Entering the Police Station, they informed the Custody Sergeant of the threats made against them. It didn't take long for an Officer to arrive to take Shay and Ruby through to the off-limits area of the Station.

What they both thought would take minutes took three hours. Ruby was taken into one interview room upstairs in the Station and Shay was taken into another interview room on the ground floor.

The Welsh Police Officer interviewing Shay was empathetic and said that he would contact Middlesex Police to advise that they should put a block on the Mercedes car being reported as stolen. As the interview continued, a text came through to Shay's phone. The text was from Connor but had been sent to Connor from Spiv. Spiv's text was asking Shay to call him urgently as Billy had paid a bloke called Ronnie for his head. Shay's world collapsed around him, the colour rapidly drained from his face when he saw Ronnie's name and he felt physically sick. Ruby had already expressed her concern to Shay regarding Ronnie. Fear hit Shay like a bolt of lightening. He sat staring at his phone, his right leg nervously jittering and the lump in his throat felt to be getting larger by the second. Could this really be happening? Shay thought. The Welsh Officer noticed how visibly shook Shay was by this text and called the Officer interviewing Ruby.

The Officer interviewing Ruby relayed the information to her. On hearing the content of the text that Shay had just received, she couldn't help but break down. She had been struggling to hold herself together during the interview and this news left her distraught. Ruby had never had any dealings with the Police in her life and even though this was voluntary, she felt scared and vulnerable as reality really hit for the first time.

The Police Officer and Ruby were then summoned to go back downstairs to the room where Shay and his interviewing Officer were. Ruby could clearly see the terror on Shay's face. She hugged him and then asked to see the text message. Ruby read the text and then read it again, still finding it hard to comprehend that Ronnie had actually been paid for his specialist services.

Handing the phone back to Shay, Ruby said what Shay already knew, "We're fucked."

The Police Officer informed them, "We deal with a lot of idle death threats, only one in every thousand are genuine threats and I think this is the one."

The Police Officer provided them with a crime reference number and said that he would e-mail both statements over to Middlesex Police who would then generate their own crime reference number and take over dealing with the matter. He tried reassuring the couple by explaining that even the Police have enormous difficulty in trying to find someone so they should try not to worry too much. His advice for them was head north and suggested that they should move hotels regularly.

Shay and Ruby left the Police Station both shocked and shaken. They got back into the car and followed the road signs for Milford Haven. There wasn't much conversation between them, each self-absorbed with their own thoughts and fears of what was yet to come. They knew they were in serious danger and the concept of returning to London any time soon were fading fast. Milford Haven was only a twenty minute drive and as the Policeman had told them, a fifteen mile radius was a very large area.

Ruby expressed her concern over Ronnie; turning to Shay she said, "You know that Ronnie is a proper nutter."

"I should have gone with Spooner and sorted this out when I had the chance!" Sounding regretful, Shay continued, "I can't believe this is happening to us! Everything was rosy and what about my work? I've got contracts, works in progress and works to commence, we're talking big money here Eyes."

"I know, I was thinking about that as well," she replied sympathetically.

They solemnly entered the coastal town of Milford Haven and as they did so, a ferry cut slowly through the water below the roadside to their left.

"That's the ferry to Ireland," remarked Shay.

"Oh is it? Perhaps we should be on it!" replied Ruby.

With the way things were, Shay thought that it may be a good idea.

Whilst driving slowly through the pretty town, they spotted a hotel and thought that they would try it. It was perfect for them, with the car park ideally located around the back and well out of sight. Before they went in, Ruby told Shay that she wanted to make a couple of calls.

Her first call was to Bungle. She told him how they had been told that someone had been paid to do a hit. Whilst explaining the current situation, she couldn't help but get upset. The cold reality of having a hit man after them was all becoming too much. Bungle quietly listened but was obviously shocked. His only advice to Ruby at that time was that Jack was not to be trusted.

He firmly told her, "Ruby, don't trust Jack, he's a snake in the grass. He's seen an opportunity now that Shay's not here and he will shit stir all he can to step into his shoes."

Baffled by Bungle's advice, she questioned him, "What do you mean? What makes you say that? What has he done?"

Bungle told Ruby that he could not go into detail but begged that she take heed of his advice.

Ruby knew that she had left two thousand five hundred pounds in her drawer at work. She knew that Bungle knew about it and knew that he would be able to get to it.

"Bungle, I need you to do me a favour. Remember that two and a half grand I got out of my savings and then locked in my drawer? I need you to get it and pay it into my bank for me. Please Bungle, I need you to do it, that's all the money I have and what money we do have is running out fast."

Bungle knew exactly what Ruby was talking about. "Of course I will, I'll have to wait 'till the coast is clear and then I'll get it. Give me your bank details now and I'll get Sharon to pay it in first thing Monday morning."

Sharon was Bungle's wife and obviously knew about what had happened.

Ruby then called Charlie. The last time she spoke to her brother was when he took her to the train station. She was happy to hear his voice and asked if he had any news. He told her that he kept being bombarded about whether he had seen or heard from her. He denied having any contact but Billy kept persisting. This was because everybody knew how close Ruby and Charlie were and that if Ruby was to confide in anyone, it would be Charlie. Charlie asked Ruby where they were. For her and Shay's safety and for Charlie's own good, she knew she had to lie. She told Charlie that they were in Manchester but moving daily.

An emotional Ruby knew that her phone credit was starting to get low. She told Charlie that she loved him and that she would call him again soon.

Ruby wiped the tears from her cheeks and called out to Shay who was pacing the car park smoking. "Shall we go and see if they've got a room then?"

"Yeah, c'mon," replied Shay as he walked over to the boot of the car to get their bags.

At the reception was a large Welsh man who looked like he had played rugby in his day. He was a bit beaten up to say the least, his cauliflower ears were the best Shay had ever seen. Inside, the building was a lot larger then it appeared from the outside. The ceilings were high, the décor was dated and even though it was a beautiful day outside, inside it was very dingy and gloomy.

"Hello mate, have you got a room for one night?" Shay asked.

"You're in luck, just the one room left boyo, you want it?" Replied the bruised receptionist.

"Yeah we'll take it."

All of the rooms were located upstairs but to get to the stairs, they had to walk though part of the bar. As they traipsed through the bar with their bags, they both noticed a guy sitting alone who watched them curiously. Suspicious of everyone, Shay stared hard into his eyes. If looks could kill, this guy would now have just taken his last breath. Was he onto them or just checking out Ruby? Shit, thought Shay, paranoia is really setting in.

They climbed the stairs up to the third floor of the pub, where the décor remained just as dingy and grim. The uneven floorboards, covered with a burgundy patterned dirty carpet, creaked as they walked down the hallway to find their room. Shay opened the door for Ruby to go through first, a gentlemanly trait of his that he always used.

Ruby entered, grimaced and declared, "Bloody wars, it's a dump in here, London. Look at the state of it. Two single beds! God I dread to think what the bathroom's like!" She stomped into the bathroom and shouted out, "It's rank in here! And we've only got one toilet roll!"

They looked at each other, no doubt their love was true but both wondered, standing in their depressing surroundings, why is this happening?

Ruby lifted back the bed throw to inspect the sheets, "Do you know the song Elvis sang called *True Love Travels On A Gravel Road*?" She asked.

"No I don't, how's it go?" asked Shay.

"Well I'm not gonna sing it but I was just thinking how true that song is. We must love each other to be going through all this shit and staying in dives like this."

Shay agreed and gave her a tight hug. "We'll be alright baby. I think I'll give Spiv a call."

"Yeah I suppose so, see what's what," sighed Ruby.

Shay called Connor to see if he was ok and to get Fred Spiv's number from him. Connor told Shay how he had had Billy on the phone, saying that he would have Shay found and killed leaving Connor without a dad. Shay advised his son to leave his phone off and for him not to go to the Police as it may put him in danger.

Shay called Fred, "Spiv, how's it going mate?"

Fred heaved a sigh and said, "Right Shay, listen to me. We can sort this out, but I'm telling you mate, Billy means business. He's paid for your head, some bloke from the old days called Ronnie and his brother are looking for you."

"What's up with him, Spiv? We could just go toe to toe instead of all this hit men stuff!" Said Shay.

"Nah, I told you ages ago, Billy's big but he's yellow. He won't have a straightener but he'll have you killed. He's been running round all morning like a nutter paying other people to find you. You've got to listen to what I think you should do."

"What's the plan then, Spiv?"

"Right, Billy's said that if you're in a hotel, you just slip away without Ruby knowing. You go and keep going. When you're out of the area you let me know what hotel she's at, Billy will then go to the hotel and get her. But when you've gone you stay gone, Shay."

Shay laughed, "Hold on Fred, there's no ball and chain on Ruby here, mate, that's Ruby's choice if she wants to go but as for me staying gone, then it won't happen. Look, we all know people, Spiv, I could just as easy turn the tables on Billy. He's got all my money and he's the one kicking off! We've done nothing wrong, he's at fault not us!"

"But you've run off with Ruby, Shay, you know how he is about her."

"The bloke's a wrong un'!" retorted Shay.

"You still in Manchester, Shay?" Asked Spiv, changing the direction of the conversation.

Shay thought. Shit! Only Jack and Spooner knew that. Had one of them turned? Someone's a turncoat, but who?

In shock and disbelief he ended the conversation by saying, "I'm off now Spiv, you just tell Billy there's two side's to that coin!" And abruptly hung up.

Shay and Ruby sat in the room and quietly discussed the fact that someone had revealed they were in Manchester.

Shay told Ruby of the deal offered by Billy via Spiv, to which she replied, "Look, if you want to do one then go but just tell me if that's what you're going to do. Don't just leave me without saying anything."

Shay quickly reacted by telling her that he would never do that, but she should also know that she didn't have to stay if she didn't want to.

"Funny innit, when the grass is cut the snakes come out!" Commented Ruby.

"Well it can't be Spooner," said Shay, "He don't even know Billy!"

"Yeah but maybe one of them told someone else, you know how word gets about. Like Chinese whispers!"

"Oh well, let them all search Manchester high and low, we're three and a half hours away. We'll have tonight and tomorrow night here. I'll ask for a better room for tomorrow night and then we can make a move on Monday. We've gotta sort something out, we won't get far on a few grand!" Groaned Shay.

"Oi, I've got that two and a half grand cash hidden in my desk at work remember that I got out for the deposit on a house, we can use that!" Ruby excitedly suggested.

"Oh yeah great!" Replied Shay in a mocking tone, "Perhaps you could ask Billy to get it out of your drawer at work and he could then get Ronnie to drop it off to us here at the hotel. We'll buy Ronnie a bit of dinner and then he can be on his merry way back to sunny Mile End!"

Ruby dismissed Shay's sarcastic comment and quickly responded, "Oi, don't start getting lemon! I told you, I rang Bungle and his missus is gonna pay the money in first thing Monday morning and then we can withdraw it from down the road."

Shay laughed. He often called Ruby 'a little Mockney' and her quick wit amused him whatever mood he was in.

Shay called Steve to get an update. Whilst Shay was making calls, Ruby started to unpack what little they had. She was in the bathroom and started to quietly sing to herself not wanting Shay to hear her. She was arranging the toothbrushes and toiletries when *Running Scared* by Roy Orbison came into her head. A relevant song, she softly started to sing the first verse,

> *"Just runnin' scared*
> *Each place we go*
> *So afraid that he might show*
> *Yeah, runnin' scared*
> *What would I do*
> *If he came back and wanted you"*

Music was a major part of Ruby's life. However she was feeling, she would relate to music. She never spoke about her feelings or troubles so listening to music was her way of dealing with those things. She was stuck in a time warp where music was concerned. She loved fifties, sixties and eighties music and all genres ranging from opera to reggae.

Ruby abruptly stopped singing as Shay called out to her, "I've been belling Steve but he ain't answering so I've left him a couple of messages. C'mon babe, we'll go downstairs for a bit and see what the apple is."

Ruby laughed. 'The apple' was new to Ruby but she quickly figured out that in rhyming slang, apple core would mean score.

"Alright, I'll just have a wee and we'll go down there," replied Ruby.

They went down to the bar and had a few quiet drinks. Mental, emotional and physical tiredness overwhelmed them. They decided to call it a night, go to bed and re-charge their batteries.

When Sunday morning arrived they moved to a better room. It was clean and all the light switches actually worked. The room was a suite of a certain kind, if you can call a pub room a suite. It had a large bathroom, a seating area with a table, television and a dressing table. The room was much lighter and had a great view looking out onto the marina. Relieved to now be staying in a half decent room, Shay and Ruby sat on the settee and watched the television. As Ruby made them both a cup of tea, Shay's phone rang, and the screen showed 'withheld' as the caller I.D.

Shay answered the call cautiously. "Hello?"

"Good Morning Mr. Sullivan," said an officious voice.

"Who's this?" Shay asked.

"DCI Turner of Middlesex Police, am I speaking with Mr. Sullivan?"

"Yes you are, sorry, I was just being wary as your call came up 'withheld,'" Shay said.

"Oh yes, I understand. I've just read your and Ms. Ward's statements. I'll be having Billy Gower picked up in the early hours of tomorrow morning for questioning. Can you give me the surname of this alleged hit man from East London please, Sir?"

"I'm sorry, we've no idea"

"Ok, best thing for you to do is to lay low for a few days. Having made some minor enquires we have found that Mr. Billy Gower is known to us. He is involved with a family called the Timbres, a family who are also very well known to us, so the best thing to do is to keep your heads low until we have made the necessary enquires and interviewed Gower. Should you hear anymore then please contact us on the main Middlesex Police switchboard number," advised Turner.

Shay took this opportunity to explain that the car he was driving was registered in Billy's name for business purposes and expressed that he was worried Billy would report it as stolen.

"What's the registration?" Asked Turner.

Shay told him the registration. Shay could hear Turner typing the registration into his computer.

"Hmmmm, well nothing's been reported as of yet but I will put a note on the system stating that if the vehicle is reported stolen, that it is logged on the computer that the vehicle is not to be stopped. Ok, you both keep safe and we will talk tomorrow." With that Turner hung up.

"That was the old bill. He's a DCI and was actually really helpful," Shay then laughed and said, "I used to be keeping them busy but now they're helping us!"

Ruby was relieved that the law appeared to be on their side and suggested to Shay, "Shall we go out today, London, and have a look about, it's really nice outside?"

They went for a drive to Haverfordwest and browsed the shops and coffee bars. They felt safe as the Police were being extremely helpful. Furthermore, Billy and his motley crew all assumed that they were both in Manchester.

They returned back to the hotel early that evening with some drinks and snacks for in the room. The night drew in and they got settled on the settee. Shay was excited to see that *Pulp Fiction* was due on TV in an hour. He had been dying for Ruby to see it as he knew that it was the type of film that she loved.

Watching the film, Ruby commented on how it used a song that she referred to as one of her and Shay's songs. They had many songs that they classed each as 'their song' and Ruby found it amusing and coincidental that Al Green's *Let's Stay Together* was in the film. Watching the film put them both in a good mood and they already felt that a certain amount of pressure had been lifted since the Police had been in touch that morning.

After having their first day of laughing and banter since last Thursday evening, Shay and Ruby felt reminded of their love for each other and spent the rest of the night showing that affection and love. For the first time, they physically made a connection that could now never be broken, despite what uncertainties lay ahead of them.

FIVE

Blue Monday

They awoke on Monday morning and the first port of call was the Middlesex Police, contacted via the main switchboard. Shay made the call and asked to speak to DCI Turner. Disappointingly, the Police Operator informed him that Turner was off duty until Wednesday.

Bemused by this, Shay said to Ruby, "Why did he say to call him today if he wasn't going to be at work?"

"Perhaps something come up, or maybe he's ill?" replied Ruby.

Shay called Connor to see how he was and if he had had any more hassle. "Morning Son, how's things?"

"I'm fine, Dad. Spiv has been on the phone again this morning though. Billy got arrested in the middle of the night. They went to his house at three am and got him," explained Connor.

"Oh that's great news. We should be back in a couple of days and then all this nonsense will be over. I'll give you a bell later on. Love you."

Hopeful and now more optimistic, Shay then called one of his main clients, "Morning Charles, how's things?"

"Shay…" A nervous Charles answered. "I'm sorry Shay, I had

46

Billy on the phone in a very threatening manner on Friday morning last week. I've got to step away from this. That man's a lunatic. I want nothing to do with this."

"Charles, I've got everything in hand, normal service will be resumed in the next couple of days, don't worry about a thing," explained Shay, shocked by his client's response.

"Sorry Shay, I run a business and have a family. I can't be doing with all this gangster stuff." And he hung up.

Shay begun the morning feeling as though he had taken a couple of steps forward, then after one conversation felt as though he had taken ten steps back. He was devastated. Charles was his best client and also a very good friend. There were numerous large contracts in progress and some larger one's to start with Charles's company. Even though a worrying recession was looming for the majority, Shay didn't have that worry, due to the fact that he had several work orders from Charles for the next twelve months.

His face showed the disappointment and upset. Forlorn, he turned to Ruby and said, "Eyes, Billy obviously put the squeeze on Charles last Friday morning, I've lost my main client, he don't want to know anymore."

"How typical of him is that? He can't just throw his toys out of the pram, he has to go that one step further! He's a bloody lunatic. He'll obviously do everything and anything to ruin us both now," she replied.

Beginning to feel the pressure once again, Shay and Ruby packed their bags and checked out, accompanied by once again, the large black cloud looming above them.

Whilst Shay loaded the car, Ruby walked a short distance to the nearby bank to withdraw her money. She was relieved to find that Bungle had kept to his word and ensured that her money was deposited.

They left Milford Haven and headed back in the direction of Fishguard. Shay suggested to Ruby that they could get some breakfast in Fishguard and then drive to Cardiff. He went on to explain what a great city it was. He had been there four times with the Chelsea Firm, having bloody battles with the Soul Crew, Cardiff City's Football Firm. This visit to Cardiff would be very different; a couple on a visit to a wonderful city as opposed to the football madness of years gone by, which Shay looked back on with shame.

As they got closer to Fishguard the phone rang again with 'withheld' showing as the caller I.D on the display. Shay answered in the hope that it may be a colleague of DCI Turner. "Hello?" He warily said.

"Is that Mr. Sullivan?" enquired a deep Welsh voice.

"Yes, speaking," Shay replied.

"This is D.S Moore here, I would like you to come into Fishguard Police Station please, Mr Sullivan, as soon as you can."

"Oh, erh… is it about the case?" Shay enquired.

"Let's just say it's better for you to come in rather than you be stopped by Traffic Police," Moore said firmly.

"Hold on!" Shay exclaimed, "Is this about the car I'm driving? Middlesex Police have a note on their system stating that we're not to be stopped. It's not stolen, if that's what your enquiry is about!"

"I know, I know. Just come in and we will sort this out, Mr. Sullivan," Moore persisted.

"Ok, well I'm in Fishguard now so I'll see you in about ten minutes." Shay ended the call.

They entered Fishguard, lost their bearings and were in a part of town they had never been in. They searched for the police station but couldn't find it and ended up going around in circles. As they drove down a side street near Fishguard dock, a parked police car with an officer standing next to it on the pavement was a great sight to see.

"Eyes, put your window down and ask him where the police station is," said Shay.

"Oh yeah, that's handy-harry, pull up and I'll ask him," said Ruby. "Hello... excuse me, can you point us in the right direction of the police station please?"

There was a slight delay in the officer's response and then he sternly replied, "Just reverse behind my car and park up please."

Wide-eyed, Ruby turned to Shay, "What's all that about?"

"Don't know, perhaps he's gonna draw us a map or maybe he doesn't want us sitting in the road while he gives us directions?" Shay said as he parked the car behind the police car.

The police officer slowly approached the car. He was in his early fifties, well groomed with a tidy beard. Walking like a stereotypical police officer; taking long, slow strides, making sure that his heel was the first part of his foot to firmly hit the pavement first.

He approached Shay's window and said, "You're under arrest, Sir, for theft of a motor vehicle. I need you both to step out of the vehicle and stand to one side."

The officer stood aside to allow Shay enough room to open the car door and get out. Shay and Ruby didn't speak. Dumbfounded, they both got out of the car and stood on the pavement. Within seconds, a large police van and three big policemen arrived on the scene, parking a short distance behind the car. They looked like they were going to be expecting trouble.

The officer then asked Ruby to step aside and as she did he announced, "You're under arrest for being a consenting passenger in a stolen vehicle."

Not knowing whether to laugh or cry, Ruby replied, "You what! You're having a laugh aren't you?"

"Hold on a minute mate," said Shay, "We were on our way to see a D.S Moore at Fishguard police station, he's just called me asking me to come in," he explained the situation and the officer listened.

The officer then said to the 'eager to get busy' policemen from the van, "It's ok boys, you can go now, I can deal with this." He then turned to Shay and Ruby, "Look, I can't let you go on in that vehicle, so I will take you to the police station where you will be for about an hour at the most. Then you can go, but you're definitely not going anywhere in that vehicle."

One of the three officers from the van took Shay and Ruby's bags from the car. Another then sat into the car and drove off.

Shay and Ruby watched the car disappear and undoubtedly thought the same thing, what the hell are going to do without a car!

Shay sensed that now the officer was aware of their situation, he'd eased up a little.

"Were you waiting here for us then?" Shay asked.

The officer laughed and said, "Yes I was. Come on, let's get this mess sorted out at the station." He came over as a decent bloke and this put both Shay and Ruby at ease a little. He obviously had to carry out what he had been instructed to do and at least he was nice enough to do it without going on a power trip.

Shay sat in the front passenger seat and Ruby sat in the back. It was very different to previous encounters Shay had had with the police. Usual form would be to throw Shay into the back of a van wearing Her Royal Majesty's bracelets. Of course, Ruby's first encounter with the police was their voluntary visit to the station last Saturday. For Ruby, to be arrested and escorted to a police station was a totally new experience altogether.

Shay could strike up a conversation with anyone if he wanted to and so started one with the officer, "Whereabouts are we actually going then?"

"Cardigan nick, Fishguard doesn't have holding cells."

"Holding cells? Are you serious! We've done nothing wrong! You can't lock us up!" Shay said.

"It will only be for an hour, boyo, nothing to worry about, it's just a formality," said the officer in a placid tone.

Cardigan was a twenty mile drive from Fishguard. The officer continued the trivial conversation with Shay, he seemed a fair and jovial man. Ruby sat in the back, numb and unable to comprehend that they had actually just been arrested and then the mobile phone rang. Shay could see from the display that it was Ruby's mum calling; how did she get this number, thought Shay. Ruby asked the officer if she could take the call and he nodded his head in response.

"Mum!" Answered Ruby, "Mum, I'm in the back of a goddamn police car, we've been arrested!" Not letting her mum get a word in edgeways Ruby continued, "Has he not done enough already? Why's he having us arrested?"

Ruby's mum told her not to worry and that she would find out what was going on. "Make sure you phone me when you can, Ruby."

Ruby told her mum that they'd only be about an hour and that she would call her when they got out.

On their arrival to Cardigan police station, the officer took their bags and led them into the custody sergeant's desk and explained that the two were no bother to him and had come quietly. He explained that he'd apprehended them en route to see D.S Moore and that the vehicle that they were driving was not stolen, more of a misunderstanding. He then proceeded to briefly explain their plight.

The sergeant looked at Ruby's Elvis holdall that sat on the floor and stood out a mile. It was loud in colour with a big picture of Elvis from his '68 Comeback Special in the middle.

He then looked at Shay, laughed and said, "I should nick you, boyo, just for having a bag like that!"

"It ain't mine!" Laughed Shay.

"You a big Elvis fan then, Miss?" asked the custody sergeant.

"Yeah, I love him," replied Ruby who would always get excitable when Elvis was topic of conversation.

"We prefer Tom Jones down here," he tittered.

"Oh yeah, I like him too," said Ruby, "You know, Tom Jones and Elvis were good friends."

Shay sighed and thought, oh this is great, standing in a cop shop having niceties about two pelvic gyrators! Hope she don't start telling her Elvis stories, has she forgotten we're getting banged up here? Shay's prayers were answered and the Sergeant moved on to booking the two of them in. The contents of Shay's pockets and all of his possessions were removed. The sergeant carried out the booking-in formalities and then advised the jailer in which cell Shay was to be locked up.

"See you in an hour, babe," said a glum Shay as he was frog-marched to his allocated cell. En route, Shay observed a big clock in the custody foyer that showed the time to be twelve fifteen pm. Good, thought Shay, we'll be out by half one to get some lunch.

For Ruby, the booking-in process was obviously a totally foreign experience. She was anxious and apprehensive as she was body-searched by a female officer. That same female officer led Ruby to her cell, which was a fair distance from Shay's. In fact, her cell could not have been much further away, located at the very rear of the building. The officer took Ruby's jacket from her, leaving her with just her strappy vest for warmth.

"Hold on a minute!" Said Ruby, "I'm gonna be cold without a coat."

The muted officer handed Ruby a blanket and shut the heavy steel door. Ruby stepped into her cell. Still standing by the cell door, Ruby looked around. It was a small, square, cold room. There was a stony floor and the walls looked bumpy, painted in a pale, grubby blue colour. Directly in front of her was a plain wall with a small barred window at the very top letting a minimal amount of light to shine through. To the left of her was another plain wall and situated at the bottom of this wall was a bed, which was just a frame with a thin, plastic blue mattress. To the right was another plain wall. Ruby walked towards the bed and sat on the edge. She unfolded the blanket, which was also pale blue and grubby looking. It was more like a baby's cellular blanket and Ruby instantly noticed the dirty stagnant smell that came from it. She put the itchy blanket around her shoulders and wondered how Shay was.

Shay had been in his cell about twenty minutes prior to Ruby being in hers. He'd removed his pink Ralph Lauren polo shirt and placed it on the dirty, blue plastic mattress. He'd been a visitor of various different cells a few times before but this time he knew it was only for an hour whilst they corrected this misunderstanding; no great shakes, thought Shay. He was more worried about Ruby who he knew had never been in this situation.

A young stocky Policeman brought Shay a cup of water. Another rugby player, thought Shay, no wonder the Welsh football team does so badly. Shay took his water and asked the Policeman, "What's the time mate?"

"Twenty five past four," replied the young Policeman.

"Twenty five past four! The arresting officer said we'd only be here an hour," an angry Shay exclaimed.

"Yeah I know, we're waiting on Middlesex Police. We're getting no answer from them and until we speak to them, we can't sort this out."

Shay explained to the young Policeman what it was all about and said indignantly, "We're sitting ducks here mate! If they inform the registered owner of the vehicle where we are, then when we leave here we're in immediate danger!"

"You're safer in here then boyo." And with that, the young jailor slammed the spy flap shut.

This riled Shay. Is he taking the piss out of me, he wondered.

Wound up with an anger that was fuelled with frustration, he paced the small cell. He was bored, hungry and discouraged at Middlesex police's incompetence. He decided to vent his anger by shadow boxing. He was a trained boxer years ago and used to have the ability to turn professional.

As time passed, Shay grew more impatient. He pressed the bell button in his cell, no one arrived, so he kicked the door repetitively.

It was dark and he guessed it was around eight pm, but it was the fact that he was being ignored that angered him most.

Shay pressed the bell button for several minutes until the young jailor came down the corridor and shouted, "Whoa steady on, what's up mate?"

"What's up! I want to know what's happening. Why are we still here? Is Ruby alright?"

"Yes she's fine, boyo, unlike you she is quiet and no bother. You keep pressing that button like that and we'll turn your bell off."

"You another rugby player?" asked Shay smugly.

"Yes, I play rugby, at quite a high level actually. You used to box?" Asked the young jailor with a cheeky grin.

"How'd you know that?"

"We've been watching you on the CCTV monitor, you've done about six rounds. So you winning then boyo?"

Shay felt embarrassed. Was this a new thing, CCTV in the cells? He thought to himself. "Yeah, very funny mate. Listen, we need to get out, we're in danger stuck here. I'm entitled to a phone call and I want to make it now, please!" said Shay.

"Ok, I'll be back in a minute. I'll go and check on your girlfriend too," replied the jailer.

The young Policeman unlocked the spy flap to Ruby's cell.

"You ok there, do you want a cup of tea or something?" He asked.

"Yes please, two sugars." Replied Ruby.

Ruby had been hearing lots of loud, repeated banging against a door and wondered to herself, oooh someone's got the hump, either that or they've banged up a nutter. Little did she know it that it was Shay who was using the steel door as a musical instrument.

Ruby had lost all sense of time. She was frustrated and tried killing time by pacing from wall to wall with one foot directly in front of the other, counting each step. When the cold became too much, she would curl up into the fetal position on the mattress.

The jailor returned with her cup of tea.

"How long is this going to take?" Ruby feebly asked as she carefully took the cardboard cup from him.

"Shouldn't be long now love." He shut the door behind him.

Feeling at her wits end and weak with the cold and hunger, she huddled herself up on the bed, sipped her tea that resembled dishwater and continued playing the waiting game.

Shay heard the clunking of his cell door unlocking, then the young jailor escorted him to the custody sergeant's desk. There had been a change of shift and a new custody sergeant was now on duty.

Shay informed him that he wanted to speak to someone at Middlesex CID. The Sergeant dialled and offered Shay the phone receiver. Thankfully, he was successful and spoke with a female CID Officer who explained that she was in the process of getting a statement over to Welsh police. She went onto explain that he and Ruby would then be interviewed regarding the car and then bailed to attend Middlesex Police Station; if they had been nearer they would have been transported back to Middlesex.

When the call was finished, another Police Officer walked by the desk, stopped and said to Shay, "I know you, I nicked you in London a few years ago!"

"I doubt you could find London mate!" scoffed Shay.

They exchanged glares and the Officer sniggered and carried on about his shift. Wind up merchant! Shay thought.

The custody sergeant told the young jailor to take Shay back to his cell.

"Hold on, hold on!" protested Shay.

Shay quickly reverted to his more charming manor, "Look, Ruby's never been locked up before, would it be out of the question to put me in the same cell?"

The Sergeant laughed loudly and stated, "We may be liberal down here in Wales, boyo, but not that liberal, you chancer you. Go on, back to your cell."

Shay needed to calm himself down, being in custody for so long was exasperating the injustice situation, but he knew that getting more wound up would not help. He decided to be calm and wait. His main concern was whether or not Billy knew that they were in Cardigan? Were Ronnie and Co. on their way to South Wales? God knows they had had plenty of time to get there.

Ruby had heard Shay's voice from her cell. She ran to the door and put her ear to the cold steel. She couldn't make out what was being said but could recognise his voice a mile off. Just to hear his voice was a comfort to Ruby who couldn't even summon the energy to try getting the jailor to let her go to the toilet. Every time footsteps came towards her cell she thought that they were coming to release her. This happened numerous times and added to her frustration when it wasn't her cell door that they came to unlock.

Hours slowly passed. Eventually Shay was taken from his cell and questioned by a traffic officer, who as it turned out, originated from Putney in London. He was a timid man and a Chelsea fan. Shay had nothing to hide and told him everything from start to finish. He was then finger printed and charged with Auto Theft, being bailed to attend a designated Middlesex police station in one months time.

As Shay signed for the release of his bag, he thought to himself, Auto Theft! What a mess. He was then released and informed that Ruby would be processed straight away. They advised Shay to wait in the police station foyer and Ruby would be out in a half hour or so.

It was now ten past three the next morning and Shay asked, "Why didn't you let Ruby out first?"

The custody sergeant barked in response, "Because she was quiet, and you were far from quiet. Go on, wait outside, she won't be long."

Shay lit a cigarette and inhaled deeply. As he continued to smoke, he turned on his mobile phone. He had several worried messages from Connor.

He saw a man asleep on the bench just inside the police station. Strange place to sleep, he thought.

Then he sent a text Connor explaining that he had just been released from a Welsh police station and that he would call him at a decent hour.

A worried Connor sent a text back asking his dad to call him. So Shay called him straight away.

Connor asked Shay, "Dad, where are you two going to go at this time of night? I'll leave now and come and get you both, you've got no wheels now!" Not surprisingly, Connor sounded extremely tired.

"Son, go back to sleep, it's the middle of the night," replied Shay. "I'm grateful, Son, but it's a long drive and you'll never make it. I'll call you at a decent hour."

Shay was worried about Ruby who seemed to be taking forever to be released. He was also very concerned that Ronnie may be lying in wait in Cardigan for both of them. He called Middlesex police and got through to CID who told him that Billy was aware that the car had been seized but the location wasn't going to be revealed to Billy for a period of one week, due to Shay and Ruby's circumstances. They also informed him that Billy had been bailed regarding the death threat charges.

The man on the bench began to stir. "Ho'way man," he said in his north east accent before wiping his mouth. "Any chance of a smoke?"

"Yeah, there you go mate." Shay passed him a cigarette.

They chatted for a few minutes. The man explained that he had worked in Wales eight months ago and that he had been picked up in Newcastle that evening and brought back to Wales for questioning and charging regarding an incident that he had been involved in during his time in Wales. Then he went on to explain that he was now stranded in Wales without money or any way of getting home to Newcastle. As the conversation continued, it turned out that he was a Newcastle United fan. He and Shay had a mutual acquaintance in Bankins, one of their top boys.

Shay waited and worried about Ruby. He decided that the madness must end. He sent a text to Janice telling her that he was waiting for Ruby to be released. He then asked her to speak to Billy and that he would call him in a few hours to put an end to the stupidity that was now effecting so many people.

A broken and exhausted Ruby appeared in the foyer at three forty five and approached Shay. An overwhelming feeling came over her when she saw Shay. They kissed and held each other tightly before she pulled away and asked Shay for a cigarette.

The man on the bench was asleep once more. Shay told Ruby of the stranger's situation. "Ahhh bless him," said Ruby. "Maybe we could leave him some money to get something for breakfast."

With that, Shay approached the sleeping man, slid a twenty pound note beneath his torso and left a packet of cigarettes on the bench for him for when he awoke.

Resembling a pair of zombies and struggling with their bags, they walked down a steep hill towards a pub/hotel. Understandably, the place was in darkness. They walked on through the dimly lit street and found another called The Country Hotel, again it was in darkness. They rang the night bell and waited for the night porter to respond. No response. Like a modern day Mary and Joseph needing a room for the night, they walked all the way back up the steep cobbled hill back towards the police station. They spotted a supermarket sign in the distance. They walked through an alleyway opposite the police station towards a twenty four hour supermarket.

Tired beyond all comprehension, they walked into the supermarket. Squinting at the bright lighting inside the store, they purchased two sandwiches and a couple of drinks. They stood outside the store and ate their food as if they had not eaten for a week, putting an end to their hunger.

Whilst standing outside waiting for morning to come, they had called every taxi firm, to no avail. It appeared Welsh taxi firms didn't operate during twilight hours.

It was now six am. Ruby and Shay watched as a car pulled into the car park. A lady got out of her car and walked towards the store. She walked passed Shay and Ruby and did a double-take.

The lady looked concerned and asked in her thick Welsh accent, "You two alright?"

Slightly taken aback, Shay and Ruby said they were fine.

"Are you waiting for someone?" the lady asked.

"Erh, no, we've been trying to get hold of a taxi but nobody seems to be about yet," replied Shay.

"Well, if you wait for a couple of minutes, I'll just run inside and then I can drop you off, if it's local," suggested the lady.

"Oh really, thanks, that'd be great. We'll give you some money for your time," said a grateful Shay.

With that, the lady went into supermarket. Ruby and Shay started to get their bags together and commented on how kind the lady was, after all, she didn't know them from Adam; they could have been anyone.

The lady was not long before she came out. "Come on then, we'll try and get your bags in the boot."

The three of them walked over to the car and the lady opened her boot, revealing a mass of cleaning products. She explained that she was a contract cleaner, the reason why she was up and about so early. Shay got into the front passenger seat and Ruby got into the back. Shay told the lady that they needed to get to a hotel and that he and Ruby had tried in the early hours of the morning but had no luck. The lady told them that as it was now six thirty, somebody should be able to accommodate them. Whilst driving to the hotel she had in mind, the lady explained that the reason she did a double take at them was because she thought she recognised Ruby. Obviously, she didn't, but she continued to say how Ruby looked like somebody she knew. They had not travelled far and they arrived at the hotel. As coincidence would have it, it was one of the hotels that Shay and Ruby had tried in the early hours, The Country Hotel. Not wanting to be any more of a hindrance to the helpful lady, knowing that she had to get to work, they said that they would get out there and try the porter again. The lady refused to take any money and wished them luck.

They took their bags and put them down at the front of the hotel and laughed at how you wouldn't get Joe-public in London being as helpful and trusting as that lady was. They walked towards the black railings that separated the pavement from the main road and each lit a cigarette. The roads now had some traffic travelling on them. It was a chilly morning and slightly overcast.

Shay stared at Ruby and said, "You're so beautiful Eyes."

Ruby looked around at Shay in mock horror. "You what! You're joking aren't you! I copped a glance of myself in the supermarket, I look like I've been dragged through a hedge backwards!"

Shay laughed and told her that she always looked beautiful to him.

They had now been up for over twenty four hours and were dead on their feet. Shay stubbed out his cigarette and walked over to the main entrance of the hotel and rang the night porter bell. Again, no sign of life. After half an hour of standing and patiently waiting, a weary and apologetic porter came to the door and took them through to the reception. He checked them into a family room, the only room available. The room was too expensive for their tight budget but their physical and mental tiredness was now unbearable and their budget wasn't their primary concern.

They entered the room. "'Ere, that geezer's had our trousers down! All that money for this!" Ruby exclaimed. The room was basic, the bathroom had barely enough room to swing a cat in and the windows couldn't be opened. Despite being overcharged, sleep took precedence. They showered and then slept until ten am.

They were awoken by a text message from Dave Timbre, Billy's mate and a member of the criminal family that knew Ronnie very well. In his message, Dave asked Ruby to call him.

"Why would I want to call him?" said Ruby, "What's he got to do with it?"

Shay had had enough and decided to call Billy. With a white towel wrapped around his waist, Shay paced the room waiting for Billy to answer the phone. Ultimately, Billy answered and Shay calmly said, "Billy, listen up and stay calm. Start shouting the odds and I'll just hang up."

Like an erupting volcano, Billy exploded, "Shay, you bastard! You listen to me! You're fucking dead do you hear me? We know where you are! You can record this call and give it to the police if you want, to be honest, I don't give a fuck anymore! I told you I'll do time for the both of you and I mean it!"

Shay interrupted him, "Stop losing it all the time, Billy! Let's just sort this out, this is nonsense!"

"Fuck you Sullivan!" Billy continued to boom down the phone. "You keep running, but you'd best keep looking over your shoulder!"

"I ain't bothered about you Billy but why'd you get this Ronnie and other firms involved? What's Ronnie's surname?"

"Never you mind what his surname is you f......" Whilst Billy was mid sentence, Shay ended the call, not wanting to give Billy the opportunity to abuse and threaten any longer. There was no way of reasoning with a madman.

Ruby had got the gist of the call from what Shay was saying but asked him what was said. Shay told Ruby word for word how the call went. She replied that he had done his best and did well to keep so calm. Bearing in mind what they had already been put through thus far, Shay proved himself to be the bigger man by making the call and trying to make the peace.

They agreed that they would have to dispose of yet another phone and purchase another one. This was more expense but they could not afford for people to know their number. This time, they would buy another pay-as-you-go and not give their number to anyone. It was still a mystery to them both how Janice and Billy had got their number in the first place.

They showered, got dressed and checked out of the hotel. The room had been paid for a twenty four hour period but they had only spent a few hours there. The porter was kind enough to return some money and let Shay and Ruby leave their bags in reception whilst they went out. On foot, they set off to the shops with the dismantled phone in Ruby's handbag. They walked by a river and Ruby got out the broken phone bit by bit. Shay disposed of the phone in various locations of the river.

Having then purchased another phone, they sat at a quaint little coffee shop by the river and had coffee, contemplating what their next move was to be.

Ruby spooned the milky foam from the top of her latte and Shay drank his double espresso. It was now a gorgeous day and the sun, shining brightly, made the river twinkle as though it was covered in a blanket of stars. Ruby thought to herself how it was a shame that they couldn't enjoy the day and their surroundings because of their unjustified situation. She sat dabbing her eye that was watering from the brightness reflecting off of the water when Shay remarked, "Now we're in danger, we should fear every stranger."

Ruby agreed and suggested, "Well, you could give Jack a call and see what kind of reception you get?"

Shay tilted his head back, drained the last of his espresso and then reminded Ruby, "But Bungle said he wasn't to be trusted, remember? I'm confused about that though. The only reason for Jack to turn is that the company owes him money for a job in Kent that I subcontracted to him. Maybe he's just waiting till he has his money from Billy? He's no one's fool, it's in his interest to keep on Billy's side really. I think we should get out of Wales, baby. I know that the police said that they wouldn't tell Billy where the car was for another week but cock ups do happen. It was because of a cock up by the police that we were banged up for over sixteen hours! Maybe we should head off to Ireland for a few days?"

"Yeah, I make you right," replied Ruby, "We can't afford to be someone else's mistake again. I'll go anywhere to be honest but let's get out of here today. I'll just go to the toilet and then we'll go back to the hotel."

Shay agreed and told Ruby that he was going to give Connor another call.

"Morning Son, did you get back to sleep alright?"

Connor was chirpy and replied, "Alright Dad, yeah, I got back off to sleep ok, cheers. I feel pretty good today actually. How are you two? Is there anything you want me to do?"

"How'd you fancy a drive to Cardiff, Con? It's a two and a half hour drive at least. If you're not able then just say so, I know it's a long way. But if you can, we'll get a train from Cardigan and be in Cardiff for about three o'clock this afternoon." Shay was reluctant to ask this of Connor, especially as he had only passed his driving test a month or so ago but his son was the only person that he trusted.

"I'll be there Dad, I've told you before, if I can do anything to help you both then I will."

"Thanks Son, see you soon and drive carefully. Just take your time, don't rush. Love you."

Shay and Ruby returned to the hotel and collected their bags. They walked about a mile to Cardigan train station and purchased two single tickets to Cardiff.

The ticket man said, "You'll have to wait half hour for the Cardiff train, boyo."

Half an hour wasn't too bad, they thought as they waited on the platform. The platform was bustling with commuters. Paranoid, they scanned everyone who awaited the imminent arrival of the train, but everyone seemed genuine.

They climbed into a busy carriage and managed to find an empty compartment with a table. Not long after the train had set off, an elderly man came down the carriage with a beverage trolley. He was smartly dressed in a dark navy blue suit and his snowy white hair was swept over to one side. Ruby thought to herself how sweet he looked, she had a lot of time and respect for elderly people. Shay and Ruby each had a cup of tea and a Kit-Kat.

"This tea's better than the tea I got given in the police cell!" Ruby remarked.

Shay laughed and said, "You're lucky you got a cup of tea! They must have liked you! All I got was one cup of water, and even that was warm!"

Shay moved down the carriage to use the toilet. As he steadily moved through the carriage, he gave each seat a glance in an attempt to determine whether each passenger was genuine or not. Billy's statement of 'we know where you are,' probably referred to Manchester. Shay hoped this was the case. Good, he thought. Let Billy's wallet get exhausted by his henchmen's expensive search of Manchester.'

Shay returned from the toilet and slid behind the table into his seat. As he sat down, he saw that a folded napkin was positioned on his side of the table. Shay looked across at Ruby who sat with a grin on her face. He picked up the napkin and unfolded it, to read *'I Love You London, Eyes x x x.'* Shay smiled and put it into his pocket. "Ahhh thank you Eyes, I'll keep that," he said with affection.

The train pulled into Port Talbot and some passengers disembarked, including a mother and her child who had sat nearby. The train the pulled away and rolled on via Bridgend.

"Not long to go now baby," Shay told Ruby.

The train pulled into Cardiff station. Connor had texted to say that he would be in Cardiff within the next twenty minutes. They knew that they had put Connor, the young novice driver, under stress with the long drive to Cardiff. Earlier on, Shay and Ruby had considered taking the train to Paddington but they felt that a return to a London train station so soon would be running a risk.

Shay replied to Connor's text and thought how precious Connor was to him. Shay loved his son dearly and admired his grace, calmness and maturity. Shay often wished he possessed the same traits.

SIX

Common Knowledge

Shay and Ruby left Cardiff train station. They walked away from the station towards The Western Pub, which Shay knew of from his visits with Chelsea. Shay told Ruby that from a slightly higher point they would be able to spot the arrival of Connor. They each enjoyed a long awaited cigarette and spotted Connor pulling into the set down area of Cardiff station.

"Ahhh look, there he is, bless him," said Ruby.

Shay looked over. "Perfect timing by boy wonder," he said and smiled with pride.

They walked at quick pace over to Connor.

Ruby found it hard to keep up with Shay and called out from behind him, "Hold on a minute! My legs are half the length of yours!"

They soon got to Connor's car, he was standing by the driver's door.

"Alright Con, you ok? You look tired," Ruby said as she gave Connor a hug.

"Nah, I'm ok cheers, Ruby," said Connor as he hugged her back.

Shay looked on at the two of them and thought how great it was that they both got on so well.

"Oi! So where's my hug, Son?" jested Shay loudly.

Father and son gave each other a tight squeeze and a peck on the cheek. "Thanks for coming to get us, I know it wasn't easy. We really appreciate it, Con," said Shay.

"I said I'd do anything for you two, Dad. I'm just glad you're both ok," replied Connor.

"I'll drive now Son," said Shay as he shut the boot of the car.

"Don't think so, Dad!" Laughed Connor. "This is my motor and I'll drive it. You've already been nicked for driving someone else's motor!"

Ruby jumped into the back seat and Shay into the front passenger seat. With Connor in pole position, he cautiously pulled out of Cardiff train station.

"So where do you want me to take you, Dad? You're not going back to London are you?" Asked Connor.

"Not quite Son, but near enough. Take us to Heathrow Airport. We've decided to get an evening flight to Dublin and spend a few days over the pond just to let the dust settle," replied Shay.

"Are you going to hire a car in Dublin and drive down to nan and grandad's then?"

"No," said Shay, "They don't need the grief. All this madness could be too much for them considering their health and age. We'll just get a car in Dublin and drive to the West of Ireland. I've never been there, it's the only region that I've never been to in Ireland, plus no one will know us there."

As they drove at seventy miles an hour on the M4 Eastbound, Ruby watched the heavy eyed Connor in his rear view mirror. She could see that he was shattered and suggested, "Why don't you stop at the next services, Con, and let your dad drive for a bit? You've been driving for hours now and you look really tired."

"Yeah, I think I will," replied a relieved Connor and he exited the motorway and drove into a service station.

The three of them had a quick coffee and snack at the motorway service station and were soon back on their travels to Heathrow Airport, with Shay now driving.

As they approached the airport, they decided that a quick drop off at departures would be best. Connor had no need to enter the airport. It was best that he resumed driving and return home to London before it got too late. There were hugs and kisses all round and Connor was told repeatedly to drive carefully.

"See you in a few days Son. Everything will have calmed down by then," Shay said as he handed Connor some money.

Ruby reminded Connor, "Remember what I said, Connor, if you get tired, just pull over." After an emotional farewell Ruby and Shay entered Heathrow Airport and made their way to ticket reservations to discover that seats were available and the flight was due to take off in three hours. They showed their driving licences as identification and purchased two tickets. They decided to change up some money into Euros and then go straight through security as it would be safer in a departure lounge as opposed to the main hub of the airport where a possible spotter could be planted laying in wait.

Walking through the airport to security was nerve-wrecking. Feeling scared, they thought that anyone who looked in their direction had followed them and were in cahoots with Billy. Paranoia fuelled them to walk speedily to security, where they could not get through quick enough.

Very relieved once through security, they decided to have a bit of dinner and found a quiet booth. Shay called Steve again but continually got his voicemail. So he then called Spooner.

"Hello mate, it's Shay."

"Alright, Shay," said Spooner, "You still up north?"

Shay laughed, "Yeah, constantly on the move, mate."

"Hmmm. That's the best thing for you, to keep moving. Jack

ain't too happy with you now, Shay. He's got the hump about the money he's owed."

Shay was confused. "What money? He's due a payment next week from the company. If I get this mess sorted out then nothing changes, if not, then Jack needs to speak to Billy."

Spooner's tone had changed. He was more aggressive in his response. "Was this all planned, Shay? Did you and that girl plan this all along? I've been trying to help you out, mate, but it looks like all this time you've been mugging all of us off! I tell you this for nothing Shay, even your own are looking for you now, as well as Billy and his crew!"

"What you on about?" exclaimed Shay.

"What am I on about? You run off with the girl fair enough, but clearing out the company's money is bang out of order, Shay," shouted an angry Spooner. "Look, I don't give a fuck about Billy! I don't even know that mug! But you gotta pay back our mutual acquaintances!"

This really got Shay's back up. Were his own mates now turning their backs on him?

"Hold the phone, Spooner!" Said Shay, "I've not taken any money out of the company! Is that what that slag Billy has put about? That we nicked money?"

"Look, do what you gotta do, but watch your back and leave me out of it! Oh yeah, and I heard a good pal of yours has just got the security of Billy's nightclub. Just give the geezer back his money, Shay." Said Spooner before he hung up.

In reaction, Shay immediately called Jack and found that his mobile was turned off. Irritated, he then called Steve once again whose phone was still going directly to voicemail. Shay gave a long sigh and looked at Ruby who had worry written all over her face as she had already interpreted Shay's conversation with Spooner.

"I'm done with this, let's just get over to Ireland and away from all this madness," said Shay. "Steve and Jack think we've stolen all the company funds, some mates they are ay!"

After such a distasteful conversation, both Shay and Ruby had lost their appetites and just ordered coffee instead. Shay decided to call Bridget, his Sister. They had always got on well and generally just have a good laugh together. Bridget loved football too, she was a Manchester United fanatic and had extensive knowledge of the beautiful game. Shay and Bridget would discuss various games and managers' tactics on a regular basis via telephone calls between England and Ireland. He knew that he could trust Bridget with his life, he felt that they shared the same integrity and neither of the siblings were interested in gossip, like many other members of the family. Bridget and her husband, Peter, had together a son, Aiden, who was married and owned a restaurant in the south of France and a daughter, Charlotte, who was living and working in Hong Kong.

Shay dialled the Irish number and waited.

"Hello," said Bridget curiously, not knowing who was calling her.

"Bridge, how's things?" said Shay in a chirpy voice.

"Shay!" Bridget was alarmed, yet relieved. "Thank God you called! Are ye ok?"

Shay felt his sister's concern and sensed that she knew something. What did she know? Or did she actually know at all?

"I'm in a bit of bother, Sis," said Shay, and went on, "I don't want mum and dad to know, and I don't want you to start worrying...."

"Shay! I already know what's happened and so do mum and dad. Where are you? Are you safe? Oh I've been so worried about you!" Her voice expressed concern.

"How do you know, Bridge? And how do mum and dad know?" asked Shay who then continued to answer Bridget's questions, "Erh Yeah, sorry, I'm fine.... Sorry, we're fine. So how do you all know?"

"Well, Tommy O'Neill heard it somewhere, somehow or other in London and the eejit called mum and told her. Mum and dad are worried sick, Shay."

"What Tommy? Dad's Nephew? How'd he get to know?"

"Yes, our cousin Tommy, auntie Kate's son. Where are you Shay?"

"Heathrow Airport. We're getting on a flight to Dublin in half an hour. I've got Ruby with me…."

"Yes we know," interrupted Bridget, "We know everything. Tommy gave mum the full run down on Saturday morning. Shay, Peter and I are flying out to the South of France first thing in the morning to spend some time with Aiden and his family so I won't be around for a week. Where are ye going? You'd better give mum and dad a call and let them know ye're ok."

"Can you call them please, Bridge, and tell them that I will call when I'm out of Dublin Airport later tonight? We'll head over to the West of Ireland and book in somewhere. I can't go near your place or mum and dad's, I don't want to bring trouble to your doors."

Bridget agreed to call their parents and then advised Shay where he and Ruby could go, "Head for Connemara or Westport in Mayo, ye will be safe there, no one will know ye. Oh, and dump that phone you have and get a new one in Ireland, then make sure you text me so I know ye're both ok. I'll save your new number discreetly."

Having told each other they loved each other and wished each other safe flights, Shay felt comforted at his sister's concern for him and Ruby.

Shay explained to Ruby that his family in Ireland were aware of their situation.

"Oh! How'd they know?" asked a shocked Ruby.

"My cousin, Tommy, who I've not seen for years phoned my parents and told them. God knows how he heard about it!"

"So is Tommy from your mum's side of the family or your dad's?"

Shay explained, "He's my aunt Kate's son, and she's my dad's sister. I've not seen Tommy since we were both kids. Mind you, I'd see his dad in Kilburn from time to time. When I was drinking in Kilburn I'd often bump into my uncle Danny, he's a right character. He's from Cork City; don't ask me what he does for a living, nobody seems to know but he's always got plenty of money on him!" Shay laughed and continued, "His nickname is Danny Good Looking, 'cos apparently he was really good looking when he was younger. You know how nicknames just stick. He's a right laugh. I used to love having a beer with him. A lot of people say he's well connected, perhaps that's how my cousin heard."

Ruby was always intrigued to hear about Shay's family, his Irish roots and the many stories that he had to tell, but they had no time to sit and chat. They quickly finished their coffees and went to the boarding gate and awaited to board the flight to Dublin.

Once embarked and bound for Ireland, they wondered how long they would be away from England and questioned if the nightmare would follow them.

SEVEN

Emerald Isle

W elcome to the Emerald Isle, Eyes! The land of Saints and Scholars," Shay announced as they exited the plane.

"Cor, it's chucking it down!" exclaimed Ruby.

Shay laughed, "Yeah, it does rain a lot here."

They hired a Volkswagen Golf and made their way out of the airport. Ruby had removed her jacket and held it over her head as they walked to the car park to find the car in its designated bay. Shay moved the seat back and adjusted the mirrors.

Ruby threw her wet jacket onto the back seat and remarked,

"Well, this is alright, ay London. Quite a nice car actually. God I'm so tired, I can hardly keep my eyes open," she yawned.

"Me too, let's just book-in somewhere near the airport tonight and head for Galway or somewhere tomorrow," suggested Shay.

Relieved, Ruby replied, "Yeah, lots of puddles and sleep!"

Ruby and Shay had always referred to cuddles as puddles, a code word they used when Shay would attend meetings at Billy's nightclub office just incase they were ever overheard by somebody. It was a word that stuck and one they used often.

The following morning as Ruby showered, she could hear Shay singing whilst shaving,

"A hungry feeling
Came o'er me stealing
And the mice were squealing, in my prison cell
And the auld triangle, would go jingle jangle
All around the banks, of the Royal Canal"

It was not unusual for Shay to sing whilst shaving, he loved to sing. He had grown up listening to his father singing and every Sunday morning would be a time when the records were played whilst his mother cooked the Sunday roast.

Ruby called out from the shower, "What's all that about then? Mice and a triangle!"

Shay laughed as he explained to Ruby that during a conversation with his father, the mere mention of a town or place would prompt Mick to burst into song and that song would be about the town or place that was mentioned. He went on to give an example, "Right, so if I told my dad that we were in Dublin, he'd probably start singing *'The Rare Auld Times,'* a Dublin song.

"Ha, not U2 or Westlife then!" Laughed Ruby as she washed her hair.

"No. He likes to sing the old, old songs!" Replied Shay.

As Ruby stepped out of the shower and reached for a towel she said to Shay, "Your family sound really nice, a good laugh."

"Yeah they are as it happens," smiled Shay.

Now more refreshed and energised, Shay and Ruby started their journey and headed for the West of Ireland. The rain continued to fall heavily and the car's window wipers went ninety to the dozen as they entered the County of West Meath. Ruby spent the entire journey with her nose pressed against the window, admiring the scenery that looked beautiful even though it was raining. She'd never been to Ireland and was excited to be there.

They found a small village called Kinnegad, and decided to stop there and stretch their legs. A pub that served breakfast was open, allowing them to get something to eat. They went into the pub, took their seats and ordered a full Irish breakfast; each with coffee. Shay always liked to start the day with a light breakfast whilst in contrast, Ruby never ate breakfast. Now in Ireland, the smell of black and white pudding, sausages to die for with lashings of Chef sauce was too much for Shay to resist. Of course, this was a new experience for Ruby who had never tried black or white pudding and had never heard of Chef sauce. The pub was quiet and they were the only customers. As they ate, they heard heavy footsteps on the wooden floor. A man in his late fifties dressed in cowboy boots, a white stetson and a leather waistcoat called over to them, "Ye on your holidays?"

"Yes," replied Shay, "We're just touring, heading off to Galway shortly."

"Is that so!" exclaimed the excited man. "I'm a Galway taxi driver! I'm on my way back to Galway now, had a drop to do at Dublin Airport this morning. Ye can follow me back to Galway if ye like."

Typical of the Irish friendliness, thought Shay. "Very kind of you but we're gonna take a slow drive, stopping here and there."

"Ok, shur no worries," said the kind Galway man. "Take my card and if ye are ever going out in Galway ye can call me. Tis a hard city to get around with all the one ways nowadays." He left with a huge wave and friendly smile.

"Ahhh, he was nice," said Ruby after just having had her first encounter with an Irishman. Shay laughed as he got up to go and pay for their breakfasts, "Yeah, a right character!"

As they left the pub they noticed a phone box.

"I'm going to call my parents, Eyes, they'll be worried. I told Bridget that I would call them last night," Shay said.

"Ok, I'll wait here and I'll phone my mum after you've made your call."

"Your mum will see an Irish number come up, can you trust her?" replied Shay as he walked across to the phone box.

"Yeah, course I can," said Ruby.

As Shay stepped into the phone box, Ruby stood outside the pub where there was just enough shelter to stop her from getting soaked by the heavy rainfall. Ruby stood admiring how old fashioned all of the buildings were, when a car pulled up. The driver got out, an elderly man, in his early seventies at least. He smiled as he approached the pavement where Ruby was standing, "Morning. Damp auld day," he said.

Ruby smiled back, replying, "Morning, yeah, it's definitely damp alright."

The old man hobbled closer towards Ruby and continued, "What are yer doing standing in the rain? Are yer enjoying the fine Irish weather?"

Ruby laughed. "I'm not getting too wet standing here. I'm just waiting for my boyfriend to finish a phone call."

The old man stood with hands in his pockets and shrugged his shoulders, "Well now, I'm going inter the butchers to get me dinner, I've no-one at home to do it for me anymore. Enjoy Ireland Miss!"

"I will, thank you, take care," Ruby replied.

She watched the endearing old man shuffle along in the rain to the butchers thinking, what a sweet old man.

Shay wiped the rain from his face and waited for one of his parents to answer the phone.

"Hello," said a chirpy voice. Shay's mother, Josie, a woman in her seventies and so full of energy that everyone would say how she looked and acted like a woman in her fifties.

"Hello, Mum," Shay replied.

"Shay! Oh, Jesus, Mary and Joseph! Are ye ok? Where are ye? Have they harmed you son?"

"Don't worry Mum, we're safe now we're in Ireland. We got into Dublin Airport last night and we're moving across the country now. I spoke to Bridget last night; did she call you and Dad?"

"Yes, Bridget called us last night. Come home Son. I've the candle burning in the window to show ye the way home. Ye'll both be safe here," pleaded the loving mother who desperately wanted to protect and help her son.

"No, Mum, I can't and won't bring trouble to your door," Shay explained.

"Head down to Kerry, you could stay with some family in Dingle or Castleisland. Ye'd be safe there."

"No, Mum, it's best we go somewhere where no one knows us."

"Ok Son. Are the Police helping ye out? Are the MFI involved?" Concern was evident in her voice.

Shay laughed to himself, he was sure his mum meant the MI5 and not the MFI. The former furniture and kitchen outlet would have no interest in Shay and Ruby's situation.

Shay held back the giggles and replied without correcting his mum, "The police are, but not the MI5, it's not that serious Mum. I will call you later on. We've gotta buy a new mobile and then we'll be in touch. Don't worry Mum, we'll keep one step ahead of them! Bye…" Shay went to hang up the receiver when he could still hear his mum on the other end.

"Hold on! Shay! Hold on, don't go yet, speak to yer father," insisted Josie before she called her husband, Mick to the phone, "Mick! Mick! Come on! Hurry, tis Shay on the phone… Come on will yer Mick Sullivan! He's in a phone box!"

Taking a long gasp for breath before speaking, Mick spoke to his son in his deep, broad County Waterford accent, "Halloo….."

"Alright Dad, how's it going?" Shay enquired.

"Jesus Shay, where are ye?" asked Mick.

"Erh some town called Kinny-gade," replied Shay.

"Kinnegad! West Meath," said Mick, correcting his son's London pronunciation before continuing, "Where are ye heading? Get somewhere out of sight, Shay."

"We're heading West, dunno exactly where yet; Mayo, Westport, or Connemara, not sure yet I don't know that region..."

Despite Shay being mid-sentence, with the mention of Connemara Mick burst into song,

"The mornings not so long ago
I bid you fond goodbye
My heart was beating in my breast
The tears rolled from my eyes
The smiling valley lay behind
The stormy seas before
And the long, long waves rolling
On the Connemara shore."

Shay loved to hear his father sing but perhaps the timing was poor, as he pumped more coins into the hungry phone box.

Josie interrupted her husband and exclaimed, "Tis is no time for singing, Mick Sullivan! Give me that phone!" A laughing Josie was now in charge of the receiver, "Jesus! That man at times!"

Shay laughed, "Oh he's alright, Mum. Look, I've gotta go, I'll call you both when I get a new mobile. Love you both."

"Yes do, please God. God be with you, Son, and that girl of yours. I'll say a prayer for ye."

"Yep, yep, ok then Mum, Bye..." He attempted to end the conversation for the second time; however, the petite Josie started another yet conversation, "Oh Shay! Wait! Make sure you phone before seven, we're going to mass at half past seven. Poor Mrs. Doyle passed away last night, may God rest her soul. You knew Mrs Doyle didn't you? She was in the hospital and..."

Shay interrupted as the money was running out, "Look, Mum, I've gotta go, I'll call you when I get a mobile." He hadn't a clue who poor Mrs Doyle was.

"Ok Shay, I love you. I'll light a candle for ye both and say a prayer at mass for ye. Bye, bye love..." said Josie.

Shay came out of the phone box and waved for Ruby to come over. He gave her some change so that she could call her mum, "I'm gonna go and sit in the car, babe, while you make your call," he said.

Ruby called her mum and jumped straight into conversation as soon as her call was answered, "Mum, Mum it's me. Look, I can't be long because I'm in a phone box and my money will run out."

Ruby's mum was surprised to hear her and asked in a concerned tone, "Ruby, are you ok? I haven't heard from you for ages, where are you?"

"We're in Ireland. Look Mum, we know for definite now that he's got people after us, that's why we had to get out and come here…"

Ruby was then interrupted by Janice, "Ruby, what are you talking about? What do you mean he's got people after you? Who told you that?"

"Mum, I'm not gonna mention names but you've got to believe me. He's paid people for Shay's head and loads of other people have been paid to find us. Mum, I've gotta go, my money's running out!" exclaimed Ruby.

"Ruby. Hold on a minute. Since I last spoke to you a few things have happened. The police are involved now. Apparently, they have a tape recording of you trying to get access into the business bank accounts."

"What!?" shouted a shocked Ruby. "What are you talking about? Why would I do that?"

Janice cut in, "Look Ruby, I know that you love Shay and that you want to be together and that's fine by me but all I ask is that you keep in touch so that I know you're alright."

By now the money in the phone box just about to run out. She told her mum that she would be back in touch and that she loved her.

She ran back to the car and they pressed on towards Galway. As they entered the outskirts of the town the rain relented and the sun attempted to shine.

Shay and Ruby purchased a new pay-as-you-go mobile phone in a supermarket. On their way out of the store, Shay noticed a DVD shop called Zhivago's. Being a movie anorak, he could not resist the urge to have look inside. "C'mon Eyes, let's have a look in here!"

Ruby found a film and waved it in the air excitedly, saying, "Oi London, look what I've found! And it's really cheap!"

Shay replied from across the aisle, "Yeah, great, we'll get it! And we're getting this as well!" He waved *Papillon* in Ruby's direction.

"Oh yeah! That's the one you told me about!" she exclaimed.

They bought the two films and returned to the car where Ruby set up their new phone.

Shay sent Bridget a text stating that they had arrived safely in Galway City. Almost immediately, the phone rang, "Hiya love, are ye ok?" asked Bridget.

Shay replied, "Yeah we're good, Bridge. Did you and Peter arrive ok?"

"Oh yeah, yeah, all went smoothly, thank God. We're staying in a beautiful hotel. It's absolutely gorgeous here, it really is. Anyhow, I spoke to Mum and I think she's arranged a hotel for ye in Connemara somewhere. You'd better call them as soon as you can. I've your number now anyway and I'll save it under another name to be on the safe side. We'll talk later love, Peter's downstairs waiting; we're going to Aiden's for lunch and we're running late. Love you darling, speak to you later."

"Ok Bridge, enjoy and I'll speak to you later, love to all," and he hung up.

"Your sister seems really lovely. You can tell you're close," Ruby continued, "What's her husband like?"

"Peter's a sound bloke, they're both sound. Bridget looked out for me when I was a kid and Peter was like an older brother to me really. They're good fun. I tell ya, they got that catering lark off to a tee. The pair of 'em make a good team. Peter's got that gift, you know… he's a natural, he can hold a conversation with anyone regarding any topic. He's a great salesman, Peter would sell a spit roast pig and pork sausages at a Bar Mitzvah and get away with it!" said Shay.

As promised, Shay called his parents, "Hello Mum, we've got another new phone, we're in Galway now."

The organised and excitable Josie replied, "Hello honey! How are yer? Right, now listen to your mother… Your father and I have booked ye into a hotel in Roundstone, Connemara. We've booked it for a week, bed and breakfast and yer evening dinners so make sure ye eat! The hotel is called The Oak Tree; a married couple have it." She started to drift away from the facts and really go into detail, "The lady sounded very nice on the phone, her name is Margaret and her husband is called Pat. They've been married for forty six years and have three children. Ye'll get on grand, they sound lovely!"

Shay was relaying the information to Ruby who was busily writing it all down.

He felt ashamed. He had always done ok for himself where earning money was concerned and never relied on anyone but himself. Now middle aged, he was being helped by his elderly parents.

"Right, hold on there Son, I'll put your father on and he will direct you, speak later love."

Mick drew a deep breath and gave a little cough, "Shay, head out toward Moycullen and then head for Ballynahinch and you should see signs for Roundstone. Tis a nice scenic drive like, especially on a fine day. You got that? Call when ye get there. Good luck." Mick very rarely said 'goodbye' instead, he would inevitably say 'good luck'.

"Hold on, hold on Mick! I need to speak to Shay again!" Exclaimed Josie.

"Erh, erh… hold on one minute, Shay, yer mother wants to talk to yer."

"I forgot to tell yer Shay, I booked ye in under the name of Keane, I know you love our little Robbie Keane," laughed Josie, "So remember, ye are married and your name is Keane, speak later darling."

As Shay took the phone away from his ear, he could still hear his mum speaking. "Oh yes, I told the woman at the hotel that you're my son-in-law and that Ruby is my daughter. I had to do that because my credit card has Sullivan on it and if I told her you were my son she'd presume your name was also Sullivan."

A grateful Shay replied, "Thanks Mum, and thank Dad for me. I'll call you when we've checked in."

Ruby told Shay how kind and caring she thought his parents were and how she felt overwhelmed at the fact they were helping her too. She thought to herself about how they would be well within their rights to shun her, especially in these circumstances, after all, they didn't even know her.

Shay and Ruby made their way to Roundstone and admired the stunning view of Lough Corrib.

They pulled into the driveway of The Oak Tree Hotel, a large Manor House surrounded with well kept green lawns and well maintained flowerbeds. It was extremely peaceful and picturesque.

As they entered the hotel hallway Ruby stopped Shay. "Who's that lady I keep seeing everywhere. Look, they've even got ornaments of her in here?"

Slightly baffled, Shay asked, "What lady Eyes?"

"That statue!" Ruby pointed to their left. "It's everywhere we go. Who is she?"

Shay looked to his left and spotted a large statue and laughed loudly, "That Lady! That's the Virgin Mary!"

"Oh right, Jesus' mum," said a satisfied Ruby.

A grey haired woman in her sixties had silently entered the reception. She asked, "The Kaenes I presume?"

This startled Shay and Ruby, they both wondered, how long was she there?

"Erh no, the Keane's," replied Shay as he corrected the lady.

"Yes dear, that's what I said, the Kaenes. Your wife's mother called and booked ye in for a week with breakfast and dinner."

A man passed them in the corridor and nodded, they nodded back, and the lady announced to Shay and Ruby, "That's my husband, Pat, and I'm Margaret. Your mother and I had quite a long chat on the phone, she said ye had just got married and were on honeymoon touring Ireland."

Margaret then glanced dubiously at Ruby's left hand. Shay and Ruby could tell by her pursed lips and slightly raised eyebrow that she had noted a missing wedding ring. They took the room key from a suspicious Margaret, ran up the stairs like naughty children and entered their room where they fell onto the bed laughing.

EIGHT

The Oak Tree

Ruby rose from the bed as Shay watched adoringly. It was time for the Ruby's usual inspection of the bathroom and bedding. Whilst Ruby entered the bathroom, Shay sat at the bedroom window, with phone in hand; one leg crossed over the other observing the lush green hilly landscape.

Ruby skipped out of the bathroom and over to the bed. Pulling back the bed covers, she gave a quick inspection. "It's immaculate in here, London, spotless," she said. "The bathroom's lovely too. Oi, guess what! It's actually got a bath! What a luxury!"

Shay laughed and replied, "Has it? We'll have to jump in that later. Eyes, I'm going to make some calls and let my family know we're here."

"Oh yeah ok. Can you pass on my thanks, please." She began the now familiar process of unpacking their bags.

Shay uncrossed his legs as he dialled Bridget's number.

"Hello," said a masculine voice. It was Bridget's husband.

"Peter, it's Shay, how you doing mate?"

"Alwite Shay, h'az it ga'ing mate?" replied Peter in his exaggerated but excellent impersonation of a London accent, often used to greet Shay.

"Not bad mate, been better."

Peter chuckled. "Yeah I heard you were in a bit of trouble, ah well, you'll rise above it!"

"How's things with you then, Peter?"

"Ah, struggling on," replied a jovial Peter.

"Nice lunch, Peter?" enquired Shay.

"Ah we did, yeah. The finest!" Said Peter in a satisfied manor and continued, "Bridget is in the kitchen talking with the chef. Oh... hold on... here she comes, I'll speak to you soon Shay, take care and behave yourself, if at all possible," said the laughing Peter.

Shay overheard Bridget in the background saying to Peter, "Is that Shay? Oh hang up Peter, tell him I'll call him straight back to save his credit!"

Still with the phone to his ear, Peter retorted, "Huh? Jesus Bridget!" Then went on to say, "Hang up your phone Shay, Bridget will call you straight back, take care now." With that, the phone line disconnected.

It rang again almost immediately. "Hiya love! Are ye both alright?" enquired a concerned but bubbly Bridget.

"Not bad Bridge," said Shay. "How's Aiden and Claudia?"

Claudia was Aiden's French wife. "Oh they're great!" said Bridget with her usual vivacious tone that would always cheer Shay up. "Honestly Shay, they're doing a great job on the restaurant here, they really are. Let me tell you, the chef is a real character, you know, he really is," Bridget laughed her ebullient laugh and continued, "I was just out the back with him, he's so funny you know, you'd love him Shay you really would. He's a fantastic chef. Anyhow, are ye ok, Shay?"

He explained that he felt as though he was on an express train and that he could not get off. He told Bridget that he was rapidly losing everything that he had worked for and that his business was doomed.

Bridget optimistically replied, "I know, I know. But you're alive Shay and that's what's important! Just lie low in Ireland for a while Shay, everything will work out, you'll see. And be positive! I know it's hard love, but you mustn't keep giving it energy. Stay calm, be positive etcetera, etcetera and everything will come good."

They said their farewells and that they would talk later.

Ruby had unpacked what few bits they had and was now laying on the bed reading a magazine, chuckling to herself as she watched Shay walk every inch of the room while talking on his phone. She always found it amusing how he could never sit still when talking on the phone. He would pace the floor and would stop every now and then for a couple of seconds to lean on the wardrobe or the wall and then set off again in another direction.

Shay called his parents and Connor. They were only short calls just to make sure that they were safe and ok.

Shay stood with his back to the window and he admiringly watched Ruby laid on her stomach on the bed flicking through her magazine. Ruby looked up at Shay who was stood grinning mischievously.

"What do you want?" asked Ruby, who already knew by his face what his answer would be.

"I want you," replied a playful Shay as he approached the bed, turning Ruby onto her back before passionately kissing her.

Clothes were scattered across the floor. After spending some intimate time together, Shay commented that the bed had been noisy and that they'd been pretty loud themselves.

Ruby laughed, "Oh no! Do you think anyone heard? Oh my God, I'm so embarrassed!" she squealed. "That's your fault, wanting to be naughty all of the time! I hope that Margaret never heard us! She's already onto us!"

After days of irregular sleeping patterns and broken sleep, Shay and Ruby couldn't help but fall asleep in their tranquil surroundings.

Shay awoke at seven pm and woke Ruby up with the creaking bed and noisy springs as he got out of the bed. Both feeling hungry, they went downstairs to the bar to have a pre-dinner drink.

Once downstairs in the small but welcoming bar, Shay said, "Hey, Eyes, do you think that they might have a DVD player here we could borrow? We could eat our dinner and then go to bed and watch *Papillion*!"

Ruby quickly swallowed her mouthful of brandy and lemonade. Sounding excited, she replied, "Oh yeah! That's a good idea! They might have one, go to the reception and ask Margaret, if she's not too busy."

With no further persuasion required, he went to enquire about a DVD player; walking out of the bar into reception.

"Evening Margaret, are you ok?" enquired Shay.

Margaret gave him a bashful eye and with the slightest of blushes replied, "Oh good evening. Yes, I'm fine and how's yerself after your tiring day?"

Shay sensed that Margaret had heard their earlier bedroom antics but unfazed, continued, "We were wondering if you had a DVD player we could borrow or hire, we've got a couple of DVD's we'd like to watch."

That same one eyebrow that made movement after glaring at Ruby's non-existent wedding ring started to rise again. "Oh have you indeed…" replied Margaret, "Well, we have no DVD machines here. Can ye not get some mountain air into yer lungs instead of watching DVD's?"

A relentless Shay continued his quest for the much wanted DVD player, "Is there a town near here that might have a shop that hires or sells DVD machines?"

Slightly flustered, Margaret replied, "Jesus! Is it that important to you? DVD's indeed… what kind of films are ye going to be watching?"

Shay held back his laughter. "Thrillers! No worries Margaret, it's not important. Thanks anyway though." He turned to return to the bar.

An indignant Margaret called out as Shay walked away,

"Thrillers! Hmmmm…. A good jog sounds more like what ye both need."

Laughing, Shay entered the bar and explained to Ruby that Margaret seemed to be under the impression that they wanted a DVD player so that they could watch porn day and night up in their room.

"She's got a dirty mind that one!" said Ruby, as they entered the dining room trying to stifle their laughter.

The dining room was small and unpretentious. The walls were dotted with various pictures and paintings of the hotel and its grounds, varying in its appearance from years ago to how it looked today.

They ate a good wholesome meal that the chef/husband Pat, had created. The food was basic but very tasty and there was plenty of it. They retired to their room and had a long-awaited bath before going to bed. They vowed to keep the noise down – not wanting Margaret's blood pressure to go through the roof.

They awoke bright and early the following morning, having intentionally left the curtains open so they could wake up to the glorious views of the mountainous scenery. Disappointingly, the rain was falling heavily at an acute angle and it was certainly no day for being outside.

They showered and made their way to the dining room that now had a paper sign stating 'Breakfast Room.'

Instantly, Shay and Ruby spotted Margaret, now in waitress mode. "Good morning honeymooners! Full Irish I presume?" She exited the breakfast room before they could even reply.

"She's like Basil!" laughed Shay.

Ruby laughed her distinctively loud laugh. "Fawlty Towers! Yeah, she *is* the female version of Basil!"

Minutes later, Margaret returned with a pot of piping hot coffee and placed it on the table. As Shay thanked Margaret and started to pour the coffee, she stood over the table, with her arms folded and enquired, "So what are ye doing today?"

"Erh, not sure. I had a look at the map last night and noticed that Westport is quite near here so we'll probably go for a drive there. We might even be able to get a DVD player!" replied the naughty Shay.

In an attempt to prevent herself from laughing at Shay provoking the poor Margaret, Ruby smothered her mouth with a napkin. "Good God, will yer stop!" said Margret, whose voice had risen in pitch. "Why don't ye go for a walk, or go down to the lake and have a swim for yourselves? Burn off some of that nervous energy ye have!"

A bewildered Ruby replied, "But it's raining!"

"Go'way! A drop o'rain never did anyone any harm!"

"But I haven't even got a bikini or anything."

A now very excited Margaret suggested, "Can't the pair of ye go skinny dipping? Shur no one will see ye!" And with that, Margaret's cheeks flushed and she quickly made her way to the kitchen.

Having laughed at Margaret's comical suggestions and having eaten a huge breakfast, Shay and Ruby returned to their room.

Whilst Ruby sat on the bed flicking through the television channels, Shay went into the bathroom. The unjust reality of what was happening returned. He thought to himself, what the hell am I gonna to do? My money? My business? My staff? Had it all calmed down? Was it just all an overreaction? The unknown left Shay angst-ridden, he needed answers.

Coming out of the bathroom, he said, "Eyes, I'm gonna give my uncle Danny a bell and see if he's heard anything." Shay called his parents to get his uncle's telephone number. He called the number straight away.

"Hello," answered a deep, Cork City accent. Even though Danny had been living in London for over thirty years, he hadn't lost his broad Cork accent.

"Danny Good Looking! How's it going?" Shay asked.

"Jasus bhoy! Tell me tis yerself Shay!"

"Yeah it is, how's Auntie Kate and the family?"

"No fear of 'em bhoy, no fear of 'em. Jasus Shay, don't tell me where you are! Best I don't know. Yer in big trouble I tell yer, you've some heavy people after yer like!"

"I'm somewhere in the old country, Danny, seems I can't trust any of me mates anymore."

Danny scoffed, "Shur I told yer that bhoy! I told you years ago they were all langers like. And all that football stuff… Shur yer wouldn't cop on. Now listen, give that fellow in Middlesex a call and try to sort this mess out. I've made my own enquiries and he's some heavy fellows onto yer. If he won't play ball, then lay low o'er there for a while before ye come back. These tings 'tend to calm down after a while like, do yer hear me?"

Shay thanked his favourite uncle for the tip and said he would be in touch.

The rain had eased up so Shay and Ruby decided to go for a drive to Westport, County Mayo. They purchased an inexpensive DVD player and had a coffee before returning to The Oak Tree. As they entered the hotel and headed up the carpeted stairs, unbeknown to them, Margaret spotted them from the lounge area as she talked to her cleaner. Ruby and Shay walked eagerly to their room to set up the DVD player so that they could watch *Papillion*.

Twenty minutes into the film, a loud knock on the door to their room startled them.

"God, that frightened the life outta me," Ruby said to Shay.

"Who is it?" Enquired Shay as he paused the movie.

The door slowly opened, Margaret's voice rang out, "I've made ye some tay and I have a few scones here for ye!" She walked through the room with the cups and saucers shaking, placing the tray on the small table by the window. She turned, stared at the television and asked inquisitively, "What are ye watching?"

Shay couldn't help laughing, so Ruby replied, "A prison film."

"Oh, I'll leave ye to it then." Making her way out backwards scrutinizing and scanning every inch of the room, as if looking for contraband.

"Thanks for the tea," said Ruby as Margaret shut the door behind her.

The day passed and the evening soon came. Time to make downstairs to the dining room. After another filling and satisfying meal, Shay and Ruby returned to their room.

Shay decided to take Danny Good Looking's advice and called Billy in one last attempt to end the lunacy.

"Billy it's Shay, we need to sort this out. Ruby and I love each other. All this nonsense needs to end." Shay had Billy's attention and felt that he was getting through to him so he continued, "I don't need this grief, nor do you, none of us do. We can sort this out. We've a profitable business together and..."

Shay was unable to finish his sentence as the mere mention of 'business' caused Billy to rumble into an explosion, "You aint got a business no more! I've made sure of that, you thick mick!"

Now offended and angered, Shay shouted back in response, "Right, you listen to me, you mug! You've got all my money and you've destroyed my business contacts! If you keep this pursuit up..."

Billy cut in and roared, "You're a dead man walking, Sullivan! Put my daughter on the phone!"

Unrelenting and determined to say what he wanted to say, Shay harshly continued, "She ain't your daughter, you fool. I'm telling you now, Billy, you stop this nonsense and get my money back to me!" He continued calmly, "You keep hunting us and barking, then I'll start biting back, I'll turn the tables on you. You seem to forget, I know where you are but you don't know where I am." Incensed, Shay hung up.

He was infuriated, and turned to Ruby who was sat wide-eyed on the edge of the bed, "That mug! I should go back and show him the left and give him the right. Fuck him…. I fancy a pint now."

Shay and alcohol were a bad mix. He'd let himself down over the years with exaggerated partying. He should have turned professional in his boxing days but had let drink scupper any chances he had. He loved to party but the actual party was the buzz, not the drink. When things had gone wrong in Shay's life in the past, he would have a drink, and if things went really wrong all hell would break lose. He liked to fight as the underdog and would often take on three or four brawlers just for the challenge of it. More often than not, he would be the hurting loser and sometimes he would be the victor. It was a self-destruct button that he would press when low; however, that was all in the distant past now. Though at this moment in time, his button had been pressed and he felt the craving for a pint of Guinness. "Perhaps just a couple to take the edge off of things," Shay suggested.

Ruby got up from the bed, walked over and took his hand.

"Don't get wound up, London, it's not gonna help the situation. Let's go out for a change of scenery. We could go for a walk and find a little pub or something. The walk will help clear your head a bit," she said.

They walked for a while in the drizzly rain and came across a quaint pub called 'Maggie's'.

As they entered the dimly lit pub Shay instantly noticed Republican memorabilia that was framed and hanging on the walls. The bar was quiet, other than five men sat at the bar talking. They turned and watched Shay and Ruby approach.

A hard faced, dark haired barmaid greeted Shay and Ruby, but in a friendly manner, "How are ye, what can I get ye?"

Shay smiled and said, "Hiya, erh, a pint of Guinness and a large brandy, no ice please."

The barmaid nodded and proceeded to fix their drinks. The men at the bar now began to whisper. Shay and Ruby thought nothing of it as they stood waiting for their drinks. Apart from the barmaid, Ruby was the only woman. She'd noticed the men eyeballing her and Shay but didn't find them intimidating. Shay turned his attention to the muted television that was showing Manchester United playing somewhere in Asia in a pre-season friendly against some unknowns. He thought to himself, Man United on the box in Ireland, always Man United! His beloved Chelsea were in action the same night and he'd hoped to catch a glimpse of them.

The barmaid placed their drinks on the bar and Shay paid for them. He turned to Ruby, "Can you play pool, Eyes?"

"Course I can! C'mon, I'll show you how it's done!" Ruby challenged.

They walked along by the bar and past the five observant men. Just around the corner, still in view of the bar, was a small room and in the centre was a pool table. Shay got some change to put into the table and racked up the balls. After Ruby had chosen her cue, she pointed out to Shay a jukebox that was fixed up on the wall. Shay continued to set the game up and the music-loving Ruby wandered over to the jukebox. "Oh, that's a shame, it's turned off!" Remarked Ruby.

The game commenced and there was plenty of banter and laughter as they tried their hardest to out-do each other. After a just few shots each, one of the men from the bar walked into the small room over to the jukebox. They both glanced at the stocky man who nodded at them both and turned away, to then suddenly boom, "Mary, will yer turn on the auld jukebox?"

Shay kept one eye on the game and the other on the man who was now selecting some tunes on the jukebox. He thought to himself that a bit of music would liven up the atmosphere. Another man then approached the small room, ducking as he walked under the beam and into the room.

The tall man, with a heavy beard and glasses approached the jukebox, sidled up to his friend to loudly exclaim, "Go'wan, put that one on! That'll educate them!"

Shay smiled inwardly and then released a cheeky grin as the music intro commenced. He instantaneously recognised it as '*Sean South*.' He quickly realised that the men had decided to intimidate the English tourists visiting their pub. As the two men paced along the uneven wooden flooring towards the bar and their three friends, they stopped in their tracks and gave a quick, startled look over their shoulders as Shay started to sing whilst tapping his cue onto the hard floor,

> *'Twas on a dreary New Year Eve,*
> *As the shades of night came down*
> *A lorry load of volunteers*
> *Approached the border town'*

Shay's sing-along caused utter confusion at the bar and provoked lots of head scratching, which turned into laughter.

"Jesus!" said one of the men who laughed and then continued, "Huh, I didn't see that coming!"

A second song then commenced from the jukebox and Shay continued his sing along to '*The Men Behind The Wire*.'

Ruby turned to Shay, enthusiastic. "Oh good, this is my favourite one!"

Shay smiled back at Ruby. He found it quite endearing given that Ruby had failed to realise that they were being bullied by a jukebox. Ruby waited for the song to end and then asked Shay if he wanted to go outside to have a cigarette. Shay agreed, so they laid down their cues and made their way to the nearby side door. Whilst they smoked, Shay explained to Ruby that the songs were played for a reason.

Standing in the wet weather, Shay and Ruby were soon joined by the two men who had been at the jukebox.

"How are yer?" said the tall man with the beard, "You shocked us all with your singing in there!"

Shay laughed and said, "I grew up listening and singing to them songs."

The stocky man quickly piped up and joined the conversation, "Are yer family from Ireland then?"

Shay turned to the man to answer his question and said, "My mother and father are both Irish, I was born in London." As a result, the two men told Shay and Ruby that they were very welcome in Connemara and went back inside.

Shay and Ruby returned to the bar, had one more drink and another game of pool before walking back to the hotel. They laughed as they re-told the night's events, "I feel a right plum not realising why they played those songs," laughed Ruby. "I was just pleased when they put the wire song on!"

Shay chuckled and took hold of Ruby's hand to hold for the rest of the walk. After such an eventful evening and exhausted from the laughter, it was no wonder that they both fell asleep as soon as their heads hit the pillows.

The next morning, they awoke to find that the weather had not improved. Shay had a shower and decided to call his parents.

His father answered "Halloo…"

"Morning Dad, you and Mum alright?" asked Shay.

"Oh we're grand Shay, yeh-yeh. Uhh… did ye sleape alright?"

Shay grinned, he loved the way that his father would say sleape instead of sleep, words like tay instead of tea and spaeke instead of speak. Shay replied, "Yeah, slept like a baby, Dad."

"Come here to me, Shay, I was spaeking wit Danny last night, he says ye are both in danger, and ye should stay in Ireland for a while. Yer mother can get you and Ruby a house in Kerry for a week and we could come down to spend some time with ye then. What do yer tink?"

"Well, Danny's in the know, so we'll do what you suggested, thanks Dad."

"Uhh… yer mother is here Shay, spaeke to her. Good luck now," said Mick as he coughed and handed the phone over to his wife.

Josie came to the phone and explained that she had arranged a house for them both in Killarney for a week after their week was finished in Connemara. Shay and Ruby agreed and were very grateful for the arrangements she'd made.

Ruby told Shay that she was going to give her mum, Janice, a call as she had promised to keep in touch. Shay gave Ruby the phone and she went over to sit on the chair by the window.

"Hi, Mum it's me," said Ruby, who didn't really get the response from her mum that she expected.

"Oh. Alright?" replied Janice in unenthusiastic tone.

Taken aback by her lack of interest and concern, Ruby replied, "Erh…. I was just calling to let you know that I was ok and to see how you were."

"Ruby, how did you get over to Ireland without your passport?" Janice was curt.

Ruby knew her mother better than her mother knew herself and Ruby could tell by her conceited tone that her she was being offhand.

Ruby didn't hesitate in replying, "You don't need a passport to fly to Ireland, I had my driving licence."

"Well that's not what Billy said!" snapped Janice. "He said you need your passport to leave the country and he's got both your passports."

Ruby was now angered by her mum who sounded to have had a personality transplant since their last phone call.

"Oh right, so he's taken my passport now as well has he! And that's alright with you is it? Well I tell you what, it's not alright, it's theft! Who does he think he is?"

"He didn't take it, he asked me for it and I gave it to him." Janice, who then in retaliation to Ruby's irritated response fired another question at Ruby, "Oh by the way, what was his problem the other night?"

"Who?" Snapped Ruby.

"That person you're with!" Janice retorted.

Now well and truly infuriated, Ruby shouted, "His name is Shay!"

"Yeah, yeah whatever. Well why did he ring Billy last night and threaten him?"

In total disbelief at her mother's spiteful tone, Ruby scoffed and asked, "How did he threaten him?"

"Well you must have been there! He was saying about turning the tables on Billy."

Unable to control her anger, Ruby cracked, "Right. Firstly, I've already told you once, HE has a name and HIS name is Shay! Secondly, yes I was there and Shay did say that and do you know what, I make him right. After what that bastard has done to us, he's lucky he didn't get a phone call before now! Thirdly, thanks for your concern Mum, you've really shown how much you care!" With that, she hung up.

Upset and shaken with rage, Ruby stomped over to Shay, now on the bed, "Did you hear that? She's obviously got both feet firmly rooted in his goddam corner!" She shouted. "I'm so angry! How could she do this to me?"

Shay beckoned Ruby to sit on the bed next to him and he calmed her down. It was understandable that Ruby was extremely hurt by her mother. "Hold on a minute...." He turned to Ruby and said, "Why did she give him your passport? Has she told him that we're in Ireland?"

Ruby's anger had now turned to tears. She wiped her face and replied adamantly, "No way! She wouldn't do that. Look London, you don't understand how it is. Yeah, she's naive but she's frightened of him and frightened of being on her own. I know her though, she wouldn't tell him where we are, she just wouldn't."

But Shay had his doubts...

The time passed slowly and the rain continued to fall heavily during their week at The Oak Tree but it did give them both time to reflect on the loss of business, money, friends and loved ones. Bridget had called Shay and told him that her and Peter had extended their stay in the South of France for another week as they had stumbled across a business deal that they wanted to look into.

On their final night at The Oak Tree, Shay and Ruby prepared to go down for dinner.

Ruby groaned, "We've got no bloody clothes, London. I feel like a right skank wearing the same things every night!"

Shay agreed, "I know, I'm really missing all my suits. I've got suits and shoes that I haven't even worn yet! Funny innit, all my money has been taken but I'm really missing my clothes!"

Luckily enough, it was a relaxed, hospitable hotel and 'evening attire' for the dining room was not compulsory. Shay wore his Diesel jeans and a Ralph Lauren lime green polo shirt with the short sleeves that allowed his Chelsea tattoo to show on his left forearm. Ruby wore her low waist designer skinny jeans with black boots just beneath her knee and a flimsy Miss Sixty black vest.

They entered the bar and noticed some new guests had arrived. In the corner of the bar were two couples in their late fifties sitting at a table. The men dressed in suits and the women wore extravagant evening dresses with their hair and make-up done just so. The two couples turned in horror at the sight of Shay and Ruby at the bar. Shay and Ruby were doing exactly what the other guests were doing, having a quiet drink and perusing through the menu, yet their presence appeared to have had a curious effect on the two couples. One of the women muttered something to the other woman whilst one of the men shook his head in disgust. Once the couples had made sure that their obvious revulsion had been projected towards Shay and Ruby, the four proceeded to leave the bar and go through to the dining room. The sight of bare skin and tattoos clearly was not to their liking.

Shay turned to Ruby, "Brandy or a water Eyes?" he asked.

Ruby looked at Shay, with a wild look in her eyes, she replied, "No thanks, I don't want either. I tell you what, I'm not having that. Let's go straight through to dinner. Who do that lot think they are? Sitting there looking down their noses at us! Did you see the two women talking about us? They've got a bloody cheek, mutton dressed up as lamb! I tell you what, if they do it again, I'll be saying something!"

They entered the dining room and Ruby immediately looked to see where the two pretentious couples were seated. Shay and Ruby ordered their meal, noticing that the two couples continued to look over distastefully at them. That was until Shay gave them his wicked eye, a look that suggested the men would do best to inform their wives that they should enjoy their meal and the evening, rather than judge what they assumed to be two vagrants. The eye had worked very effectively and the supercilious couples finished the meal, knocked back a bottle of wine, and then promptly ordered another.

Shay and Ruby ate their meal and decided that they'd have a quick drink in the bar before going up to bed. They left the dining room unnoticed as they passed the rather inebriated couples, now very loud and having a great time for all to hear.

Shay and Ruby had been sitting in the bar for around twenty minutes talking quietly. The silence was abruptly broken by the boisterous return of the two couples who were laughing at full volume and being playful with each other.

Ruby had her back to the foursome but Shay could clearly see them and said to Ruby, "Look at the judge and jurors! A sniff of the barmaid's apron strings and the snobbery has turned into a free for all touch up."

Ruby laughed and replied, "Oh really! Well, their heads didn't stay stuck up their own arses for long!"

The intoxicated couples moved to a secluded area of the bar and were now no longer visible. Shay and Ruby sat and listened to their now comical conversation.

"Go on, go on, feel it!" said a female voice.

"Go on Joe, feel her, Dave won't mind," said another female voice.

"Ok, I will so!" said an excited male voice.

"That's it! Yes! There! Feel it! No, no! Harder! Harder! Use two fingers!" shrilled one of the women.

"Let me do it!" said another eager male voice.

"That's it, you got it! Just there! Shur let Mary have a go now!" Instructed the woman. "Mary come on, you feel it. You use three fingers though, the men have bigger fingers than us! That's it you've found it straight away Mary! Well done. Shur it took both husbands forever to find it!"

By this time Shay and Ruby were near to collapsing on the bar floor in hysterics. As she wiped the tears of laughter from her eyes, Ruby said, "All the dirty looks they gave us, making out they're so high-brow and all that. A few bottles of wine, and they turn into a bunch of swingers!"

With their sides aching from laughing so hard, they made their way out of the bar. On their way out, they noticed that the couples were merely playing a harmless game of trying to feel each other's pulses.

NINE

A Killarney Cocktail

Ironically, on their day of departure, the sun shone for the first time during their short stay in Connemara as they pulled out of the Oak Tree Hotel. It was a beautiful day and Shay wore his sunglasses for the exhilarating drive to Kerry. He explained to Ruby that his mother's family were Kerry people. He laughed and fondly described how his grandmother would address him as 'Boyeen' when he was a child. He went onto enlighten her on what a beautiful County Kerry was. Ruby listened attentively and admired the stunning scenery, so picturesque in the sunlight. So that she wouldn't miss a thing, she put her sun visor down so that she could glance into the mirror and get a view of behind. Shay laughed at Ruby, and her energetic alternation from looking out of her window to then using the sun visor. From that moment on, Shay gave Ruby a second nickname, 'The Periscope.'

They made good time to Galway City and continued their journey through Gort and into the County Clare. "Well Eyes, now we're in the Banner County," explained Shay.

They stopped in Ennis to replenish their cigarette supply and had coffee and a light lunch.

They resumed their journey to Killmer and drove onto the car ferry for the short crossing to Tarbert, County Kerry. Though the journey on the car ferry was short, this was another new experience for Ruby.

They continued on toward Tralee, Shay explaining to Ruby that his grandfather had enlisted in Tralee during the times of trouble in Ireland. Ruby always paid attention when Shay told her stories, whether they were about his family or the history of Ireland. She never realised that he had such an extensive knowledge about Ireland. They continued on to Killarney and finally found the house where Shay's parents had arranged for them to stay.

They'd had a great day and were so excited about being in Kerry, so they decided to have a night out in the busy little tourist town.

They went into a cocktail bar that was within a hotel called, The Goss Hotel.

Shay and Ruby sat at the bar on high leather barstools, which were more like chairs, and admired their stylish, trendy surroundings. They decided to have a fun night out and relax with a few cocktails.

Shay perused the cocktail menu, whilst an excited Ruby asked, "Oi, London, do they have mojito's here? I love them!"

He scanned the menu. "Hmmmm.... yeah! You're in luck, Eyes, they've got 'em." Shay was still undecided and couldn't make his mind up on what to drink. "Right, I think I'll go on a tour!"

Ruby laughed and asked, "A tour of what?"

"A tour of the cocktail menu! Let's do one of each and decide what's the best!"

"Nah, I like mojito's so I'm sticking to them. I don't wanna mix my drinks either, I'll be ill if I do! C'mon Son! Shout 'em up!" joked Ruby.

They sat at the bar sipping their drinks, having a great time laughing and telling each other stories; intermittently popping outside for a cigarette. The cocktail bar was rapidly filling up with people; obviously a popular venue. After a game of 'people watching' Ruby spied two women the other side of the bar. They were in their early fifties but had attempted to dress as though they were in their twenties.

Ruby chuckled, nudged Shay in his side with her elbow and said, "Ere London, them two over there have got their eye on you! Oh! Oh! Did you see that? The brassy one just gave you a smile!"

Shay looked over and one of the women winked at him, Shay laughed and said, "Shit! I think they think I'm here on me own! Stand up for a bit, Eyes, maybe they can't see you," joked Shay.

"Ha ha, funny man," quirked Ruby sarcastically who couldn't blame the two women for giving her boyfriend the eye as he sat there with his tan, blue eyes, dark hair, wearing a black shirt. He's so handsome and he's all mine, she thought to herself.

After Shay had completed his tour of the menu and Ruby had had her fill of mojito's, they agreed to leave the swanky bar.

On their walk home, they heard live music coming from another bustling bar. Intrigued, they entered. The venue was dark, packed to the rafters with people having the craic. Shay walked ahead of Ruby reaching back with one arm to hold her hand so that he could lead the way through the sea of people.

They eventually made it to the bar and squeezed in along side the other punters so they could order their drinks. Whilst waiting for their drinks, a man in his late twenties approached the bar and stood next to Ruby, unashamedly admiring her. He was smartly dressed, good looking but had let himself down with a new wave hairstyle. Shay and Ruby didn't attempt to have a conversation as the music was too loud. The admirer was still firmly rooted next to Ruby and made it very apparent that he wasn't there to order a drink, he was there to ogle Ruby.

The audacity of the man didn't sit too well with Shay who stepped forward, lent in close to the man and asked, "Do we know you mate?"

The man grasped that Shay wasn't trying to be sociable; he promptly left and made his way to the dance floor.

After a long wait, the bartender brought Shay and Ruby their drinks. Not wanting to fight through all of the people whilst holding their drinks, they decided to stay at the bar. Ruby carefully surveyed the room and observed everyone, quickly coming to the conclusion that the majority must have been there quite a while as everyone seemed to be very merry. As Ruby happily looked on at horrendous dance routines and swaying observers, Shay started to tug at Ruby's jacket. She lent in and strained to listen, "Oi, Eyes, have a look!" said Shay. "That old boy sitting there is out for the count!... Well, I hope he's asleep anyway!"

Ruby lent forward and saw an old man in his seventies slumped in a chair at the bar. He was dressed smartly in trousers, a blazer and a peak cap, fast asleep. Having a soft spot for old people, Ruby lent into Shay and kind-heartedly said, "Ahhh bless his heart. Is he on his own? Do you think he'll be alright?"

Shay also had a lot of time and respect for old people, so he turned to a man who was standing by the sleeping old man and asked, "Excuse me mate, is he alright? Does he need any help getting home?"

He laughed and said "Jesus no, he's sound." The plump Kerry man knew the old man. "He comes here every night, sits in that same chair, has a couple of Guinness's and goes to sleep! He only lives down the road. He'll wake up later and try finding himself a young lady to walk him home."

Shay laughed and relayed the conversation back to Ruby.

Shay and Ruby finished their drinks and danced their way through the lively crowd to the busy smoking area outside. They both got talking to different groups. Ruby spoke with some girls from Killarney, whilst Shay was approached by two men in their late forties, "Alright mate," said the more sober man who was a cockney from England.

"Hello mate, how's it going? Is your mate ok, he looks like he's had enough," laughed Shay, as the drunk man staggered towards him. The drunkard looked at him and mumbled; Shay had no idea what he'd said.

The soberer man said, "Oh he's alright, he's my brother, it's been a long day. We brought our mum over for her birthday, she comes from here but ain't been here for twenty two years. Name's Harry, what's yours mate?"

Shay shook his hand. "Ah that's nice," he said. "I bet your mum's made up. Mind you, bet she's noticed a few changes after twenty two years." Shay was purposely evasive and ignoring the invite of giving his name.

"We're from Enfield mate, where you from?" asked Harry.

Shay wondered to himself, is this bloke for real? It's like being on a chat show, and then replied, "Oh, erh, I'm from West London."

The drunk brother then slurred, "Oh yeah… nice… we go over the Spurs, you into football, mate?"

Shay was quick to reply and said, "Not really mate, not my thing to be honest."

The two brothers laughed loudly. "Bollocks!" Harry said. "You're Chelsea! We both said it as soon as you came out here! Why you pretending, you nutter!" Playfully slapping Shay's back.

Shit! thought Shay, that's all we need! Getting recognised from the old days by two loud drunks!

The drunker brother piped up again, and garbled, "Yeah… it's definitely you! I see you out with Keith and erh… erh… what's his name? Grips…and Dec. They're top boys over the Spurs. They got a lot of respect for you and say you're alright even though you're Chelsea. I've see you up the West End with 'em!"

Uneasy, Shay replied, "Look, that fucking football stuff is in the past yeah, you got me. Keep it down right, I'm here with me girl, she don't need to know about all that. Anyway, I'm off to bed now boys, we could meet for a beer tomorrow night?"

Obviously Shay had no intention of meeting them again but didn't want to rile them in any way.

"Yeah! Nice one mate! Meet us in here tomorrow night at seven,"

Harry said enthusiastically as he supported his intoxicated brother.

"Yeah, will do. Look forward to it chaps." Shay shook their hands and beckoned to Ruby that they were leaving.

As they walked back in the darkness to their temporary house, Shay explained to Ruby that the two brothers were ok, but they had recognised him.

Shay considered his shameful fame with football and stated that bars were a no go from now on, just to be on the safe side.

Next morning, Shay awoke excited as his parents were coming from County Waterford and he hadn't seen them for six months. Ruby on the other hand, was very nervous and apprehensive about meeting Shay's parents for the first time.

Josie called. "Morning Son, how are ye?" she asked. "We'll be down to ye about two o'clock and we have a surprise for you!"

"Oh yeah, what's that Mum?"

Unable to keep it as a surprise, Josie erupted with excitement. "Well I'll tell you now, we're collecting Connor from Farrenfore Airport at half past one! He misses you and I know you miss him, so have the kettle on for two o'clock, Son!"

"Ah Mum, that's great, thank you. The kettle will be on."

"Ok honey, we'll see ye soon, please God. Bye, bye"

The arrival of the three loved ones was very emotional for Shay and nail-biting for Ruby. Shay's mum and dad greeted Ruby and appeared to be genuinely pleased to meet her, despite the circumstances.

Ruby and Josie sat in the lounge whilst Shay, Connor and Mick sat in the kitchen talking.

Ruby sat on the edge of the settee fiddling nervously with one of her rings whilst Josie started off the conversation. As Ruby sat and listened to Josie, she couldn't get over how young and attractive she looked for her age and also how much Shay looked like her. Blimey, it's Shay in a dress! Thought Ruby.

Ruby really struggled to try and keep up with the conversation. She found the Irish accent hard to understand and it didn't help that Josie spoke so quickly. There were also words and expressions that Ruby had never heard before, which threw her a bit. They discussed the situation and talked about Shay. At no point did Josie make her feel uneasy or unwanted. Ruby was overwhelmed at how lovely, kind and sympathetic Josie was and pleasantly surprised at how well they got on.

After a couple of hours of light hearted conversation with Shay's parents, Ruby found that in comparison to his extremely energetic wife, Mick was the complete opposite. He came across as more of a listener than a talker but Josie more than compensated for that. Whereas Josie would fly around the room at a hundred miles per hour, Mick would move very slowly, it was more of a shuffle than a walk and he would always take his time.

Excited to back in her home town, Josie was eager for them all to venture out for a drive.

Before they left, Shay caught Ruby on her own upstairs to ask her how she got on with his mum, "So how'd you get on then, Eyes? Did you two get on alright?"

Ruby smiled and replied, "Yeah she's really lovely. I can't believe she's seventy-two! I found it a bit hard to keep up with her but I'll get used to it I suppose. You look just like her!"

Shay laughed and told Ruby that he was glad they got on so well.

They went out for a drive to the Gap of Dunloe and to Muckross House. The amazing scenery was complimented by the late afternoon sun. They had dinner in Killarney and finished the evening off with a tour in a horse drawn jaunting car.

After breakfast on the Saturday morning, Mick and Josie got ready for the drive back home to County Waterford with a planned return to Killarney midweek. There were big hugs given and a fond farewell and Josie splashed Shay, Ruby and Connor with her holy water that she'd brought with her.

Shay, Ruby and Connor spent the day at the house and in the evening watched movies and ate snacks. Sunday came and passed, as they made the most of the glorious weather and toured the lakes of Killarney.

On Monday morning Ruby dealt with washing what little clothing they had whilst Shay and Connor created a tennis court in the garden using chairs as posts and a rope as a net. They played football tennis, a game that they had played since Connor was able to kick a ball. Shay had introduced the game to enhance Connor's natural ability with a football and now Connor was older, the five sets of football tennis would be seriously contested in the two-touch game. They commenced the third set, having won one set each, and Shay's phone rang. Breathless, Shay answered with a panting "Hello."

"Shay, tis Dad here. I've had your uncle Danny on the phone. Jesus Shay, ye have to get out of Ireland. Danny said that bad bastard knows ye are in Ireland and ye are being hunted over here!"

Shay listened in disbelieve and silently questioned, will this nightmare never end, so replied to his father, "Do you know what Dad, I've had enough of this shit! I'm gonna go back to sort this out once and..."

Mick interrupted Shay, "Huh! I wouldn't do that if I were you, Danny said for ye to get out for a while. Yer mother and I was tinking... you'd planned to make yer money and go to California to set up a life in the sun, would yer not go now?"

"Yeah, that was the plan, Dad, but with half a million in my pocket! I've lost all my money now and I'm half million short of that target," Shay replied pessimistically.

"Look, yer mother and I have savings, we don't have much but we could give ye ten t'ousand Euros and with the exchange rate, that'd give ye about fourteen t'ousand dollars, shur that would get ye going. I spoke to your cousin Mickey Sullivan o'er there this morning, he said if ye went out to California he'd help get ye going," explained Mick.

Shay thought long and hard. It had been his dream to return to California following the visit he'd had in the nineties and he'd remained in touch with his cousin, Mickey. Shay was well travelled, he'd visited five different continents but loved the Californian life. It was his goal to spend his next three years reaping the benefits of his successful business with the view of leaving England to start a business in the sunny state.

"I can't take your money, Dad, I already feel ashamed that I'm becoming reliant on my family. The thing is ..."

Mick interrupted again, "Jesus Shay, I don't want to bury yer! Shur ye can pay us back when ye have it. Danny said tis serious, he tinks ye should go tomorrow."

"We can't, Dad! That nutter's got our passports!"

"I know, I know. Look, give Bridget a call, she's an answer to that problem and then call me back. Good luck."

After hearing that news, the first call Shay was going to make was to his uncle Danny, knowing he'd explain things a bit better than his elderly father.

"Alright Danny," said Shay.

A logical Danny recognised it was Shay and went straight to the facts, "Now, listen to me bhoy and listen up good. There are no facts as to what has gone on with ye and yer man but the word is out that you ran off with Ruby and that you stole that langer's money. Now, I'm not saying you did take the money, shur you know I only work on facts but people are saying ye had cheques washed and used official documents like. You know I don't care who done what but I don't want yer mother and father harmed or being worried. Shur I don't want you harmed! But you're in big danger altogether, the Dempsey's are after ye."

Shay would never interrupt Danny as he respected him a great deal, so he allowed him to finish before he responded, "Right, firstly Danny we did not take a penny. He's the one that's got all my money! And who the hell are the Dempsey's?"

"Huh, the Dempsey's are people yer never want to meet bhoy! They are highly organised and they're all o'er the place. Disappear to America for your sake and the sake of yer family. If the Dempsey's find yer they'll kill ye both!" advised Danny.

A petrified Shay pleaded with his uncle, "I did nothing wrong but fall in love. I've lost everything…"

Danny quickly interrupted and boldly corrected Shay, "Not everything Shay. Yer alive bhoy, yer alive! I've made enquiries and the contract for ye is paid. We can't stop it like, get out to California and ye'll be safe. I'll see to it that Connor and the rest of the family are safe. I'll miss yer Shay, shur yer like a son to me. Now yer mother and father and Bridget needn't know about the Dempsey's, they'd be worrying more than they are already."

After an emotional goodbye to Danny Good Looking followed by some time to gather himself, Shay called Bridget.

"Alright Bridge."

"Shay! Jesus, ye need to act quick! Now listen to me, you can get an Irish passport as Mum and Dad are both Irish but Ruby needs a British passport. Anyhow, there is no need to go back to London, ye can drive to Belfast. Make an appointment for a same-day passport and as ye are up there together ye can get one each or Ruby can just get her one; I think that you'd be better off travelling with an Irish passport."

"I can't believe this is happening Bridge, what about Connor? He's my life. And what about Mum and Dad? They're getting on and neither are in good health. And then there's you… when will any of us see each other?"

"Look Shay, you'll only be a flight away. You'll be alive and in the states exccetra, exccetra, which is better than yer being in the grave yard. Anyhow, you were always going to go to California, I know it'd have been under different circumstances but it's like I've told yer before Shay you know, all things happen for a reason."

Shay thanked Bridget and agreed that he and Ruby would go. He explained that he'd found his love in life just like Bridget always said he would. He also said how it was a great shame that he would be gone before Bridget returned to Ireland from France.

Shay had to let Ruby and Connor know what had happened. He sat them both down in the kitchen and explained what his uncle Danny had found out. Ruby was shocked and a little shaken but reminded Shay that she'd go anywhere with him as long as they were together and safe. She looked on as Shay became very emotional as he told his son how he loved him so very much. The strain and hurt was easy to read on Connor's face. He was and always had been very close with his dad who was now going to live in California, but he was also close with his mum. His life was undoubtedly in England.

The following morning Ruby called Middlesex Police and spoke to DCI Turner. He expressed his concern with regard to the case and stated that he was powerless as no-one had come forward with a statement. He agreed that they were in terrible danger and admitted that he was frustrated with the lack of progress following his enquiries as everyone had clammed up. Turner also told Ruby that he wouldn't want her and Shay returning back to England yet because if anything was to happen, he wouldn't want it on his conscience. He asked if Connor would give a statement and be a witness. Ruby explained that Shay wouldn't allow his son to be put in danger and would therefore advise Connor not give a statement. Turner stated that he would send an e-mail to Belfast passport office. The content of the e-mail would explain Shay and Ruby's case, theft of their passports and reasons for lack of birth certificate documentation. Ruby was anxious at the fact that DCI Turner was so concerned but was thankful that he empathised with their situation and that he was going to do all he could to help.

Ruby then called Belfast passport office and made an

appointment for ten thirty am the following morning. She updated Shay on the two phone calls that she'd made but was stopped mid-sentence when the phone rang.

Shay answered the phone to a crying Josie, "Shay, oh Jesus Son, will I ever see yer again? Once ye're out there ye will never come back yer know. That basket in England has ruined us!"

"We'll sort something out, Mum. You know you can't get rid of me that easy!"

"Yer father and I will book ye yer flights for Thursday from Dublin to Los Angeles. We can meet ye in Dublin tomorrow night please God." Josie fought to hold back her tears and continued, "We'll stay in a hotel for our last night together as a family…" Josie lost the battle in holding back her tears and then sobbed "…We'll bring Connor back wit us. Jesus, Mary and Joseph, that poor lad. He'll miss yer as much as I will."

TEN

Killing Time in Belfast

In the early hours of the morning Shay, Ruby and Connor set off from Killarney for the long drive to Belfast. For Ruby and Connor it was a new experience. Due to their age, they were not aware of the troubles and Shay gave them a narrative of the difficult history of Ireland. However, the account of past events only helped in sending Connor to sleep in the back of the car.

They drove in the morning darkness and didn't take a well earned refreshment or toilet break until they arrived in County Laois, stopping in the quaint town of Abbeyleix. Whilst they drank their coffee, Shay joked that Ruby had already been to more counties in Ireland than some of his proud London Irish cousins.

Back in the car, Ruby was sitting in the front passenger seat and Shay appointed her as his co-pilot and handed her a map to read. They continued their journey and passed by The Curragh, County Kildare. They then bypassed Dublin, scrambled for change at a toll booth and continued to bypass Drogheda and Dundalk, and finally crossed the border into Newry.

Connor awoke and suddenly exclaimed, "Oh, my phone's gone back to a UK network, that's weird."

"I know, it's mad isn't it?" agreed Shay.

By now, Ruby had also been appointed as the D.J. as well as the co-pilot. Whilst she flicked through the various radio stations, she commented on her observations. "'Ere, London, there's a lot of Union Jacks about. Look at the start of some of the road junctions, it's lined with Union Jacks, why's that?"

Shay replied mischievously, "It's their marching season. They march with their tin whistles and all that," he laughed and continued, "Some would say the butchers apron, not the Union Jack. You'll see plenty of Irish flags soon. We're in a car with a Dublin plate, we've got cockney accents and two of us are plastic paddies, as they would say. No-one's gonna welcome us!" joked Shay.

They entered Belfast in great time. They parked in the city centre and with forty five minutes to kill, they went and had breakfast.

They attended the passport office for their half past ten appointment and found the staff to be very helpful and sympathetic following the official e-mail from Middlesex police. Shay decided to get a British passport to kill two birds with one stone.

The lady in the passport office told them, "These will take a wee while, if you come back at half past four, they'll be ready for collection."

It was now eleven thirty and they had plenty of time to view the city. They went window shopping around the impressive city centre and Connor bought himself a pair of training shoes that he had been wanting for some time. Shay and Ruby agreed that there was no point in them buying any clothes until they got to California.

The day passed slowly and the weather became very overcast and damp. They decided to tour west Belfast by car. They drove past The Hospital for Sick Children and then up the Falls Road to view the many painted walls that were covered with Republican murals.

They were amazed by the remarkable, lifelike artwork and they took several photos using a disposable camera. Again, Shay took this opportunity to voice his knowledge and explained the reason and message behind the murals and who and what each one was about.

They eventually returned to the passport office and after a short delay they received their passports.

The return journey was much shorter as they had arranged to meet Josie and Mick in a hotel in Malahide, Dublin for their last night together as a family. It had been a very long day and they all felt sleepy. They had only been travelling fifteen minutes when Ruby looked back and noticed that Connor had fallen asleep again. With his mouth wide open and his head bouncing off of the window, she rolled up her coat and carefully put it under his head.

They arrived at the hotel and parked. They entered the hotel, noticing Josie and Mick drinking tea in the bar. As they quietly approached them, they heard Josie, "Will yer take off yer cap Mick Sullivan! Jesus, if my father could see yer, the Lord have mercy on him. You wear yer cap outside! Not indoors!"

An obedient Mick removed his cap and smirked. "Jesus Josie, will yer stop," he said in his usual appeasing tone,

"Hello Mum, alright Dad?" Said Shay with a big smile.

"Oh heavens preserve us! Ye're back safe from up the North, t'anks be to God! Did ye get yer passports?" asked Josie.

"We did yeah, no problem," said Shay as he shook his father's hand and cuddled his mother.

Josie held onto Shay in the same fashion she did when he was a child. Shay could feel the anguish in his worried mother's hug and thought that how his parents could do without this stress in their twilight years. Josie did the rounds and cuddled Ruby and Connor with all her might, sobbing "Jesus, that man in England has wrecked this family, the fecker!"

Shay, Ruby and Connor checked into the hotel and explained to Josie and Mick that they would be down shortly. Mick wagged a finger at the three of them and joked, "If ye're not having a cup of tay will ye hurry up, me belly tinks me t'roat has been cut!"

"Ah, Mick, will yer stop! Leave them alone," exclaimed Josie. "Jesus, that man constantly tinks about his belly!"

As Ruby and Shay prepared to leave their room to go down for dinner, Josie and Mick came up and ushered them back inside, closely followed by Connor who had just put his bag in the room adjacent. Josie offered a large brown envelope to Shay, "There you are, Son. That's for you and Ruby to start a new, safe life with." She welled up with tears and said with her voice trembling, "Yer father and I want ye to have it, just promise us ye will look after each other and love each other…"

The emotion was too much for Josie's breaking heart so Mick stepped in. "Go easy with that money now… Do ye hear me… Ye'll be safe in California," Mick said emotionally.

Shay struggled to hide is emotion in his response. "Thank you both, from both of us." With that he broke down.

Ruby hugged Josie, "Thank you so much Josie, you've both been so kind. I promise you that I'll look after him."

Shay embraced his father who began to weep, "There's fourteen t'ousand dollars in that, that will get ye off to a good start, Son. Go easy on the money now."

Collectively, they wiped away the tears and then went down to dinner.

They had a fun meal together laughing and joking, followed by tea and coffee in the empty lounge.

"Did ye do any shopping in the North? Did they have a Marks & Spencer, I love Marks," Josie said enthusiastically.

Connor replied, "Yeah. I got some trainers. Dad and Ruby just looked about, it's cheaper in America so they'll get some clothes out there hopefully. If not, a plastic surgeon will have to remove Dad's jeans for him!" he joked.

"I've always wanted to go up there shopping, tis cheaper, they all say," Josie said.

"You were up there before, Shay... or were yer?" enquired Mick.

"I was Dad, yeah. I was in Belfast and Derry back in the nineties," said Shay.

With the mention of Derry, Mick closed his eyes and quietly began to sing in his fine voice,

> *"As the train pulls out today from Derry City*
> *A t'ousand memories linger in my mind*
> *Why do I need to go, it's such a pity*
> *And all the dear old friends I leave behind*
>
> *As I gaze beyond the harbour I'm recalling*
> *Familiar names like Doherty and Coyle*
> *From misty eyes I feel the teardrops falling*
> *Goodbye to my old home town on the Foyle*
>
> *The spire of St Eugene seems to vanish*
> *In the distance o'er the City, oh so high*
> *And my childhood thoughts , I never want to banish*
> *When I wondered if it reaches to the sky*
>
> *Many t'ousand miles I travel on my journey*
> *To a new home on the wild Australian soil*
> *But never can I hope to lose yearning*
> *To return to my old home town on the Foyle"*

This song of exile left everyone with damp eyes as Mick went on to explain, "I worked in London wit the man that wrote that song many moons ago."

With an early start to the next day looming, they finished drinking their tea and jadedly retired for the night.

ELEVEN

The American Dream

The morning arrived hand in hand with a tearful departure at Dublin Airport. Through their tears, Shay and Ruby watched the elderly Josie and Mick standing and waving goodbye before boarding a coach back to Waterford. Their love had been unconditional. They looked so old and frail and should have been relaxing at home, not getting upset and facing a long coach journey. A tearful Connor stood with them, also confronted with the long, tiresome coach journey and then a return flight to London the following morning. When would Connor see his father again? They were so close yet California was so far away. Would Shay and Ruby ever see Josie and Mick again? Ruby was upset at the sight of Shay hurting. He looked as though he was having his heart ripped out and there was nothing she could do or say to console him.

Shay and Ruby boarded the Aer Lingus flight to Los Angeles in economy class, far from the first class seating Shay had become accustomed to. They shuffled down the aisle and found their seats. Ruby slid in and sat down whilst Shay put their bags in the overhead storage area before taking his seat. They were in a three seated section in the centre of the plane, with Ruby in the middle seat next to a middle aged man with long hair and glasses. Whilst the airhostesses wandered up the aisles checking that the passengers' luggage had been stored correctly, Ruby asked Shay, "So what's your cousin Mickey like then?"

Shay laughed affectionately, "Mickey's a right character. He was born in New York but grew up in California. He's the all American guy you know, he has the sun tan, the muscle, the moustache and the perfect white teeth. He never married and has no kids but I don't think he's ever alone in his bed at night."

Ruby giggled, "Oh really! He sounds like a bit of a playboy!"

"Yeah he is! He's a good guy though and is extremely proud of his Irish roots. He always claims to be one hundred percent Irish in his Californian accent," Shay said.

"Hark at you saying *guy*! You're talking like an American already!"

They both laughed loudly, which alerted the passenger who sat next to Ruby writing something into a notebook.

"Hi, I'm Greg. You guys on honeymoon?" asked the smiling passenger in his strong American accent.

Ruby ceased laughing and answered, "No, what made you think that?"

"Oh I dunno….. you both seem so in love!"

Shay lent forward. "We're just off to visit some family in southern California, we're thinking of relocating out there. Good to meet you Greg, this is Ruby and I'm Shay."

"Great to meet you guys!" Greg shook their hands. "You from London?"

"Yeah, we are," said Shay, as Ruby sat back and quietly paid attention to their pleasant conversation.

"Irish roots though, right?" Greg asked keenly.

"My parents are both Irish, Ruby is English. So do you have Irish roots then, Greg?"

"Yeah man, I *am* Irish! I was born and live in San Diego but I'm Irish. My grandfather was a Dublin man and my grandmother was from County Wicklow. I'm just writing a journal about my third visit to the old country. When my kids are older they'll enjoy reading about their roots," Greg continued, "Hey, so where are you guys heading to in Southern Cal?"

"Well, Rancho Cucamonga as a starting point but we hope to see it all really. We need to find some work so we'll settle where the work is, to be honest."

"Oh gee man! You sound like my ancestors! It won't be easy to find work though, we're in a recession and you'll need a social security number to get employment. Hey, you gotta see San Diego, it's the greatest city in the U.S.A.! It's cooler than Rancho Cucamonga, wow man, it's way too hot up there, late nineties, often over a hundred degrees this time of year! Down in San Diego it's nice, you know, high seventies, coastal breeze, cool people. Oh, and you gotta see the Gas Lamp Quarter. We also a have Mardi Gras in San Diego, you'll love it there, check it out, you'll have a blast!"

Shay waited for the animated Greg to catch his breath and then took his opportunity to respond. "Wow, sounds great, Greg. My cousin will help us with the legal side of things and with employment."

"Well, good luck to you both and enjoy Cal!" said Greg as he resumed writing his memoirs.

After a long, tiresome flight they finally touched down in Los Angeles. Before disembarking, they shook hands with Greg, who'd been a great ambassador for the USA and in particular, San Diego.

They stepped out of the plane and gasped with joy at the intense heat.

"Wow, at last! I love the heat," Ruby said.

Greg overheard Ruby as he stood behind them in the queue. "Man, if you think this is hot, you wait to you feel the heat in Rancho Cucamonga! If you like the heat, you'll love it there!" Fortunately enough, both Ruby and Shay were sun worshipers.

After collecting their baggage they made their way to the arrivals area where Mickey would be waiting to collect them.

"I'm really nervous, I hope Mickey likes me," Ruby said anxiously.

"I'm a bit nervous myself, babe," said Shay, "I've not seen Mickey for eighteen years, not since I was last out here."

They entered arrivals to be met by a sea of people. Shay immediately spotted Mickey who in turn had spotted Shay. They embraced and an excited Mickey exclaimed, "Hey Cuz! I'd forgotten what a big guy you are! You still boxing the heads off of guys?"

The heartfelt embrace came to an end and Shay said, "Nah, I'm too old for all that nowadays. Mickey, meet the beautiful Ruby."

Mickey took a dramatic step back. "Oh gee! She looks like a real Californian Gal! Hey Ruby, welcome! You're gonna fit right in here!" Mickey said.

Ruby gave Mickey a kiss and a hug and thanked him. She thought to herself how Shay had been accurate with his description of Mickey and how he looked like a movie star with smouldering good looks.

As they walked through LAX car park towards Mickey's Hummer, Ruby stopped to light a very long awaited cigarette. Mickey eyed Ruby's slim, toned figure, turned to Shay and said, "Hey Cuz, is that what all the shit is about? Hey man, I'd take a fucking bullet in the arm for her, she's stunning dude!" Mickey patted Shay's back firmly as Shay cried with laughter.

They set off in Mickey's Hummer with the air-con keeping them cool.

Mickey asked "Hey, shall we call Uncle in the old country and let them know you both arrived safely?"

"Yeah, lets," replied a weary Shay.

As Mickey dialled from his in car-phone he said, "I just love that fucking guy! Gee, you know, my uncle Mick is my favourite uncle! I miss my old man, you know since he passed away life's been real different…" He stopped as the call connected. "Hey Uncle! I have Shay here with me, and the stunning Ruby! How you doin' Uncle?"

"Huh…" Mick coughed before continuing, "Mickey, how are ye?"

"We're great Unc, I have my cousin and his gal with me now. Hey man, Shay will be running this fucking town within a week! I'm telling you Unc, we're gonna take over this goddam state now Shay's here!" joked Mickey.

Suddenly, Josie came to the phone and without coming up for air said, "Hello darlings, are ye ok? Did ye have a good flight? Is it hot there? Are ye tired? Have ye eaten yet? T'ank God ye arrived safely."

"Everything's just swell Auntie Josie, don't you be worrying no more, you hear me. I got their backs now!" said Mickey.

A tired Josie and Mick thanked Mickey for his help and told Shay and Ruby that they would speak to them tomorrow.

They drove down the busy freeway with Shay noting the changes to California. The conversation was continuous as Mickey mentioned familiar names such as Burbank and Pasadena. Mickey asked about London knowing that it was something Shay loved to talk about. Ruby sat in the back listening to the pair of them, taking it all in. When Ruby heard Shay refer to Ladbroke Grove being in 'downtown London', she couldn't control her laughter.

"What's so funny, Eyes?" asked Shay.

Eventually Ruby managed to curb her laughter and catch her breath and said, "I'm laughing at you! You plum! Downtown London! You've been in America less than an hour and you're already using their lingo!"

Shay scoffed at Ruby and said quite adamantly, "I didn't say that! I didn't say downtown! I just said London!"

Shay's denial only fuelled Ruby's laughter even more.

Mickey laughed at their repartee as they continued on the freeway and took the 105 to the 605 and finally the 10 east.

They arrived in scorching Rancho Cucamonga and Mickey suggested that they should check into The Chilton just for the one night as it was expensive. The next morning he would introduce them to a website called Priceline, where you could bid for hotel rooms and car hire. Mickey went onto explain that you could bid for virtually anything on it and get a really good deal.

They checked into the hotel. "I guess you guys are tired and need to chill for a while," suggested Mickey. "Hmmmm, let's see, it's four thirty pm now, you should try to keep going till night time to beat that jet lag. Get settled in here and I'll come and pick you up at seven. We'll get a bite and then you can get some sleep. Tomorrow I'll get you set up with a hotel, car and a laptop. You gotta get some work Cuz."

Shay and Ruby took the elevator to the fourth floor and found their room. Shay made sure that the air-con was on full blast before they both collapsed onto the bed, exhausted. Ruby couldn't even summon the energy to carry out her routine inspections. They cuddled and lay there for a few moments in each other's arms, feeling safe and out of harms way and knowing that Danny Good Looking would see to it that no-one would harm any of the family members left behind.

Having spent hours travelling, they decided to freshen up with a shower, to energise them and keep them awake until the night time. Mickey was right, it was the only way to adapt to the time zone change.

Coming out of the bathroom, Shay noticed Ruby sitting at the table and chairs on the balcony with a towel wrapped around her head and another wrapped around her body.

She called out, "Oi London, come out here, it's so hot! I've got a pot of coffee here and the cigarettes."

He joined her for coffee and a smoke. They admired the cleanliness of the surrounding streets and landscape; agreed to take it easy for the night and the next day but to start seeking employment and an apartment on their third day in California.

Mickey collected them at seven thirty and took them to a barbeque chicken restaurant. It was a chilled out meal with no heavy conversation as the tiredness was overpowering. Mickey was aware of their exhaustion and said, "Hey, let's kick back and tread those boards early in the morning. My dad would always say to me, hey, time to get up, tread those boards, gotta earn a dollar! My work diary starts at ten am, so I'll join you both at eight am, we'll get some breakfast and get you guys set up!"

Later, Shay and Ruby lay in bed reflecting on how nice Mickey was. They both fell asleep thrilled at the prospect of a new life in California.

TWELVE

Californian Dreaming

Shay and Ruby awoke at seven the following morning, feeling refreshed and raring to go. Today was the start of the rest of their lives. They took their coffee and cigarettes to the balcony and enjoyed the early morning sun. The temperature, already in the seventies, hit them like a brick wall as they stepped out onto the balcony. Full of anticipation and enthusiasm for the day ahead of them, they made their way down to the reception and checked out, to wait outside in the parking lot at the front of the hotel for Mickey to arrive. As they Ruby stood absorbing the powerful rays of the intense sun, Mickey pulled up in his shining black Hummer. With his window open and one hand on the steering wheel, Mickey lent out of the window and called out loudly in his attempt at a posh English accent, "Hallo mates! Tally ho!"

Shay and Ruby laughed and picked up their bags. Mickey reverted to his energetic Californian accent and shouted, "Hey guys! Jump in! Let's go kick some ass!"

They jumped into the Hummer and made their way back to Mickey's chic apartment. Not yet accustomed to the intense heat, Ruby and Shay were relieved to feel the blast of the cold air-conditioning as they travelled on the already very busy highway.

Mickey was excited to show Shay and Ruby his bachelor's pad and led them up to the door of his apartment. The area was spotlessly clean and peaceful.

"Welcome to The Love Shack, guys!" announced Mickey as opened the white front door. Shay and Ruby walked into the apartment with their mouths wide open in admiration.

"Wow! This place is the nuts, Mickey!" exclaimed Ruby.

Mickey laughed as he closed the door and asked, "Nuts...? Does that mean good or bad?"

"Nuts is good Mickey, same as the dog's bollocks," she said.

"Oh yeah, I heard the dog's bollocks before me old china! Tally ho mate!" joked Mickey. He loved to mimic their English accent. Then, he got serious, "Ok, you guys, you wanna work in here or out by the pool? We could take the laptop out to the patio if you want. I'll fix us some cold juice first though. Hey Cuz, set the laptop up outside on the table and I'll be right out. Hey, the password is 'love machine' – all one word, Cuz."

Ruby and Shay walked out onto the patio, sat at the stylish table and chairs and were blinded by the sun bouncing off of the very inviting swimming pool that was framed with various tropical plants and palm trees. Over by the far side of the pool was a huge, extremely modern barbeque that looked like it'd never been used. Ruby didn't have any sunglasses so she moved her chair and turned her back to the dazzling water of the pool.

"This is definitely a bit of us, London!" laughed Ruby.

Mickey arrived with a tray and three glasses of freshly squeezed orange juice and plenty of ice, accompanied with a vitamin bar each.

"Right then guys, let's get down to business. You guys can have this laptop 'till you get set up. You need to get familiar with a website called Priceline.com; for example you choose an area and bid for car hire, you set the daily rate and see if it gets accepted. The same applies to hotels. You're better off in hotels for now and then look at getting an apartment once you find work," he explained.

Shay was intrigued by the website and asked, "Is that Priceline good then Mickey?"

"Fuck yeah! Hey you paid what…? A hundred and sixty dollars last night, right? Well you go on Priceline and say bid fifty dollars a night for a hotel in Ontario, Cal and you might get that same room in the same goddam hotel for a third of the price! Go on man try it!"

As Ruby wondered at how Mickey's teeth became even more white in the sunlight, Shay logged into Priceline. He typed in a bid of fifty dollars for a hotel in the Ontario, Cal region. Mickey was quick to get up off of his seat and he stood over Shay's shoulder as they both waited for the results. "There you go!" Said Mickey, "One week at fifty dollars a night at the Chilton! Gee, you're saving money already man. Now try for car hire, Cuz!"

"Yeah, this website is really good! Let's try and get a Mustang!" Said an excited Shay.

"Hey, a Mustang is about eighty dollars per day, if you do it through here, you'll get it for… Hmmmm let me see…Try seventeen dollars, Cuz," suggested Mickey.

"Sweet! A Mustang for seventeen dollars a day! What a touch! Thanks Mickey."

"Hey, I told you guys, we're family and I love you guys! Shay, you'll be running this town by the end of the week, man! Let's go get you both a cell phone and collect your car. Didn't you guys say you wanted to go shopping for clothes? Well, once you get your car you can get a Sat Nav, check into your hotel and go shopping at a place called Victoria Gardens. You'll love it there," Mickey finished his glass of orange juice and looked at his watch. "Hey, it's nine thirty and we're done. Let's go get them phones and that Mustang, then I'll go to work and see you guys tonight. You just give me a holler if you need anything."

The process of collecting the hire car was quick and simple. Shay and Ruby sat into their bronze Mustang and admired its smooth lines and the sound of its sporty engine.

"I've always wanted to drive one of these! I hope I manage to stay on the right side of the road, it's been over eighteen years since I last drove out here!" Shay joked as he revved the car before driving out of the parking lot.

They set off to find a store where they could purchase a Sat Nav that they then used to lead them in the direction of Archibald and Haven, which eventually led them to Victoria Gardens.

They were pleasantly surprised to find that Victoria Gardens was a beautiful shopping village, as opposed to a mall. It was modern yet imposed a traditional feel with lantern lights for street lighting. The entire shopping village was beyond measure and had every outlet they could have wanted. It was clean and obviously well maintained. There were stylish benches dotted around and beautiful hanging baskets on the corners of every building.

As Shay and Ruby walked hand in hand along the spotless pathway in the scorching heat, they felt as though they were on a film set, not in a shopping village. Shay soon purchased three pairs of jeans and six tops, "Ere Eyes, it's cheap as chips here!" He said. "This lot comes to one hundred and twenty dollars, back home it'd be four hundred sheets at least! Right, now I need to get shoes."

Shay liked to dress well and took pride in his appearance. He'd struggled with the lack of clothing, a struggle that was exacerbated by not having access to a washing machine. At his place of work he loved to wear snappy suits and designer shoes but presently, jeans and t-shirts would suffice.

Ruby took her time to browse around the shops and was a little more calculated than Shay, who just wanted to get in and out of the shopping area and back to the hotel to change outfits. Ruby perused the shops like a predator hunting for the best prices. After having scoured the shops without actually buying anything, she suggested that they have a coffee in order to consider her findings. The coffee order was simple, it was always the same, it never changed. Shay ordered a double espresso and a latté. Ruby loved a latté but unexpectedly called out to Shay, "Erm, London, I think I'll try a frappuccino instead please." Soon to become a drink that she'd fall in love with.

They sat outside in the shade and sipped their coffee; away from the hysteria, feeling safe from the clutches of the Dempsey's and all of the other hit men that Billy had employed. Easy to decide that Ontario was the place for them and feel that here they could be happy. Whilst Ruby sucked every last drop of her frappuccino through the straw, they decided that all they needed to do was to purchase Ruby's clothing before returning to the hotel to seek employment on the laptop Mickey gave them.

Ruby actually purchased her clothes from the first shop of many that they went in and they made their way back to the hotel.

Back in the cool, air-conditioned hotel room, Ruby prepared both her and Shay's resumés and uploaded them onto various employment websites. Then they checked job vacancies and applied for numerous vacant positions; both felt confident that they'd have employment within a week.

It was early evening by the time that the laptop was shut down and when Mickey called, "Hey Shay, how'd it go today, man? Did you apply for work?"

"Alright Mickey, yeah we've put our resumés out there and applied for everything that's going in this area and in Orange County," replied Shay optimistically .

"There you go! Good job! I knew it, you're gonna love it here, man. Hey, you wanna go out and grab a bite?"

"Yeah ok, but we'll buy you dinner tonight though, it's our spin."

"Sure, hey do you guys have TGI's in the UK? We could go there. Meet me at the one that's at Victoria Gardens, and Cuz, I'll have a friend with me. She's a beautiful gal, her name's Reagan and she can't wait to meet you guys!"

"That sounds good to me. What time do you wanna meet then?"

"I'll see you both there in twenty minutes," continued in his exaggerated English accent, "Tally ho mate!"

Shay packed the laptop away into one of the drawers and informed Ruby of what plans had been made, "Right, Eyes, Mickey wants us to meet him in twenty minutes at TGI's for something to eat. Apparently he's bringing some bird with him called Reagan."

"Oh right. I'd better quickly go to the toilet and then brush my hair. I wonder what this girl's like?" said Ruby as she hurried into the bathroom.

Shay and Ruby entered the restaurant and were pleased to hear the music pumping. The restaurant was buzzing with people and they were unable to immediately find Mickey and his friend. They continued to shuffle amongst all of the people in the large restaurant/bar trying to seek out Mickey, when they heard a loud shout.

"Hey! Ruby, Shay, get over here! We got a booth!" They followed the shout and saw a smiling Mickey waving his arm, beckoning them over.

Shay and Ruby made their way over to Mickey who was sat with a nervous looking Reagan. They slid into the booth and sat opposite Mickey and Reagan.

"How's it going?" Shay asked them both.

Quickly followed by Ruby, "Hiya, you alright?"

"Oh my God Mickey! I just love those British accents!" said Reagan animatedly. "Wow, this is awesome! How you guys doin?"

She appeared to possess the same enthusiastic and energetic traits as Mickey. She was attractive and looked younger than Mickey. Even though they were sitting down, she seemed to be a very tall girl.

Everyone had settled, drinks had been ordered and there was good conversation. As Ruby sat picking at her beer mat, she felt Reagan looking intently at her, and then out of the blue, Reagan stated, "Gee! You're so pretty Ruby. You know, you're gonna fit right in here!"

Mickey added, "Hell yeah, that's for sure! I tell ya, as soon as Ruby turns up for an interview, they'll hire her! Who wouldn't? And this guy, my cousin… fuck man! He'll be running this place!"

Ruby was never one to accept compliments easily, not even when they were given by Shay; so at this point she felt more than a little embarrassed and proceeded to tear at her beer mat. On the other hand, Shay was much better at accepting compliments, proudly smiling with his hand on Ruby's leg.

Their drinks came and Mickey took a gulp of his cold Budweiser. As he wiped the froth from his moustache, he said, "Hey Shay, I spoke to some guys today. You know my real estate business is pretty quiet right now, so I told some other guys I know about you and proposed you for an air conditioning or a management job. Fuck man, they're all feeling the slump right now, but you know, something will turn up. Right?"

"I've no doubt Mickey," said Shay. "There are loads of jobs that I've applied for on the websites, so I'll get a spin somewhere. Is there any way we could get a bank account? We're carrying all of our cash around with us, we need to bank it really."

"Yeah, no problem Cuz. I'll call my guy in the morning, we'll have you guys set up by midday.

Reagan lent over to Ruby, "Hey Ruby, you wanna go shopping to the mall with me sometime? We could go cruising down to the beach too, it'd be so cool! All my girlfriends will love you!"

Slightly taken aback by Reagan's forwardness Ruby replied, "Erh… yeah ok, sounds good."

"Oh great! We'll have a blast! Hey, is this your first time in America, Ruby?"

"Well, it's my first time in California but I've been to Memphis before."

"Memphis in Tennessee? Wow… So you like Elvis then huh?" He was so handsome!"

"Yeah, I've loved him since I was a child, so I went there with a friend a couple of years ago. We went to Graceland and Beale Street, it was the nuts. I can't wait to go again."

"Gee, you must really love Elvis to go all the way to Memphis!" laughed Reagan.

The four continued to get along well and enjoyed their meals, not noticing how late it'd got. Shay settled the bill and they all left with full stomachs.

After breakfast the following morning, Shay checked his and Ruby's e-mail in the hope of having had some response from the many jobs that they'd both applied for.

"Ere, great news Eyes! A company in Riverside are interested in interviewing me for a contracts manager role!" exclaimed Shay.

Ruby shouted out from the bathroom, "Wow, that was quick, when's the interview?"

"The e-mail says I've gotta call them this morning to arrange a time. I'll do that right now." Eager, Shay started to dial the number.

"Good morning, Cool Air, how may I help you?" answered a female voice.

Shay went on to explain who he was and why he was calling.

"Great accent, you Australian? Oh by the way, I'm Jordan," said the lady.

"No, I'm from London as it happens," Shay said.

"Oh gee, London, England! Awesome! Ok Sir, how long have you resided in the United States?"

Shay turned on the charm and said, "We've only just arrived, Jordan. I worked here in the nineties so here I am, I'm back now for good in your beautiful country."

"Oh that's awesome. Welcome back Shay. Can I take your social security number and then we'll get you in today to meet the boss," Jordan sounded very keen.

"Oh... erh... well I don't have one yet. I'll be arranging one very soon, we..."

Jordan promptly interrupted, "Oh that's a shame. We can't employ anyone without a social security number. Geez, that's a real shame, it would have been great to have you work here. The lines are getting busy, sir, but you make sure you call back sometime." With that, Jordan hung up.

Ruby was now stood with bated breath next to Shay. He turned to her and said, "Shit, that didn't go too well. That woman said they don't employ anyone without a social security number."

"So how do we get them?" Ruby asked.

"Don't know to be honest, I'll call Mickey."

He called Mickey, "How you doing Mickey? Hey, I had a company interested in me but they lost interest when they found I didn't have a social security number."

Disappointed for Shay, Mickey replied, "Oh shit man, that's bad luck. I told you some company would love to take you on, with those British accents you'll have no trouble. Just keep trying, Cuz, but in the meantime find an immigration attorney. We'll go and see one and sort this shit out."

Ruby frantically searched the internet and found many attorneys but was drawn to one in Palm Springs. She called and booked an appointment for the following day. She then called Mickey who said he would also attend to support them. He then explained that he'd arranged for them to meet his banker at one pm that afternoon to open an account.

The bank account was opened without hassle and they were relieved that they were no longer having to carry cash around. They spent the rest of the afternoon at the hotel by the pool, sun bathing and enjoying the high temperatures.

The next day Mickey collected them to take them to Palm Springs for the appointment with the attorney.

As they travelled, Mickey gave a weather forecast, "Gee, I tell ya guys, it gets mighty hot in Palm Springs! It's in the desert in The

Coachella Valley, it'll be around hundred and twenty degrees up there. Fuck…"

Shay and Ruby laughed. They loved Mickey's enthusiasm and how he would explain something and finish the sentence with his usual 'fuck', which he said very slowly and drawn out.

They arrived and immediately felt the intense, dry heat that Mickey had described.

They entered the small but impressive reception area and were then summoned into the attorney's office by a very organised secretary in her late fifties with miniature glasses perched on the tip of her nose.

The attorney stood up from his big leather chair and held his arm out offering Shay and Ruby the smaller leather chairs positioned in front of his desk and said, "Hi there, welcome. Wow, we have three of you," he unenthusiastically attempted a chuckle. "Ok, first things first. My consultation fee is one hundred dollars, in advance please. If you pay now, we can begin."

Shay offered a one hundred dollar bill with his right hand, which the attorney accepted with his left hand whilst his right hand patted Shay's right forearm.

"That's swell, sir, now let's begin. I guess you guys have a story, you two are from London, right?" The attorney then looked over at Mickey, who was slumped in the leather couch that was positioned to the right of Shay and Ruby. "And you sir, are an American citizen?"

"Wow, you're good!" Said Mickey, "How'd you know where we're all from?"

The attorney, now seated, undid the buttons of his suit jacket and replied in a sarcastic tone, "A lucky shot I guess."

Shay and Ruby grinned at each other knowing that Mickey couldn't look more American if he tried.

Unexpectedly, Mickey sat up and proudly announced, "Well, we're a hundred percent Irish actually!"

134

The attorney lent back in his big chair, looked at Mickey and scoffed, "Yeah, sure you are," he then picked up his pen, turned to Shay and Ruby and asked, "Anyway guys, what's the story?"

Shay explained the story as briefly as he could to the sharp attorney who was listening intently.

"Well now, if you're on the run from these gangsters, perhaps you should inform the police department. As for gaining employment, that's impossible. And as for gaining a Green Card, that's also a no go. You have a ninety day Visitors Visa; it's illegal to work on that but you can stay on vacation for a period of ninety days and then you gotta go back home to London."

Disappointed, Shay replied, "We've got a return flight to Dublin actually."

"Ok, ok, then you gotta return to Ireland," the attorney replied indignantly.

Mickey, now comfortably slumped back into the couch with his hands linked behind the back of his head, said, "Hey, my father has passed away, God rest his soul, but he and my mother went to New York from Ireland in the sixties and moved to California in the seventies. My mother and sister live here like I do, so couldn't I get my cousin in through sponsorship?"

The proficient attorney was quick to correct Mickey, "No I'm afraid it doesn't work like that. It has to be a parent of theirs, or a sibling perhaps," he checked his watch and then talked even faster, "I take it neither of you have a parent or a sibling here, plus you are also two separate cases as you're not married."

Shay realised by the attorney's mannerisms that the meter was ticking and asked if there was another way around it.

The attorney explained, "On the east coast there are quite a few Irish and British who have... shall we say, gone under. They're now stuck in the US, they've overstayed their ninety day Visa and they work cash in hand. And in California, many Mexicans also do this," he then burst out laughing and said, "You guys sure don't look Mexican to me though! Hey enjoy your vacation, or go marry

American citizens!" Said the mocking attorney as he rose to shake their hands. They left his office feeling disappointed and frustrated.

Mickey thought it would be a nice idea for them all to visit his mother and sister, Shay's aunt Mary and cousin Kathleen, who both lived in Palm Springs. Shay remembered his aunt Mary from his visit in the nineties and that he was very fond of her. There, they spent the afternoon looking at old photos whilst Mary cast her mind back to life in Ireland.

After a week in Rancho Cucamonga with no joy on the job hunt and an unfortunate visit to the attorney, Shay and Ruby decided to go further south in search of employment.

THIRTEEN

Cool San Diego

Before heading off to San Diego, Ruby and Shay changed their Mustang for an economy car. Having bid fourteen dollars per day, the same rental company issued them with a standard car that they hired for four days.

They checked out of their hotel and drove down the freeway 15 to San Diego. The journey was short and the temperature got cooler and more comfortable as they drove. They found their pre-booked hotel in the city and checked in.

They walked through the city centre hand in hand and instantly fell in love with San Diego. "Seems as though Greg was right about this place, Eyes."

"Who? The geezer on the plane? Yeah he was, it's really lovely here. The temperature is better too, a bit of a breeze makes a difference. Do you fancy a coffee?" Ruby suggested.

They found an internet café and Ruby set up the laptop whilst Shay ordered the frappuccino and double espresso with danishes. He joined Ruby at the low set antique table and gazed round the room. It was a big place with high ceilings. Large settees were scattered around the room, covered with brightly coloured throws and lots of patterned cushions. In contrast, the furniture looked old and worn. It definitely had a hippy look that in turn, provided a real chilled out feeling. With young and middle aged people sitting and quietly chatting, San Diego had an air about it that they both loved.

Shay and Ruby began to search for work. They were both work-aholics and were positive that they'd get a lucky break soon. They searched the online job vacancies in San Diego and uploaded their resumés. They each had several replies via e-mail in response to applications they'd sent to various companies located in San Bernardino and Los Angeles but all replies requested a social security number. They thought they'd try their luck anyway and so intermittently stepped outside of the café to use their cell phones to call the various employers who had replied. Many of the employers were interested in Ruby and Shay but the lack of the social security number stopped any further interest. They sat in the café all day and relentlessly called various job advertisements from the newspapers but constantly found themselves up against the same problem.

They left the internet café somewhat discouraged but not beaten. They decided to have their dinner in the Gas Lamp Quarter that had the Mardi Gras feeling to it, as described by Greg on the plane. It seemed that Greg, a great ambassador for the USA, had been very accurate in his description of San Diego.

Shay announced, "Well, Greg's got everything right so far. Look Eyes, we'll get employment by hook or by crook!"

After a peaceful nights sleep, Shay carried out the routine calls back home to Connor in London, Josie and Mick and also to Bridget's house in Ireland as she'd now returned from France. All of Shay's family were encouraging and agreed that he and Ruby should continue their search and that all would come good. Their kind, hopeful words perked both Shay and Ruby up. They knew that if they were going to get a break, they would have to keep persisting.

The entire day was spent searching for employment and it was late afternoon when Shay decided to take a different approach. "Eyes, back in the day when the Irish went over to England, they would go to Irish pubs to find work because they always tried to help each other out. You know I've always run my own business and this is all new to me, I've always been the employer not the employee. And you've always managed the accounts for Billy's nightclub and never had to do this this either. I saw a lot of Irish pubs and one English bar when we were walking about yesterday. If we went back there, we might meet someone who could help us."

"Hmmmm… that's actually a good idea. Plus, you can talk the talk, sell snow to the Eskimos and all that. Talking directly to people might get us somewhere instead of e-mailing!" Ruby now sounded playful, "C'mon, let's get changed and go out for the evening. C'mon on London, chop chop!"

"Yeah, let's get right on it! A couple of cheeky drinks, a laugh and two jobs would make a good night out," and he laughed.

They got a taxi from the hotel to The Green Field, an Irish bar. Entering the bar they received a welcome with a friendly atmosphere, and great music was playing in the background.

About an hour had passed when a man sitting reading a newspaper at the bar and drinking what looked like whisky, turned to Shay. With an Irish accent with a hint of American, he asked,

"You on yer vacation from London? Although I'd say yer have the head of an Irish man!"

Shay laughed at the man's bold statement. "Me mum and dad are Irish."

The sociable man chuckled and replied, "Ah… yer a plastic paddy! Ah well, you'll fit in here alright. This place is full of plastic paddies."

Shay smiled and held out his right hand, "Name's Shay and this is Ruby," he said as he shook the man's hand and continued, "We're over here looking for work as it happens."

"Good to meet ye both, I'm Kevin, welcome! So, looking for work ay? Well, yer in the wrong city, in fact, you're actually a long way from finding any work here. This city is full of immigration police because we're so close to the Mexican border. You'll get no work around here without a social security number."

"Yeah, we've heard that, but surely there's a way around it." Shay said, with a wink.

"Ah yer right, there's always an angle! Well there used to be, fellows years ago would buy false numbers but they've put a stop to that."

Shay explained that they'd been to see an attorney a few days ago but had no joy.

Kevin laughed and replied, "Jesus! I'd keep away from them fellows if I were you, all they're interested in is taking yer money. The Olympics are on at the moment, if you can run the hundred metres in under ten seconds then they'll give yer citizenship and welcome yer with open arms but otherwise, they'll just take yer money and send ye on yer way. If ye want to stay, ye could go under but I'd advise ye to go to San Francisco. The place is full of Irish and English, ye will no hope in this town."

Shay and Ruby spent another hour in the bar, had a few more drinks and exchanged stories with Kevin who had clearly been in the States for many years.

The following morning Bridget called, on a terrible line, "Hiya love, how are ye getting on? Any luck yet?"

Struggling to hear her muffled reply, Shay asked, "Is that you Bridge?" Shay continued, "It's a really bad line, Bridge. We're doing ok, it's not as easy as we thought. We're learning the do's and don'ts out here."

A shocked and very disappointed Bridget replied, "Oh Shay!

That's no good! Ye will get nowhere behaving like that! I'm shocked, Shay, I really am."

Extremely confused, Shay asked, "Why are you shocked Bridge, what's up?"

"Well love, ye are out there to start a new life. What's made you get on the booze and dope? Ye will end up…"

She was stopped mid-sentence by Shay's roar of laughter, "I said do's and don'ts! Not booze and dope!"

Bridget could not stop laughing. "Oh Shay, I'll call you back, I'm gonna wet meself!" She hung up.

Bridget eventually called back and thankfully the line was a lot clearer as they both giggled with regard to the mis-understanding.

Shay told Bridget about Kevin who he had met the night before. Bridget advised him not to go under, just as Kevin had already advised. She told Shay to continue to stay positive and it would all work out.

Shay then called Mickey and told him of Kevin's advice.

Mickey replied, "Fuck that man! Hey, I got you a break, Cuz! A friend of mine in Orange County has a two month air conditioning contract in Nevada that's coming up at the end of next week. He can start you on that. If you do a good job like I know you will, you'll roll right on to the next one! We'll find something local for Ruby May, you'll see. Fuck going to San Fran man! That's eight or nine hours drive from here! Fuck…" Since learning at the bank appointment that Ruby's middle name was May, Mickey liked to call her 'Ruby May'.

Shay couldn't thank Mickey enough. An overwhelming sense of relief came over him and the dark, heavy cloud had shifted. Finally, they got a break. Shay told Ruby straight away and she was equally as ecstatic.

They decided to check out of the hotel and return to Rancho

Cucamonga, stopping at Newport Beach for a day of sun bathing. Newport Beach made them even more reluctant to leave. To Shay and Ruby, Newport Beach and San Diego were faultless and completely idyllic. Nevertheless, their priority was finding employment, the job was what determined their destination.

FOURTEEN

The Proposal

Shay and Ruby arrived back to the red-hot climate of Rancho Cucamonga and checked into the Lindigo Hotel, which was a boutique hotel that they found via Priceline.

Now very used to the routine of unpacking their bags on a regular basis, Shay and Ruby soon settled into their stylish room. Whilst Ruby carried out her habitual room inspection, Shay sat on the bright purple, modish leather chair by the desk and called Mickey. He asked Mickey if they could meet later on in the evening as he wanted to talk to him.

Mickey, as keen as ever, said, "Yeah man, I'd love to meet up! Hey, d'ya mind if I bring a friend of mine? Her name's Cassidy, she's a beautiful gal!"

"Yeah ok, you don't have to ask me, Mickey. 'Ere, is she a hundred percent Irish?" Bantered Shay, who personally found the question quite amusing.

"Nah man, she's not, but I know some gals that are! Would you guys prefer I bring an Irish gal?" Mickey had obviously taken Shay's question seriously.

Shay was unable hold back his laughter, which prompted Mickey to realise that Shay had asked the question in jest.

Mickey laughed with Shay and continued, "Well actually, I

could bring a Mexi... or anything come to think of it! You know, this place is full of chicks and I know 'em all!"

All four met at a steak house and Mickey introduced Shay and Ruby to the blonde haired, plastic surgery loving Cassidy who was in complete awe of the British accent. After only spending a short time in Cassidy's company, Ruby and Shay took to her bubbly personality. They both thought how it nice would be to meet her again, but it seemed like Mickey had a conveyor belt of chicks and there were probably a lot more to meet before Cassidy came along again.

The mood was upbeat and they decided to move onto a bar for music and have 'a cold one' as Mickey called it. Shay and Mickey discussed the forthcoming work in Nevada and Mickey told Shay of the hourly rates, which pleasantly surprised him. Ruby and Cassidy were also deep in conversation and Ruby was finding out where the best shops and nail technicians were from the informative Cassidy.

Cassidy went on to talk about Mickey and said to Ruby, "You know, Mickey's such an exciting guy! He rocks! And... he's awesome in the bedroom!"

Ruby laughed her distinctively loud hysterical laugh and thought to herself, oh my God, I can't wait to tell Shay that one later on, he'll piss himself!

Seeing that the girls were engrossed in their own conversation and laughter, Shay pulled Mickey to one side. "Mickey, I'm going to propose to Ruby, no one knows, so keep it quiet."

"I'm so happy for you Shay, I really am!" He hugged Shay and continued, "You two are swell together, congratulations! Hey, I get married every night but I wake up a single guy in the morning!"

Ruby and Cassidy danced and chatted whilst Mickey and Shay discussed the family. Mickey spoke about the loss of his father, which still hurt him deeply. Shay saw his pain and told Mickey that his dad had lived an eventful life and had earned everyone's respect.

"You know, I love stories about our family from the old

country. My dad used to tell me that Danny, Aunt Kate's husband, was a real character. What's he like, Shay?" Mickey asked.

Shay simply replied without hesitation, "Danny Good Looking is a top bloke. I'm really close with him."

Shay and Mickey fondly discussed how it was strange that they had grown up on different sides of the Atlantic yet they felt like brothers.

It was a fun, lively evening but was filled with kind, fond memories.

The next morning, Shay suggested that Ruby went to get her nails done at the place that Cassidy recommended whilst he would go and buy some work clothes and boots. Shay had an ulterior motive for wanting Ruby to get her nails done, so after he'd dropped Ruby off he went on his secret mission.

He drove to a huge jewellery outlet. Inside, he sat at the counter on a high stool drinking a bottle of water as he waited for assistance.

Shay smiled and introduced himself, "Hi, I'm Shay."

An oriental female trader swaggered seductively towards Shay and said, "You fwom London honey? I'm Mia, how can I help you today?"

"I need to purchase an engagement ring."

Tray after tray was viewed until Shay eventually made his choice and purchased a ring after a long bartering session.

"Be sure come back and buy wedding wings here honey, I give you vewy, vewy good discount Mister London," Mia said flirtatiously.

Proud of his new purchase, Shay sat in the hired car in the parking lot and scanned through the Sat Nav in search of an Italian restaurant. Having found several within a five mile radius, he drove around surveying the restaurants. He settled on the third restaurant, a romantic looking place called Luigi's. Knowing how much Ruby loved Italian food, he happily made a reservation for eight o'clock that same evening.

The evening soon arrived and Shay suggested to Ruby that they should go out to an Italian restaurant as he was fed up of the themed restaurants.

Ruby stood and admired Shay in his black shirt as he did up the final button leaving the top two open and said, "Mmmm... I love it when you wear that shirt. I'd better go and make myself half decent!"

The two set off in the car with Shay concealing the engagement ring in his pocket. He wasn't nervous; after a life of failed romances he knew in his heart that he'd found his soul mate in life. Their love was real and they'd given up everything to be together. Shay felt no need to wait to marry Ruby and he would suggest a Vegas Wedding, not ideal in his opinion but with work commencing shortly in Nevada, he felt they should marry before they got too busy.

They entered the romantic restaurant and were met by a short, stocky man, who definitely looked the part with his dark skin, black hair and moustache; wearing black trousers, a crisp white shirt and a black bow tie.

Shay smiled and said, "Buongiorno!" in his best Italian accent.

Ruby laughed at Shay and the waiter replied, "Hi guys, sit anywhere you like, I'll be right over with menus," and he quickly scurried off.

Shay chuckled and wondered if he'd made the right choice. They seated themselves into a quaint corner in the restaurant that only had one other functional table, which Shay studied for a moment. There were a couple in their sixties and a man in his late fifties sat eating and quietly talking. The man in his fifties was clearly an Elvis fanatic as he sat there with a mass of blue black hair and huge side burns styled as Elvis had his in the seventies. He wore a loud shirt and two massive replica rings; one was Elvis's TCB ring and the other was of Elvis's horseshoe ring that was studded with diamantes.

It didn't take long for Ruby spot the Elvis-Wannabe, "Oi, have you seen him over there? I saw loads of blokes like that when I was in Memphis. Ah bless him, he obviously thinks he really looks the part!"

Whilst Ruby sat and cleaned her cutlery with the mint green napkin, as she always did, she commented on how nice the restaurant was. The clean white walls were decorated with tasteful paintings and there were indoor plants dotted around the restaurant. Shay felt comfortable with the imminent proposal, and very pleased that Ruby liked the restaurant he'd chosen.

The waiter quickly approached their table and dropped two menus on it, "Can I get you guys a drink?"

"Have you got a wine menu please?" enquired Shay.

The waiter let out a sigh and stomped the ten feet to the counter in order to supply Shay and Ruby with a wine menu. Shay selected a cold bottle of Rosé as he knew that Ruby liked it. The waiter returned with the wine in an ice bucket and simply left it on the table, unpoured, before scurrying back off to the kitchen. Unimpressed with the waiter's lack of etiquette and enthusiasm, Shay did the honours and poured the wine.

The waiter returned and took their order. Ruby ordered Mozzarella for her starter, to be followed by Carbonara, Shay ordered Calamari to be followed by Spaghetti and Meatballs.

Shay decided that he would propose in the twenty minute interval between the starter and main course. He tried to ignore the fact that the waiter was not at all to his liking or satisfaction and to remain focussed on the job in hand, vowing to himself that he would not stray from it.

The waiter brought over their starters in his careless manner. The food was well presented and had been cooked perfectly, so they both agreed the chef knew his stuff. They had literally only been eating for three minutes when the little chubby waiter rushed over to their table with a trolley of food. As Shay and Ruby sat looking at him in total disbelief, he managed to squeeze their main courses onto the table and then started to walk away.

Shay called out to him, "Erh, excuse me. We've only just started our starters!"

With that, the waiter returned. "Ok, ok! I'll get chef to put them under the lamp 'till you finish your starters."

"Under the lamp?" scoffed Shay, "I don't think so, you're not that busy! We'll have new main courses cooked, please, during an interval."

The flustered waiter apologised and removed the main courses from the table.

Prior to this incident, Shay had discreetly removed the ring from his pocket and placed it between his legs on the chair but during his animated complaint, he had somehow managed to knock it off of the chair. Inconspicuously, he searched for the ring with his right hand, desperately wanting to make the proposal before the waiter intruded any further.

"What's up, London? You got an itch or something?" Ruby asked.

"No... I erh... I dropped my wallet on the floor," stammered Shay as he scooped up the ring from the floor next to Ruby's feet.

With the ring now back in place, Shay took Ruby's hand,

"Eyes, you know I love you and that I've never felt this way about anyone. We've both sacrificed an awful lot to be together and together is how I'd like us to remain. So, my beautiful Eyes, will you be my Wife?" and he offered the ring.

Shocked and tearful, Ruby accepted the ring onto her finger.

At the peak of the romantic moment, she couldn't resist a joke. "Erm... nah. I don't really fancy getting married." Then she laughed, wiped her eye and continued, "Of course I'll marry you.

You know I love you more than anything. I'm shocked. You're so sweet. I love you."

They lent over the table to kiss and the waiter returned, removed their empty plates, smiled and said, "Wow! Congratulations Guys! Gee, you're a lucky guy!"

As Ruby sat transfixed staring at her ring, the waiter returned with the main courses that were freshly cooked and apologised for the earlier mishap. They ate their meal and avidly discussed a Vegas wedding and a new life in the States. Ruby was so excited about going to Vegas and reminded Shay every ten minutes that Vegas was where Elvis had got married. They talked about their positively happy ending and how something so good had come from such a terrible situation, even though it was still far from over.

As they talked contentedly, the waiter rushed past their table and slipped their bill onto the table like an Olympian relay runner passing the baton. Shay had had enough of the waiter and his discourteous behaviour and called him back, "Hey! What's that?"

"That's your check, sir."

Stunned, Shay replied, "What is this? A fast food restaurant or what? We're still eating our main course! We've not even had dessert or coffee yet. You do know I just proposed don't you?"

The bemused waiter replied, "Yes sir, I do. What's the problem?"

Riled by his ignorance, Shay retorted, "Look mate, I could have proposed at a McDonalds drive through and got more romance!"

Still totally oblivious to Shay's problem with the poor service provided, the waiter replied, "Well I'm sorry all was not to your liking, sir."

"Go away mate. I'm telling you now, do your health a favour and stay in the kitchen 'till we're gone!" Shay said firmly.

"C'mon, let's just finish our mains and then go. Don't let that mug wind you up," Ruby said as she took Shay's hand.

They didn't hesitate in settling the bill and left, laughing about the not-so romantic Italian.

The next morning, Shay and Ruby agreed that they would go to Las Vegas the following day. Shay called Chuck who had the contract to start in Nevada. Chuck explained that they were all set to go in two weeks and that he had more work in Orange County to go onto. He told Shay how he was glad to have him on board and part of the team.

Shay and Ruby had breakfast and then set off to Victoria Gardens to purchase their wedding outfits. They went their separate ways, each in pursuit of their outfit. After two hours, they met up at the same coffee shop that they'd drank at before, both concealing their outfits as best as they could.

Shay called Mickey and told him that they were off to Las Vegas the following day to get married and would be back in three days.

Mickey was pleased for them both. "Hey, that's great news Cuz," he said. "You'll have a great time! Hey, when you're back we'll go out to dinner to celebrate. I'll bring my friend Shania… she's hot man! You guys will love her!"

Shay then called Connor, his parents and Bridget who were all delighted for them both with regard to the marriage and the work that Shay had obtained.

They went back to the jewellery outlet where Shay had purchased Ruby's engagement ring.

"Hey Mister London! You back! Wow! She must have said yes huh? She beautiful lady," Mia said.

"Hiya Mia, I'm back for the deal on the wedding rings you promised," Shay said.

Whilst Shay and Ruby carefully chose their two gold wedding bands, Mia lent on the glass counter and explained, "Hey, Mister

London, I was thinking…. you wanna live in California? Well, I have weally nice girl, she marwy you for five thousand dollars! She so good, you stay with her for two years, get citizen, divorce and marwy your England girl!"

Flabbergasted, Shay and Ruby didn't take offence at Mia's suggestion, on the contrary; they couldn't contain their laughter. Here they were to purchase their wedding rings and the retailer seemed more intent on selling them a bride so that Shay could gain citizenship.

They bought their wedding rings and Mia gave them the agreed discount.

Having left the jewellers Shay and Ruby went back to their hotel room and looked for another economy car from Priceline, to find that the accepting hire company was the same one as they had hired their current car from.

They parked their car at the drop off bay and went inside to the car hire reception. Ruby went and sat at the nearby seating area and Shay walked the very short distance to the reception counter. He immediately noticed that once again it was Tina on reception, an African American who had always been extremely helpful and jovial. Shay decided to try and use his charismatic side with Tina as Ruby had often mentioned that she loved Cadillac's, as did Elvis.

"Hey Tina, my favourite Californian girl, how you doing today?"

"Hey! Y'all back again! Smiling and trying to sweet talk me again," laughed Tina.

Shay leant over the counter and whispered, "Tina, we're off to Vegas to get married tomorrow. Any chance of a Cadillac for a week at the same rate of an economy car?"

"Get outta here!" she laughed loudly. "Coming in here like Prince Charming giving me those eyes!"

"Tina, c'mon, do us a deal. This is our third car from your company," he pleaded.

Tina grinned, stood with one hand on her hip and looked at

Shay out of the corner of her eye. "Y'all getting married huh? Show me the rings, if you're telling the truth I'll do you a brand new Cadillac for eighteen dollars per day for a week, how's about that?"

Shay produced the wedding rings and true to her word, Tina did them the deal.

FIFTEEN

Midnight Run to Nevada

It was late evening and Shay and Ruby sat in their hotel room excited about their drive to Vegas the following morning.

"I won't sleep tonight, London, I'm too excited to sleep! Not only are we going to Las Vegas to get married just like Elvis did, we're going in a Cadillac!" squealed Ruby.

"Me too, Eyes… Hey, let's go now! D'ya fancy a midnight drive, baby?"

"Are you serious? Really? Go now? Oh my God! Yeah c'mon, let's go!"

It was eleven thirty pm when Shay and Ruby left Rancho Cucamonga for Las Vegas, utterly elated with the prospect of a night drive through the desert to Vegas in a Cadillac.

They took the freeway 15 to the 66 that would take them all of the way to Las Vegas. As they drove, they listened to the radio. Ruby was flicking through the numerous stations, each playing songs from a particular decade. As she flicked between the fifties and sixties music channels, Ruby was happy to hear her favourite Gene Pitney song, '*Something's Gotten Hold Of My Heart*', which was then followed by Petula Clark's '*This is My Song*'. Shay loved that song and held Ruby's hand whilst he drove and sang along. Despite the extremely late hour, the adrenaline pumping through them both was keeping them energized.

The temperature quickly rose as they entered the desert regions, which shocked Shay as he'd thought that the desert temperatures cooled off at night. Ruby stuck her arm out of the window and referred to it as feeling like a hairdryer was being held on her arm.

They had been travelling for a couple of hours and started to feel hungry. Shay took an exit at Yermo and found a nineteen fifties diner called 'Peggy Sue's', which disappointingly was closed. Ruby loved the fifties era so Shay suggested that on their return journey that they would stop there to eat.

They continued the night drive for a short while and took an exit that was signposted 'Ghost Town' as their hunger and the name of this town was too much to resist. They found an all-night diner and parked outside.

As they walked into the large diner to choose where to sit, they were spoilt for choice. It was a large diner and its size accentuated the fact that there were only a handful of customers. They sat in a booth that was back to back with another booth where an older couple were eating. The only waitress there came over to Shay and Ruby's booth and stood in the dim light of the low-level hanging lamp.

"Hi my name's Mandy and I'm your waitress tonight. What can I get you guys? Do want some coffee whilst you decide?"

They opted for large mugs of coffee whilst they read the menu. Shay then ordered steak and eggs and Ruby ordered sausage patti's and scrambled eggs.

Eagar to finish the remainder of the journey, Shay and Ruby finished their breakfast and left the diner to hit the dusty trail.

The remainder of the journey was painstaking. Because it was so dark and the fact that they were driving through the desert, it felt as though they were getting nowhere fast. Ruby was dying to get a glimpse of the bright lights of Vegas. Mainly because of her love for Elvis, she'd read and watched so much about Las Vegas. It still hadn't really sunk in that she was going to be there.

At three thirty am, the famous lights were in sight. Shay drove slowly to allow Ruby to take it all in. Ruby stared wide-eyed in total disbelief at what she was seeing. She came over very emotional and couldn't help but shed a couple of tears, completely overwhelmed, and it all felt too much. The themed hotels were so big that they seemed to touch the stars and the dazzling, colourful lights appeared to cover every inch of every building, emphasized by black night sky.

The traffic was heavy and there were people everywhere. Shay had been driving for four and half hours and started to feel drowsy. They pulled into the Monte Carlo Hotel to find it was fully booked. The receptionist explained that most of the hotels were fully booked but she offered to make some enquires on Shay and Ruby's behalf. She made a call to the MGM and found that there was one room left. She requested that the last room be held for Shay and Ruby and explained they would be over at the MGM within ten minutes. Shay was pleased to be staying at the MGM, as he'd stayed there before a few years ago.

They arrived at the MGM and after checking in, wanted to go straight to bed and get some sleep. As they walked through the hotel, the tables were still busy and the slot machines still being played. During the drive to Las Vegas Shay had explained to Ruby the rules of blackjack and gave some tips on when to hit for a card or when to stay. She'd never been to a casino before and thought how the gambling lingo that Shay used was like a foreign language, the rules of Blackjack went straight over her head.

They found their room. It was spacious and clean with a large bathroom filled with fluffy towels and complimentary soaps, shower gels and body lotions; all covered with the famous MGM emblem. Shay was relieved to finally lie in bed and shut his heavy eyes, whilst Ruby lie drifting off to sleep feeling like an ant in a gigantic fantasy world of make-believe.

After a long sleep, they both got up at eleven am and went to the impressive buffet to eat. Ruby felt lost amongst the chaos in the huge hotel. This wasn't Shay's first time in Vegas and without thinking, took on the role of being Ruby's personal tour guide. Whilst eating, they decided to get their marriage licence.

They got a cab from outside the hotel and went to the Clark County Court to obtain a marriage licence. It was a short, painless process and they soon returned to the MGM and booked their wedding for the following day at four pm .

With time on their hands, they were able to make the most of the superb hotel. Whilst Ruby popped back to the room to safely put away their marriage paperwork, Shay took the opportunity to book a surprise for her. He'd heard that Tom Jones was appearing in the hotel and knew that Ruby would be in raptures if they'd got tickets. Shay was successful and managed to buy two tickets to see Tom Jones that evening.

After Ruby got back from the room, they made their way to a blackjack table. Feeling like a fish out of water, Ruby agreed that Shay would play for an hour or so whilst she would watch and learn the game. After two deals were complete, Ruby confidently decided to join the game. It was an upbeat table with three guys playing who were from New York on a stag weekend. Shay liked a table with a positive vibe. He liked to be vocal whilst playing and to involve the dealer in conversation, trying to break the dealer's concentration. Hit after hit would take Shay over the maximum twenty one and each time he stayed would leave him below the dealers score. He felt the atmosphere was good and vibrant but the cards were not coming for him and the three New Yorkers. Ruby on the other hand, was having the time of her life. Shay's fear of Ruby's inexperience was unwarranted, she played her own hand using her own system. Shay had previously explained that if she had a hand showing twelve and the dealer was showing a five that she should stay, as law of averages would predict that the dealer would have fifteen and she shouldn't take his bust card. Nevertheless, Ruby played her own way; she hit and pulled a six taking her to eighteen, giving the dealer a king, which busted him. The cheers and praise from Shay and the three New Yorkers got louder and louder as Ruby continued to win again and again. After three hours of playing, Shay was two hundred dollars down and Ruby was five hundred dollars up and nicknamed Lady Luck. The time had flown by, so they left to go back to their room and get ready for dinner, three hundred dollars better off, thanks to Ruby.

Ready for the evening and just before closing their hotel room door, Shay pretended to panic and told Ruby he'd forgotten something and rushed back into the room. When she asked what he'd forgotten, he pulled out two tickets for the Tom Jones concert. Ruby screamed with excitement and flung her arms around him. She was shocked to say the least, but at the same time completely over the moon.

They impatiently entered the venue where the concert was to take place, both surprised at the size of the room and how intimate it was. It felt more like they were going to a private performance, not a concert. They ordered their drinks and eagerly awaited the performance, of in their opinion, a Legend.

Tom came on stage and his presence was electrifying. His energy was contagious and his powerful voice and provocative dance moves were mesmerising. He had the men at the concert green with envy as the female contingent screamed for more. He pounded out hit after hit making it impossible for anyone to stay still in their seats. Shay got emotional when Tom sang, '(It Looks Like) I'll Never Fall in Love Again' and 'Green, Green Grass of Home.' Ruby got up and danced to 'Kiss,' 'Delilah,' 'Sex bomb,' 'What's new Pussycat' and many more. It was clear that nobody wanted the night to end. Everybody had a fabulous evening of entertainment and left on a high.

Shay and Ruby decided to return to the Blackjack table before bed and had a great night of blackjack after blackjack. Ruby was still on a winning streak, as was Shay in this session. Everyone at the table was amused at how, coincidently, Shay and Ruby were often dealt the exact same cards. Whilst playing, they met an African American man from Kansas and between the three of them, they had the dealer under pressure.

Shay and Ruby happily went to bed twelve hundred dollars up.

Today was their wedding day. They received supportive calls from Shay's parents, Connor and Bridget. Bridget spent a particularly long time speaking to Ruby and was very compassionate on a day that every girl needs her mother and family with her. Ruby told Bridget that today was about her and Shay and that was all that really mattered. She remarked how the situation wasn't any of their doing, and it wasn't just her that didn't have family there, Shay didn't either. And to them, all of the material things were irrelevant.

They spent the day by the crowded pool of the hotel. Wanting to look their best for their wedding, they decided to spend some time topping up their tans. The heat was intense and the humid air was still. They left the pool giving themselves plenty of time to get ready.

Back in the hotel room, Shay and Ruby compared tan lines before getting showered. When Ruby was in the shower, Shay secretly rang down to reception and ordered her a dozen red roses and a bottle of Rosé. By the time she'd got out of the shower, the hotel bell boy was knocking at the door with Shay's romantic surprise. She was choked with Shay's gesture and was grateful for the wine. She felt like a bag of nerves, and thought a glass of wine while she got ready would help to calm her down.

It was arranged that Shay was to be at the wedding chapel fifteen minutes before Ruby got there. By quarter past three Shay was ready. He looked striking, dressed in a black suit, ivory shirt, ivory tie and black shoes. Ruby couldn't take her eyes off of him as he walked around the room and she repeatedly told him how handsome he looked. Ruby remained in her dressing gown as she didn't want Shay to see her in her wedding dress until they were both at the chapel. Shay announced that he was leaving. He told her that he loved her very much and would see her shortly.

Now that Shay had gone, Ruby was left by herself with her nerves and thoughts. She had another glass of wine and lit a cigarette. She sat at the desk and wished she could listen to some music. Listening to Elvis would help calm her down and dismiss the wishy-washy feeling in her stomach. She put on her dress, her shoes and made final touches to her hair. Being accustomed to usually having Shay's opinion to reassure her that she looked ok, she now had to assure herself. She stood and looked at herself in the full length mirror. Her long, black strappy evening dress draped down onto the floor. It was fitted and nipped in at the waist. The front was wrapped across from under the bust and had a black satin trim. She stood and fiddled with the straps and let out a sigh. She knew that Shay couldn't wait to see her dress and wondered to herself whether or not she looked ok. When she'd spoken to Bridget earlier in the day, Bridget reminded her that she needed something old, something new, something borrowed and something blue. For something old, Ruby had her bra. For something new, she had her wedding dress. For something borrowed she had something from Shay. He gave Ruby a five dollar bill, which on it he wrote the date of their wedding followed by, 'Eyes, This is a loan. I will borrow this to you. You have my heart forever! Love always, London x x x x x *x.*' For something blue, she had a royal blue little mesh bag that Shay had her engagement ring in. She put the five dollar bill inside the tiny bag and hid it inside her bra.

Soon enough, it was time for Ruby to make her way to the chapel. As she checked herself one last time in the mirror, she fought to reject any thoughts of her family that entered her head. She held her dress up on one side as she walked down the long corridors heading for the lift. In an attempt to stop her apprehension and combat the shakes, she hummed to herself a song of Elvis's called '*Something Blue.*'

Ruby approached the main door to the chapel reception area and noticed the sign that indicated that a wedding was in process. She entered the reception area to be greeted by the two women that she'd met earlier in the day. The ladies told Ruby how beautiful she looked and handed her the bouquet, made up of ivory roses and which stood out against her elegant black dress. She was ushered into another room where she was soon greeted by the Reverend, who explained in brief how the ceremony would go. After only a few minutes, which felt like hours, one of the two ladies from the reception area entered the room and told Ruby that it was time. Those two words 'it's time' were as though somebody had just pressed a panic button.

Ruby gripped her bouquet tightly as she stood outside the white chapel doors. She heard the music start. She had wanted '*Air On The G String*' by J. S. Bach, which was her much loved, favourite piece of classical music. Unfortunately, they didn't have that particular piece of music but now, standing outside the chapel about to get married, the music was unimportant. Ruby was ushered by the two ladies into the chapel. Ruby was frozen still.

"Ruby, it's time to go in. You look beautiful," said one of the smiling ladies.

"What, now…? Sorry… I'm just really nervous!" said a shaky Ruby.

With a few more kind, reassuring words from the empathetic ladies, she plucked up the courage to step through the doors.

Ruby saw Shay standing at the alter. He looked more handsome than he did in the hotel room, standing proudly with an ivory rose in his button hole. With his arms held down in front of him with one hand on top of the other, his face beamed as he watched her walk towards him. Hating being centre of attention, Ruby felt as though she wanted to run to him but instead had to walk slowly and gracefully, trying not to trip on her long dress. They exchanged their vows and the ceremony only lasted quarter of an hour, before they walked out of the chapel hand in hand to be congratulated by the staff waiting in the reception area.

They were introduced to their photographer who took them into another room for the photo session. They had photos taken together and individually and were to collect them the next day.

Now man and wife, Shay and Ruby went and ate in the Italian restaurant inside the MGM, had a beautiful meal and drank fine wine. They then returned to the blackjack table in an attempt to top up their winnings, vowing not to go back to Rancho Cucamonga at a loss.

They played for hours, but as Shay often reminded Ruby, you lose all sense of time in Vegas. They had stayed even, when suddenly Shay received a pair of aces. With a black one hundred dollar chip on the table he doubled his stake. Now, he had two hundred dollars on each hand riding. The dealer then produced Shay's next card, another ace; great cards, another two hundred dollars. He had six hundred dollars riding on this hand and with the dealer showing a two, this was almost a guaranteed win. The other players at the table were excited for Shay and were being very vocal. He'd also attracted quite a few passer-by's who stood by the table to watch.

The dealer called out to the pit boss, "Six hundred dollars down!" He then said to Shay, "One card on each only, sir."

Shay hit the first ace and received a two, on the second ace received a five. Hmmm, not great, he thought.

On the third ace he received a three. "Shit!"

"C'mon! Bust it out dealer!" shouted out the man they'd previously met from Kansas.

The dealer turned his discreet card. Shay sighed with relief at the sight of a ten, which took the dealer to twelve and an imminent bust. A third card from the dealer showed a three taking him to fifteen.

"Oooh... high card! He's gonna bust that out man!" roared the Kansas man.

Shay sunk to the table as the dealer turned a six, beating Shay's three hands that were a sure thing in his and everyone else's minds.

"Damn! Shit man! The devil played his fiddle and you danced, that's bad luck. I aint never see cards like that! You were on a winner, that's a real shame! Hey, I'm off to bed. Goodnight y'all and congratulations on your marriage buddy. You're a lucky guy, your wife is beautiful, man." The Kansas man reached an arm out and touched fists with Shay.

With a sour taste in his mouth, Shay had had enough of cards and decided to cut his losses and quit whilst ahead. As they made their way out of the casino area, Ruby still had some chips left and said, "Oi look, that table's empty, let's play that one."

Shay agreed but said that he'd watch. As Ruby placed her bet, an American man sat down at the table to play. Shay noticed that he watched Ruby more than he watched the cards or the dealer. Already riled by his bad luck, he thought to himself, is this bloke playing or just here to eye up Ruby?

As Ruby watched her cards, the American watched Ruby and Shay watched the American. Shay was becoming more and more frustrated with this man who was sat blatantly ogling his new bride.

"You here on your own, mate?" Shay asked.

The startled American replied, "Erh no, my wife's upstairs sleeping."

"Oh really, that's good… I tell you what, give me your room number and your key and I'll go upstairs and stare at your wife!"

"Oh… Erm… I meant no offence, sir. I was… erm… just admiring what a good looking couple you are," said the embarrassed American.

Ruby looked at Shay and knew it was time to go. She suggested that they leave the table and go and get something to eat. It was now early morning and they were both hungry. They ate in the hotel before going back to their room.

The following morning they packed their bags and started the journey back to Rancho Cucamonga, as Mr and Mrs Sullivan. The drive back was long, hot and mundane, in the daylight the desert scenery never seemed to change.

They stopped at Yermo to get some lunch at Peggy Sue's diner, as Shay had promised. They entered the fabulous nineteen fifties diner and felt as though they were stepping back in time. The décor, fixtures and furnishings a replica to what a nineteen fifties diner would have been like. It was obviously a popular venue as they struggled to find somewhere to sit. The typical food of that era was fantastic and the milkshake was the best they'd ever tasted.

Ruby was intrigued to find that even the ladies toilet had the fifties theme, including lots of Elvis Presley memorabilia.

They were back in Rancho Cucamonga by late afternoon and went straight to Mickey's apartment. Shay had spoken to him on their journey back and Mickey had asked them to drop by to see him.

Shay and Ruby knocked on the door and were greeted by Mickey and his wide smile. "Alright Mickey, how's it going mate? Allow me to introduce you to the wife!" Shay said proudly.

Mickey gave them both a quick hug and told them to go inside.

Ruby sensed that something was up. "What's wrong, Mickey? You don't seem yourself?"

"Gee, you guys ain't gonna believe the bad luck."

As the three sat down on Mickey's large leather corner settee, Shay asked, "Why? What's up, Mickey? You been blown out tonight by one of your chicks?"

A low-looking Mickey looked up from the floor, "Man, I had Chuck on the phone this morning. The main contractor for that air-con job has gone and given the job to a Nevada based company, as Chuck only has a Californian licence. I know you had it in the bag, Cuz, I'm sorry man, you're back to square one."

Shay jumped up from the settee and angrily paced the living room. "Fuck it! What a mug I've been. We've spent money that we wouldn't have spent 'cos I had that job. For fuck's sake! Well, we've gotta get jobs or we're really gonna be in the shit!"

Mickey heaved a sigh and said his usual long-drawn out "Fuck…" which he then more positively followed by saying, "Hey c'mon guys, something will come up. It's hard at the moment, you know. When the election is over, things will pick up for sure!"

"Fuck that, we can't wait that long! We'll have to take the advice from that geezer in San Diego and go up to San Francisco," Shay insisted.

Ruby sat quietly twiddling her new wedding ring feeling let down and disheartened at this blow, following on the day after their wedding day.

Their bubble had been burst but just like all of the times before, Shay and Ruby would wipe their mouths, dust themselves down and try another avenue.

SIXTEEN

The Streets of San Francisco

Having accepted their situation for what is was, Shay calmed down and Mickey perked up. Mickey, Shay and Ruby collectively cooked a meal and ate barbequed steak and tossed salad out on the patio. They discussed the wedding and the trip to Las Vegas and Mickey was eager to see their wedding photos. They turned their frustration and desperation into positive thoughts and all felt certain that a break would come soon.

Shay and Ruby stayed the night at Mickey's playboy pad and planned to set off early the next morning for San Francisco.

They left Mickey's at five am the next morning. During their drive, Shay and Ruby decided that they should make a call to DCI Turner in England for an update. Since Shay was driving, Ruby called Middlesex Police but was told that DCI Turner was not on shift, she was then put through to one of his colleagues. This colleague informed Ruby that due to lack of evidence, the Crown Prosecution Service had decided not to charge Billy Gower, negative news that was not what they wanted to hear. For all Shay and Ruby knew, if Billy wasn't going to be charged, he would be free to carry on running around paying his underworld contacts. Had being arrested incited him even more to have Shay killed? Would Billy now think of himself as being untouchable? How far would he go to ensure that the contracts were carried out? Would he stoop so low as to lean on any of Shay's family members?

Shay drove with his head held in one hand, sighed and began to despair, "Where's the justice in that, ay? Let's have it right!... Here we are, running around America because he's made it impossible for us to stay in England or Ireland, we've lost everything and that slag gets away with it! We've done nothing wrong and we're the ones that are suffering! I tell you what Eyes, I don't know how much longer I can keep this positive thinking up. Yesterday we find out that the job in Nevada's been cancelled and then this morning we get another kick in the bollocks. I'm gonna have to ring Danny and see what he knows, he'll probably be more help than the police have been."

As it was currently six am in California but ten pm back in England, he refrained from calling Danny Good Looking for an update, and decided to wait for a more appropriate time to call.

They had an eight or nine hour drive ahead of them. They didn't want to spend all those hours getting stressed about the charges being dropped on Billy. On a more positive note, so far, all had been quiet and no one had heard anything from Billy, Ronnie or more importantly the Dempsey's.

Once they had got north of Los Angeles the landscape turned into a burnt red colour. This scenery was monotonously consistent for several hours, making the journey tiresome and uninteresting.

After five hours of constant driving, they pulled off of the deserted freeway and found a shop/diner called The Willow, a mile from the freeway. The place was extremely quiet and they wondered if it was even open. Thankfully it was, and when they entered they found that they were the only customers. To get to the actual diner, they had to walk through a large shop that sold homemade fudge and various other gifts and keepsakes. In the diner, there were many tables and booths to choose from; however, they decided to sit on the high stools at the counter.

A young, friendly dark-haired lady greeted them holding her order pad and a pen, "Hi, how you guys doing? You want something to eat?"

Shay and Ruby smiled at the pleasant young lady and ordered a slice of apple pie and a mug of coffee each.

Whilst they drank their coffee and ate their homemade pie, Bridget called. "Hiya love! Congratulations! Now listen, give me yer American bank details… Peter and I want to give ye a little wedding gift!"

Shay was taken aback by Bridget and Peter's generosity, "Ah Bridge… you ain't gotta do that, we're…"

Bridget abruptly interrupted. "Look, yer going to do what yer big sister tells you ok! Anyhow, we'd do exactly the same if ye had got married in Ireland."

Shay thanked his sister and went on to explain that the Nevada job had been cancelled and that the police had dropped the charges on Billy due to lack of evidence.

"Well, all is quiet here, Shay. I'm sure everything will be ok," Bridget went on to pacify him, "Don't waste your energy thinking about him or worrying about us, just concentrate on finding work in San Francisco. Anyhow, I love you and know that ye will be alright."

Shay and Ruby resumed their long journey and eventually reached the outskirts of San Francisco. The Sat Nav lead them to their pre-booked hotel in Oyster Point Waterfront, Veterans Boulevard. Both relieved that the journey was over, they got out of the car and stretched.

Ruby rubbed her arms and said, "Bloody hell, it's a bit nippy here!"

Shay laughed. "Nippy! It's freezing! Look at all the fog rolling in from the bay and the mist coming over the hills." He put on his hoodie and Ruby put on a jacket.

They got their bags from out of the trunk, entered the hotel and made their way over to the reception counter to check in. The receptionist was of Asian appearance and had an unidentifiable accent.

As soon as he made eye contact with Shay, Shay handed him the booking confirmation number provided by Priceline and said,

"Hi, we've got a room booked for two nights."

The receptionist typed the relevant details into his computer, "Oh yes… here we are. So where are you guys from?"

"Have a guess!" Replied Shay, assuming that the receptionist would guess Australia, as most people did.

"Oh awesome!… Wow, how exciting. What's the weather like there?"

Ruby smothered her mouth but couldn't disguise her laughter. Bemused, Shay smiled as he took their room key. They both laughed hysterically as they made their way to the elevator. Their room was large but very basic. They dumped their bags and decided to check out the city.

As they set off for a drive, Ruby entered various locations into the Sat Nav. They drove in the darkness around the hilly streets to Union Square, China Town and Fisherman's Wharf. Ruby then entered 'Irish Pubs' into the search system and they chose a place called Durty Kelly's as their first point of call.

On entering the bar, Shay commented on how he felt like he was back in Ireland. There were thirty or forty drinkers inside the small, dimly lit bar and the atmosphere was relaxed.

They sat in the corner and read The Irish Herald newspaper searching for jobs. They felt more positive and that their chances of actually getting somewhere were better in San Francisco. They sensed a real European feel to the city by the bay.

After spending some time reading the papers and people watching, they became exceptionally tired, left the pub and returned to their hotel to sleep with the intention of getting off to an early start the following day.

Shay awoke when he heard Ruby talking and laughing on the phone.

"I'll pass you over to him now, Peter, hope to meet you soon, take care." Ruby said as she passed the phone Shay. Heavy-eyed, he manoeuvred himself in the bed and sat up, rubbed his eyes and took the phone from her.

"Hello," he said.

"Alwite mate! Did I wake you?" Peter asked mimicking a cockney accent.

"Nah, nah… I just woke up. How's it going Peter?"

"Ah, struggling on Shay! I paid four t'ousand dollars into yer account today. Will yer check to make sure it's there? Let me know if it is, yer know how these banks make errors."

"Yeah, course I will! Why have you done that, you didn't have to? It's a bit much, Pete."

"Ah, tis from myself and Bridget and we want to hear no more about it. Forget about what you had and just get yourself going out there."

Shay thanked him and asked him to convey his and Ruby's appreciation to Bridget.

Shay and Ruby ordered a cab at the quiet hotel reception, but waited a while before it arrived. Shay sat in the front and asked the cab driver what region of the city they should go to for Irish bars.

The middle-aged cab driver pulled slowly out of the hotel entrance. "If you want an Irish bar guys, I could drop you in the Financial District," he said. "There's one or two Irish bars there. That'd be a good area to start."

It was only a short distance to the Financial District. Shay paid the cab driver and the cab driver pointed them in the direction of the Irish bars.

In the overcast weather, they walked along the busy sidewalks and eventually found an authentic Irish bar called The Bankers Bar. It was a large venue and customers were sparse. It was dark inside, there was a lot of dense mahogany woodwork and the perimeter of the room was framed with dark emerald green leather seats.

The Irish barmaid, a tall lady in her thirties dressed in a black and white uniform was standing behind the bar and greeted them.

"How ye doing, ye wanna wee drink?"

"Please yeah, we'll have a Guinness and a brandy no ice," Shay said.

"Ye over from London? You've the head of a paddy so you have. Are your mammy and daddy Irish?"

"Yeah, Mum's a Kerry woman and my dad's from Waterford. Where are you from?"

She placed the pint of Guinness to one side to settle, and replied, "I'm from Tyrone, been here t'ree years now so I have. I love this place. I'm Sinéad by the way, what's yer names?"

"I'm Shay and this is Ruby. We just got married in Vegas and now we're looking for work in San Fran."

"Jesus, dat's great! I'd love to go to Vegas! I'm a big Elvis fan, shur he was married there was he not."

Pleased as ever to be in the company of a fellow Elvis fan, Ruby swallowed her mouthful of brandy and joined the conversation, "Yeah he did! On the first of May nineteen sixty seven at the Aladdin Hotel. Mind you, that's not there anymore and neither is the International Hotel, he was contracted for performances there in the early seventies. It's a shame, I'd have loved to have seen those hotels. Have you been to Graceland?"

Sinéad leant on the bar as she and Ruby continued their conversation about The King.

After serving another customer, Sinéad wandered back over to where Shay and Ruby were sitting and went on to explain that for accommodation they should use a website called 'Craig's List'.

"It's not cheap to rent so it's not. Maybe ye'd be better off sharing for a wee while 'till ye get settled. For work, yer better off hitting all the Irish bars in the Richmond District. Just get talking to the lads up there and yer bound to get hooked up."

Shay and Ruby took Sinéad's advice and got a cab that took them through the tram filled streets to Richmond District, where they got dropped off at Geary Boulevard.

"This is like being back in Kilburn or Cricklewood in London. Look Eyes, there's Irish pubs everywhere. This is much better, we'll get work off someone here," Shay said with optimism.

They entered an Irish bar and noticed the Republican memorabilia that was mounted haphazardly onto the walls.

As they both sat at the bar on the high bar stools, Ruby announced, "This is like the place in Connemara that we went in. I wonder if they've got the wire song, I like that one!"

Shay laughed. The barman was looking at Ruby out of the corner of his eye with a bemused look as he poured their drinks.

Shay corrected Ruby and said, "It's called 'The Men Behind The Wire', you nutter! Not the wire song!"

The barman clearly overheard Shay correcting Ruby, he couldn't contain his amusement and asked, "Do yer like the Rebel music then dar'lin?" He shook their hands and introduced himself as Sean.

Shay took Sean's friendliness and sociable manner as an opportunity to enquire about work. "Is there of plenty work in San Francisco? We're desperate for work. You know the score, we've no permits but people do work without permits over here, don't they?"

Sean stretched out both arms and leant on the bar, "Shur most fellows here have gone under, that's not the problem, it's actually getting the work, yer know what I'm saying. What do yer do, lad?"

"Air conditioning or anything construction based really."

"Jesus, the construction business is quiet altogether! Yer know this election needs to finish 'cos this country needs an injection of life, t'ings are tough at the moment like! Go down to Eileen's bar, tis down the road. She's a Kerry woman and she'll hook yer up with someone."

Shay and Ruby thanked Sean and left to head for Eileen's bar.

They walked up Geary Boulevard taking a left on twenty third to Eileen's Bar. Inside the small bar, they felt as though they had walked into a time machine and gone back fifty years. The first thing that they noticed was the smell of smoke. Most of the dozen drinkers inside the bar were smoking cigarettes, generally not permitted in all of the bars. It was very basic, the bar was long and almost the length of the entire room; there were very few tables to sit at and a pool table was in the middle of the room.

Ruby and Shay acknowledged the male drinkers as they positioned themselves at the bar. Ruby tapped her bar stool with her foot in time to Johnny Cash singing '*Ring of Fire*' that was being played on the jukebox on the far side of the room. They both felt welcome and admired the authenticity of the old-fashioned 'Speak Easy.'

Down at the far end of the bar was a petite lady in her sixties. She called out to an elderly Irish man and asked if he wanted another drink.

He replied, "Ah… Go'wan! Stick another one in there, Eileen!"

Obviously, the lady behind the bar was Eileen, the Kerry woman that Sean had told Shay and Ruby to speak to about work.

Eileen soon made her way down the bar towards Shay and Ruby and greeted them with a welcoming smile. "Hi, how are yer. Tis nice to see new faces in here. Where are ye from?"

Shay replied, "Well, I was born in England but both my parents are Irish. Mum's a Kerry woman and my dad's from Waterford."

Eileen placed a clean ashtray on the bar for them both and then asked, "So where's yer mum from in Kerry?"

"Dingle," he replied.

"Well, I'm a Killorgin woman meself but I've been here for t'irty two years now, so this is home!" she laughed.

As Eileen wandered down the bar to fix their drinks, a young man called Kieran approached to ask, "Hey, you wanna shoot some pool?"

Shay accepted the young mans invite and they played three or four games. It turned out that Kieran's parents originated from Kerry and Wexford and he was an extremely proud American Irish man and wore his grandfather's peak cap with pride.

Whilst Shay played pool, Ruby sat at the bar looking at the collection of cobweb covered pictures and postcards displayed on the wall behind. Eileen seemed to be glad of some female company and spent some time chatting with Ruby. Ruby explained her and Shay's desperation to find some work.

Shay came back to the bar for his drink and Eileen said, "I'd like to help ye both, ye seem like a nice couple anyways. Pop in tonight at about seven o'clock, Shay, I'll introduce yer to Andy, he's a Limerick man and he's sure to have some work for yer."

After a couple of hours, Shay and Ruby left Eileen's Bar and went to Clement Street between fifth and sixth to an English pub, which had only one man drinking in it.

As they ordered their drinks the man called over, he had a Yorkshire accent, "You alright mate, you from London?"

Shay looked over and replied, "Yes mate, where you from?"

"Sheffield. Colin's the name. You's on your holidays or living out here?" Coming over to shake their hands.

A smiling Shay introduced himself and Ruby, then went onto explain that they were hoping to live there but needed to find some work first.

"That's easy mate, you gotta form an American company. Then you get a Business Visa, which allows you to stay. You'd hafta keep popping back home but it's the easiest way to do it," Colin explained, as he stood holding a bottle of Corona.

Colin looked like he was in his mid-thirties. He was casually dressed in a zipped up hoodie, jeans and trainers. His dark hair was purposely styled to looked messy and every so often, he would sweep his fringe out of his eyes.

Shay was pleased to discover that Colin was also a big football fan and enjoyed an in-depth conversation over a couple more drinks. Ruby quietly sat on the bar stool sipping a glass of tonic water, listening to their conversation.

Having spent two hours exchanging stories and gathering information from the informative Colin, they left the English bar to return to Eileen's.

Eileen gave Shay and Ruby a huge welcome as they entered the bar. She gave them both a drink on the house and then called over to a man sitting in the corner, "Andy! Come over here please, this is the couple I was telling yer about!"

After a long conversation with Andy they decided to return to Rancho Cucamonga the next day. Andy explained that nearly everyone was working two days a week because work was so scarce. He went on to enlighten Shay about the reality of life in San Francisco for people who had gone under. Andy was only a young adult himself and missed his family in Ireland very much. Due to the fact that he couldn't leave America, his very elderly father and older brothers would have to make the long, hard trip over to San Francisco to visit him. However, the most poignant fact that Andy made was that there was no work there.

Again, now taunted with the feeling of utter despondency, Shay and Ruby saw no point in staying at the bar any longer and decided to return to their hotel.

Once settled back in their room, Ruby told Shay that she was going to call her brother, Charlie. The last time that the siblings spoke was when Shay and Ruby were in Wales, Ruby knew that he was bound to be worried.

Ruby dialled Charlie's number and anxiously waited for him to answer. "Hello…" answered Charlie.

"Charlie it's me!" Ruby replied, feeling emotional at hearing her brother's voice.

"Ah Ruby! Hang on a minute, let me just turn the music

down... Sorry Rube, right, I'm back now. Why's it taken you so long to ring me? Where are you? Are you both alright?"

"I know Char, I'm really sorry but things had really gotten out of hand. Did you hear that Billy hired that bloke, Ronnie, from Mile End and another firm called the Dempsey's to kill Shay?"

"What? Nah I didn't hear that! Bloody hell Ruby, are you two both alright?" He sounded shocked.

"Erm, yeah. We're not bad. We're still just moving around from place to place," Ruby then asked, "So you haven't heard a thing then?"

"Nope, not a word.... Well, not about hit-men anyway! I've only heard the usual bollocks, you know, like how you two have done one and left everyone in the shit. Mum just keeps crying about it all and keeps asking me to move back in... Same old shit different day really. So are you sure you're both ok?"

"Yes Charlie, honestly, we're fine. I just wanted to call you to see how you are. Look, I'm gonna have to go because my credit is gonna run out. I'll phone you again soon though, ok. I love you... bye." With that, Ruby hung up the phone feeling better, now having spoken to her brother after such a long while.

Shay couldn't sleep that night. He stood on the balcony feeling lost and depressed. He looked out over the city feeling like an alien. Though he was well travelled, this was so very different. This wasn't a holiday, far from it. As he smoked his fourth cigarette, he thought about how he and Ruby were trying to find work illegally and do so by trying to impose friendships with people they didn't even know. He reflected on the business he'd built up over a number of years and all of the money that he'd invested; along with time, blood, sweat and tears. It was all gone now. He'd lost everything overnight and in vain, was trying to start again in a country struggling with a poor economy. At his lowest ebb, he felt dejected but safe as whilst he and Ruby were in America the threat of the Dempsey's and Billy was non-existent. He decided that Mickey had been correct in saying that they should remain in Rancho Cucamonga and that something would turn up. All this constant moving around in such a huge state was senseless and costing money; the money that his parents had given them to get a fresh start in life.

They set off the next morning both feeling very tired and hung over from their non-productive time spent San Francisco.

Whilst Shay drove his cell phone rang, it was Bridget. "Shay, I had a phone call from a man this morning." She was traumatized and became choked and struggled to get her words out.

"Bridget, calm down, who phoned you? What was said?"

Bridget took a deep breath to compose herself before she continued with her trembling voice, "He, he, he… he said that I'm harbouring you and Ruby. He said that he's got my address. If ye don't go back, he said that they would visit here and they'd hurt me instead. Shay he really meant it. He really scared me."

"Shit! I thought all this was over! What we gonna do?" Shay said as he banged the steering wheel.

"Well, I've spoken with the Garda and they're on alert. We've good security here so if anyone tries to get in, they'll have a struggle. They've also put a trace on our phone line so if we get anymore calls from a with-held number, they'd be able to trace it."

"Bridge, I'm so sorry, I don't know what to say," he sighed. "I've brought this grief to your door. I'm really sorry, Bridge."

"Don't be silly Shay! Yer not to blame for the actions of those nutcases, ye are victims too. How are ye getting on in San Francisco?" Bridget asked, in an attempt to play down her distress for Shay's sake.

Hearing from his distraught sister that she'd been threatened, Shay was seething with anger and feeling as though it was his fault. He now had no enthusiasm to discuss his and Ruby's time in San Francisco but perhaps a change of subject might help Bridget to calm down. "Ah there's nothing doing there, Bridge. We met loads of Irish and English people but the majority of them are working a two day week. It's difficult to get anywhere here to be honest."

"Shay, ye should stay in San Francisco. Ye won't get any breaks moving from town to town, ye should be in one place."

"Nah, I can't stay in San Francisco. It's just pub after pub after pub and boozing. We'll sort something out in Rancho Cucamonga, we should never have left there."

"I hope so Shay, yer need to get working. Ye definitely can't come back here though, Peter and I have made some enquires through some official people we know and these Dempsey's are very dangerous. Uncle Danny was right about them. Anyhow, good luck but make sure ye both get something going, England and Ireland are not options for ye anymore."

Ruby had sat listening intently to Shay's part in the conversation. She knew that something bad had happened and that as soon as the call ended Shay was going to be livid when telling her what had happened.

The call ended. The mobile phone was thrown into the footwell of where Ruby was sitting. Shay exploded. "That fucking low-life piece of shit has rang Bridget and threatened her! She's terrified! Who the fuck does he think he is?"

Ruby was shocked and also enraged. "He's threatened your sister! What a bastard! That's 'cos he got off with it! If the police had charged him like they should've done, this wouldn't have happened!"

They had been driving in slow traffic for two hours, both tense with anger and stunned that the monster had reared its ugly head again. Shay had had enough of driving and knew that both he and Ruby needed some time to calm down. He pulled off at the next exit having no idea where it would take them.

They stumbled across a charming town called San Juan Bautista, a mission town full of charm and character from the past. They slowly drove through the dusty town that resembled a movie set from a John Wayne film. The place seemed deserted until they spotted an old fashioned looking restaurant that had a hand painted wooden sign outside saying *'Welcome! We are open.'*

Shay pulled into the designated car park next to the restaurant and commented on what a pretty town it was. "This is the nuts here Eyes. If we're lucky, we might see a couple of cowboys and Indians!"

Ruby laughed and responded with her attempt of a John Wayne impression, "Yeah we might do! Get off your horse and drink your milk!"

They approached the pretty restaurant that was called Mariposa House Restaurant. A brilliant white building; a perfect background for the colourful flowers that hung and garnished the old fashioned house. Inside, the décor and furniture was just as quaint. There were old, framed family photos scattered around the room and delicate white doyleys were precisely placed on the shelves and sideboards. Such humble, unpretentious surroundings made Shay and Ruby feel as though they were intruding in somebody's home.

Shay called out and asked if anyone was there. Within seconds, a lady came into the room, a tiny woman in her early sixties. Her grey hair was neatly pulled back and pinned in a bun. She wore a floral dress and frilly white apron. The smiling lady looked just as traditional as the restaurant house.

She welcomed Shay and Ruby and asked if they would like to sit inside or outside in the garden. They chose to sit outside in the garden where they enjoyed a Mariposa House Restaurant garden salad. Whilst waiting on them, the bubbly lady introduced herself as the owner and enjoyed hearing where they'd visited so far in California. Shay and Ruby asked if there were any hotels nearby where they could stay for the night. She recommended the Posada De San Juan Hotel. She told them to go to the hotel and say that she had recommended them and that they'd have no trouble with getting a room for the night.

Shay and Ruby parked outside the hotel, becoming amused at

the chickens that were running around the car park.

They entered the large hotel that was once a grand house and had been converted. It was consistent with the town being full of character, tradition and charm. The floors were carpeted throughout, the ceilings were covered with time-honored beams and, much to Shay's liking, the room key was actually a proper key and not a card. They had booked in for one night before their return to Rancho Cucamonga the following morning.

That evening, they could not resist returning to the Mariposa House Restaurant to enjoy the fantastic food and humble hospitality once more.

SEVENTEEN

Luck in Los Angeles

Back in Rancho Cucamonga, they met with a relieved Mickey who was pleased that they had returned. "Hey, I missed you guys! You gotta listen to me, here's where it's at!"

Shay agreed with Mickey. "We gotta cut down on costs though," he said. "You know when we first arrived, we should have bought a second hand car and rented an apartment instead of renting cars and paying hotel bills."

"Ok Cuz, take my laptop again and get on it tomorrow. We'll return your car now." Mickey could see the logic in what Shay was saying.

The following morning Ruby searched for work using Mickey's laptop and put their resumés out again on every employment website. She spent the entire day and evening searching for work. Shay was at a loss and was having a real low day again thinking about the irretrievable loss of his money and business and the threat made to his sister.

At around eight pm that evening, Shay's cell phone rang. Ruby passed the phone to him and he answered the call.

He was shocked to hear an English accent on the other end of the phone, "Hello mate, Ian here. I've been looking for a contracts manager for my air conditioning business and found your resumé on a website. You still looking for work?"

Slightly dumbfounded yet very excited, Shay replied, "Yes, still looking Ian. Well, a contracts manager is what I am, so look no further!"

"Great stuff, Shay. I've got loads of work in Beverley Hills, the clients up there love that English touch. I'm winning twelve jobs a week and to be honest, I'm struggling with managing it all. From looking at your resumé, you seem ideal for my company. It says that you're based in Rancho Cucamonga but willing to relocate... Could you get up to LA tomorrow so we can meet up for a chat?"

"Yeah, that's great, mate. We'll leave here first thing in the morning. What time and where do you want to meet up?"

"Erm.. not sure yet Shay. I'm in San Francisco at the moment so I'm a long way from home. I've been here on business but I'm heading back to LA in the morning. Best thing to do is give me a call when you're settled in somewhere tomorrow. You said 'we', so are you married then?"

"Yeah, I am as it happens. My wife does accounts."

"Oh does she? Great! Bring your wife to the meeting as well, I should be able to help her out with some work too. Like I said Shay, call me tomorrow and we'll all meet up." He hung up.

Shay and Ruby jumped for joy around their hotel room.

"At last Eyes!" Cried Shay, "Beverley Hills here we come! And, another Londoner to work with! Happy days, Eyes! Happy days!"

Ruby was thrilled, this was just the break they'd been waiting for. Knowing Shay, she knew that a job offer would be the only thing to get him out of the dark place that he started to visit more and more often in recent days.

"Oh my God! That's the nuts, I can't believe it! We're gonna be alright now aren't we. Let's tell Mickey, he'll be made up!"

Mickey was delighted for them both and this was reflected in his loud, enthusiastic reaction. "I fucking told you, guys! Hey,

Hollywood will love you! Fucking-ay! You finally got your break huh, I'll drive you guys up there tomorrow, I'll pick you up at eight o'clock sharp!"

The call ended, Shay settled into the chair positioned in front of the laptop. He logged onto Priceline and booked an inexpensive motel in LA. It took a few minutes for the booking confirmation to come through with the name and full address of the allocated motel. When it did, Shay burst out laughing. "Erh Eyes, come here a minute..." Ruby skipped out of bathroom and he continued, "We're booked in at the hood! Compton here we come! Shit, I thought we'd get something further uptown though. We should be alright there, shouldn't we?"

Ruby giggled. "Oh! That's like boys in the hood territory!" She then proceeded to sing a line from Dr. Dre's *Next Episode* whilst imitating rappers hand signs, *"Na – na – na – na nah! It's the motherfucking D. R. E. Dr Dre motherfucker!"*

Shay leant back on his chair and laughed at the comical sight of his rapping wife.

Whilst Shay and Ruby were packing their bags ready for the early start the next morning, Mickey made a surprise visit to their hotel to congratulate them both, as he hugged Ruby he said, "Hey Ruby May, I bet'cha some big movie producer spots you in Hollywood and signs you up."

Shay jested, "It would seem that rapping is Ruby's thing, not acting."

He then called Connor to tell him the good news. In high spirits, Mickey took the phone from Shay to speak to Connor,

"Hey Cuz! Get your ass out here! Man, the chicks will love you! You'll be so fucked from getting laid you'll be too tired to go back home!"

The following morning Mickey was true to his word and arrived at seven forty five ready to depart for eight o'clock. He helped load their bags into the car and they set off on their journey to pursue their imminent new life in America.

They arrived in Compton and found their motel using Shay's Sat Nav. Their room was very plain and very dated. They settled in and Shay called Ian several times but only got his voicemail.

Mickey, being his usual upbeat self, said, "It's Saturday, Cuz! You know, you might not even see that guy till Monday. Hey, it's midday now, let's go get a cold one!"

Mickey drove them to Santa Monica and parked by the beach. Shay and Ruby were both stunned at the beauty of the large scale beach. They strolled along the beach and then headed to the main street to find somewhere to get a drink, and found an English bar that had lots of people inside eating and drinking. They were lucky to find three vacant bar stools at the bar. Shay sat in-between Ruby and Mickey and happily watched English football on the widescreen television. He got talking to the barman about football, he was sociable, in his early thirties and had a distinct Dublin accent.

Mickey sat hunched over his pint of Budweiser watching the barman like a hawk, fascinated by his dark hair, brown eyes and tanned skin.

Mickey slyly turned his head to Shay and whispered, "Hey Cuz... did that guy there say he's Irish?"

"Yeah, he's from Dublin," Shay said.

Now far more indiscreet, Mickey threw himself back in his chair and exclaimed, "No fucking way man! He's a goddam Hispanic! Fuck man... why's he saying he's Irish? Fuck that, look how dark he is!"

"No, he is Irish, Mick. A lot of Irish have the tanned skin and brown eyes." In his attempt to pacify his cousin, he continued, "The Spanish Armada sank off of the coast of Ireland; hence, the dark skin and brown eyes."

"No way, I tell ya, he's up from Mexico! He aint Irish! Fuck, we're a hundred percent Irish!"

Ruby was laughing in hysterics at the indignant Mickey whilst Shay began to feel a little uncomfortable with his outbursts as the friendly barman was only a short distance away from them.

The barman approached Shay, Ruby and Mickey to refill their drinks. "Jaysus, tis hot out there today, whah," said the barman in his strong north Dublin accent.

Shay agreed and went on to ask him if the pub would be showing the Chelsea game on Sunday.

"Jaysus yeah! We're open at seven in the morning, the place will be packed. Yer should come in to watch it, it'll be a great craic, whah."

Mickey stared intensely him and decided to challenge the Dubliner, who in his opinion was definitely a Mexican impersonating an Irish man. "Hey man, I've been to Dublin. What part of Dublin you from?"

The barman simply replied, "North Dublin."

"Oh yeah... So what's your name then, buddy?" Mickey asked in a conceited tone.

The Dubliner looked at Shay and discreetly gave him a naughty wink as he replied to Mickey, "Raul."

Having given his humorous one-word answer, the barman walked away to serve the next customer. A satisfied Mickey screamed and slapped the bar with both hands. "Goddam it! I told you! He aint no Irish man! Who ever heard of an Irish man called Raul! Fuck... we're a hundred percent Irish, he didn't fool me for one minute!"

Shay decided it was best to agree with Mickey, as opposed to explaining to him that the barman had clearly overheard Mickey's doubt and had decided to wind him up.

Now feeling ever so righteous and very vocal, Mickey stated,

"Hey, you know once you guys get settled here, me and you, Shay, will fly over to the UK. I tell yer, I'll take a baseball bat to that mothers hit man, then we'll go and see him and say, hey motherfucker! Now your muscle's gone, what'cha... gonna... do... now, you fuck!?"

The three laughed. Shay and Ruby looked at Mickey with affection, he was such a funny guy. They had a fun day in the bar and then went on to another English bar located in Sunset Boulevard before Mickey went back to Rancho Cucamonga and Shay and Ruby returned to their hotel.

On Sunday evening Shay received a call from Ian. "Alright Shay? Sorry, I got delayed on business in San Francisco, you in LA yet?"

"Yeah, we got here yesterday morning."

"Good, can you both meet me tomorrow evening? I could come to your hotel room. Where is it you're staying?"

"Erm…. We're staying in a motel on Sunset Boulevard, Hollywood. We could meet at your office or at a restaurant? Our motel room is pretty cramped to be honest." Shay had thought on his feet and felt no need to tell Ian that they were staying in Compton.

"Oh… erm… ok. Well I tell you what, we could meet at the chicken restaurant on Sunset Boulevard at five o'clock tomorrow evening instead."

The meeting was agreed. Ruby and Shay spent the remainder of their Sunday night watching very bad movies in their dingy motel room.

Monday morning arrived and Shay and Ruby walked to an ATM to withdraw some cash to get some breakfast. As Shay pocketed the withdrawn money, a black man in loose jeans and a large white t-shirt approached them and shouted, "Hey!"

Startled, Shay stopped and said, "Yeah, what mate?"

The stranger replied, "Y'all from London? Wow, that's great, Europeans in the hood! Shit man, you gotta cigarette I could bum?"

Shay laughed to himself as he delved into his pockets for his box of cigarettes. The guy looked threatening but on the contrary, seemed really nice. He handed him a cigarette and then lit it for him.

"Thanks, man. Y'all enjoy LA now you hear! London huh, shit man, I'm gonna get me a gal from London if they do be looking like your gal, homey!" Joked the harmless man as he walked away smoking his cigarette.

Shay and Ruby walked to a diner called Polly's Bakery Café and devoured the best breakfast they'd had so far in California.

They returned to their motel room where the day passed slowly in anticipation of their meeting with Ian at five o'clock. They sifted through what clothes they had to find something half decent to wear for the meeting.

Ruby sighed and grumbled, "This is ridiculous. We've hardly got any clothes as it is but when we can't even wash anything for weeks on end makes it ten times worse! We have a shower and then get dressed in dirty clothes. I don't even feel like I've had a shower once I'm dressed. Right, well I'm gonna jump in there now."

Ruby showered, Shay stood at the sink shaving and singing *'Strange Town'* by The Jam, but was interrupted by a call to his cell phone. Shay dried his face and ran to the bed to answer his phone.

"Shay, listen up, tis Danny here. They're onto yer bhoy, they know ye are in the States. There are four of them o'er there and they've seen yer work experience on a website like, so…"

Shay interrupted Danny, which he rarely ever did, "How'd you know that Danny? Who…?"

Danny Good Looking stopped Shay mid-sentence. He wanted to convey all of the facts before Shay asked any questions. "Will yer stop and listen to me. Now, the Dempsey's will call ye up offering you work, they'll arrange a meeting wit ye, and if ye go they'll kill ye both bhoy…"

Shay was panicked and interrupted Danny once again. "We've had that call! A Londoner has arranged to meet us in three hours."

"That's the call bhoy! My man never gets it wrong. Ye'll have to come back to Ireland, Shay. I'll meet ye in Cork, we can't interfere with the Dempsey's at the moment as we have business wit them. But we can keep you safe shur. Move hotel tonight, get rid of them phones ye have. I'll call your mam and dad and let them know ye'll be home. I've already spoken wit Bridget and yer to call her when ye get to Dublin. She'll pick ye up and bring ye down the country. Now Shay, get the next available flight to Dublin."

"Erh Dan... the bloke who phoned me said he was in San Francisco, which is where we were. He said he was there on business but he's back in LA now. To be honest, I never thought anything of it." Shay was now distraught.

"I know shur, we know everything. Ye were in San Francisco last week were you not? They've been tracking ye for the past five days. Ye left San Francisco just in time bhoy! Now listen to me, tell yer cousin, Mickey, to lay low as they may squeeze him for some info like. Go'wan now, God bless and I'll see ye in Cork next weekend. We'll sort this out once and for all."

Ruby was hysterical as they both sat on the edge of the bed in total shock and disbelief, Shay explained everything that Danny had told him. He sat with his head held in hands as Ruby solemnly said,

"You know we would have been killed only for Danny calling. We're fucked!" Ruby became more frenzied as she continued, "We'll never get away from these people, Shay. We've travelled thousands of miles and they still found us! Can I ask you something?... What is Danny Good Looking? How come's he always knows what's going on? And who's 'we'? You said that he said 'we have business with the Dempsey's.' Who's he involved with?"

"I told you before, he's connected. Nobody knows what he does but trust me, he's the real deal."

Shay called Mickey and told him what Danny had said. "Fuck those fuckers man! What's up with these motherfuckers?!" Mickey said angrily.

"Listen Mickey, we're gonna do one. Danny Good Looking said they might put the squeeze on you."

"Fuck them man. Any fucker that comes near me or my family will be dealt with," Mickey affirmed.

After an emotional farewell over the phone with Mickey, Shay disposed of both cell phones. A process that both he and Ruby had thought was well behind them. They decided to remain in their motel in Compton that night as thankfully, Shay hadn't revealed their location to Ian. Paranoia had obviously been instilled in them from the start and it was paranoia that was going to help keep them alive. Ruby didn't hesitate in booking their flights online for the following day at four pm using Mickey's laptop, which they'd arranged to leave at reception for Mickey to collect.

With flights booked, they decided to spend the entire night at LAX airport knowing that inside the airport security would be stringent and that they'd be safe. The night passed slowly, it was torturous.

At five am Shay called Bridget in Ireland where the time there was one pm, "Alright Bridge, Danny said…"

Bridget interrupted. "Shay, oh my God! Are ye both ok?"

"Yeah, we're fine. We spent the night at the airport."

Bridget began to sob and struggled to get her words out.

"Shay… I've had Auntie Mary on the phone… Mickey and some girl are in hospital… Someone broke into Mickey's house and attacked him and a girlfriend of his. Mickey's stable but… Oh Shay, I can hardly bring myself to say it."

"What?! What is it, Bridget, just tell me!" Shay exclaimed.

"They tortured him. They… they severed both of his thumbs and his toe nails are gone."

"What do mean… gone?"

"Apparently, they pulled them off with… with pliers. The girl is fighting for her life. Oh God Shay, they won't stop till yer both dead, what are we going to do?"

Shay's heart sunk. His cousin was laying disfigured in a hospital bed and all he had done was try to help out his family. "I can't believe this is happening. This is all my fault! I'd better call Auntie Mary."

"What time are you landing at Dublin, Shay?" Bridget asked.

"Nine am your time, I gotta go Bridge, I gotta call Mary." Shay was struggling to hold back his tears.

"Shay, yer in shock! Just get out of there. Uncle Danny will be over and he'll sort this mess out."

Ruby approached Shay at the telephone box. She grabbed hold of him as he stood with tears streaming down his face, breaking his heart. She hugged him tightly and he explained, "They've hurt Mickey and some girl who was with him. They've hurt them badly, Ruby. Those fucking bastards. I swear, I'll go back to London and do Billy some serious damage."

Inconsolable and no fit state to make anymore calls, Ruby said that she would call his aunt Mary. Ruby spoke with a friend of Mary's who informed Ruby that things were not looking too good and that Mary was at the hospital waiting for news on Mickey and his girlfriend, Cassidy.

EIGHTEEN

Tenderness and Treachery

R uby and Shay boarded the flight from LAX to Dublin after a long, emotional and silent wait. They both felt riddled with guilt and felt that they were to blame. Mickey had given them so much of his time and help and now he and Cassidy lay in hospital beds seriously ill.

They eventually touched down in Dublin after a nine hour flight, which seemed to take a lifetime.

Bridget was cautiously waiting for them both in arrivals. She ran towards them and hugged them both tightly. It was the first time for Ruby and Bridget to meet. Despite this, Bridget showed Ruby just as much affection and concern as she did towards Shay. Ruby was taken aback by Bridget's kindness and was instantly put at ease. She felt an emotional connection with her, like she already knew her.

Bridget was watchful and said, "Ok guys no delaying, airports are dangerous places to be, let's get going."

Once safely inside her BMW X5, Bridget explained the latest on Mickey and Cassidy's conditions, "Mickey's girlfriend, Cassidy, is out of danger. Her jaw is wired and she has a fractured skull with multiple bruising. Mickey is very badly beaten and in excruciating pain. He has both of his arms in a cast but they were unable to reattach his thumbs as the paramedics arrived too late. All they can do for him is help with pain relief. Apparently, Mickey hasn't told anybody anything. He's still deeply in shock but there's talk of having a psychiatrist assess him. "

Then she started to dial a number into her car phone, Danny Good Looking's number.

"Yer have to speak to him," she said.

Danny answered within seconds, "Hello Bridget dar'lin, are yer alright?"

"Uncle Danny, I've Shay with me here to talk to yer."

"Oh ok Bridget, take care now and remember, don't yer be worrying like. Shur you know I won't let anyone touch a hair on yer head," said Danny.

"Alright Danny?" Shay said.

"Hello bhoy, now we won't talk too much on the phone. Ye are to go to your parents house, ye'll be safe there like. I've spoken to some people and yer parents won't be bothered by anyone. Ye can stay there for t'ree days and then meet me in Cork City on Saturday. Go'wan now, tis no good talking on the phone." He hung up.

After time spent struggling to get through the Dublin congestion, Bridget suggested that they stop for a quick snack and a drink.

They resumed their journey and eventually arrived in the small, pretty village in County Waterford where Josie and Mick lived.

Readily waiting at the door to greet the weary travellers, Josie squeezed both Ruby and Shay whilst Mick stood in the background looking on awaiting his chance to greet the couple, which he did do, once Josie moved on to hug Bridget.

All five of them made their way into the house and sat round the large table in the kitchen. As Josie hurriedly started to boil the kettle ready for some tea she updated Shay and Ruby about

Mickey and his girlfriend, with her slightly confused version of events.

"Now then kids, Mickey and his girlfriend are going to be ok, thanks be to God. Jesus, Mary and Joseph, that man in England is a bad basket!" Josie said.

Mick sat in his chair at the head of the table and Shay sat opposite him at the other end. Whilst Josie, Bridget and Ruby prepared a huge fried breakfast, Mick expressed that he couldn't see a way out of this and asked if Shay had a plan.

"For once in my life Dad, I don't have a plan. I'm going to meet Danny in Cork at the weekend and see if he has any ideas."

As they sat and ate breakfast together, the house phone rang and Josie left the kitchen to take the call in the hallway.

Within three minutes, Josie had returned to the kitchen. "Oh Jesus, may the Lord rest his soul… Jon-Jo Ryan passed away last night, Mick."

"Huh? Who? Jon-Jo from the Glen? Oh Jesus, when's the funeral, Josie?" asked Mick.

"Tis tonight at seven, shur we'll be going." Josie went on to explain at great length that how going to funerals was a very important thing in Ireland. Then, standing by Ruby's chair, asked, "Would yer like to come to the funeral, Ruby?"

Ruby was unsure of what to say and looked over at Shay with a face that said 'help me!'. So Shay quickly intervened, "We never even knew the bloke, Mum, and funerals aren't really a good omen for us at the moment."

"Ah, shur we didn't really know him either but we'll go anyway," Josie said as she seated herself back at the table.

Shay laughed. "Christ Mum, where do you get your kicks on a Saturday night? At casualty?"

Everyone laughed but Josie pursed her lips and glared at Mick who knew by her look that he was to stop laughing immediately.

After everyone had eaten, Shay telephoned Connor, "Alright Son, how's it going? You been down the Chelsea?"

"Hi Dad! Yeah, I'm going to every game. Loads have been asking where you are. Billy's turned the entire firm against you, they all think you nicked his money. Oh yeah, and some bloke called me about five minutes ago, said he was a mate of yours and that he could help you."

"Oh yeah, what's his name?" Shay asked.

"He wouldn't say, he was a wrong'un. Obviously something to do with Billy cos he started getting irritated saying that if I didn't tell him where you were then he couldn't help you."

"Listen Connor, all this will be sorted out soon, Son. Just be vigilant…" Shay went on to explain that Mickey and a girlfriend of his were in hospital in California.

After Shay had finished his call to Connor, he went outside the house to have a cigarette and noticed Bridget sitting in her car talking on her mobile. Shay walked through the landscaped rear garden and sat on a bench to wait for her. He was soon joined by Bridget who sat beside him.

"Listen Shay, I just called Danny. He's flying into Cork on Saturday and he wants you and Ruby to meet him in a pub called The Hurlers in the city centre at one o'clock. He's going to help ye out. Yer must take Ruby though because he needs some information from her. This madness has got to stop and Danny thinks he can help ye."

As Shay and Bridget continued to sit talking, Ruby walked towards them holding one hand up to shield her eyes from the sun. Ruby told Shay that she was going to call her mum. Even though the last phone call Ruby made to her ended on a sour note, Ruby held some hope that maybe she had come to her senses. After all, it'd been some time since they last spoke and they used to be so close, surely she would be glad to hear from her daughter and want to help her. Shay gave Ruby the phone and reminded her to with-hold the number, just to be on the safe side.

Ruby wandered through the garden back towards the house. She changed the phone settings and with-held the number. Apprehensively, she dialled her mum's mobile phone number. She listened to the ringing tone waiting for her mum to answer, she lit a cigarette and began to pace up and down the driveway.

"Hello…" Janice said.

Ruby took a deep breath and responded, "Mum… it's me."

"Oh… Alright?"

"Erh… I wanted to ring you, Mum. The last call ended badly and I wanted to see how you were."

"Yeah it did. I'm alright. So where are you then?" Janice nonchalantly asked.

Ruby purposely avoided saying where she was, instead she began to tell Janice her news before she heard it from somebody else.

"Mum, I have something to tell you, I'm married now."

Janice's uninterested tone rapidly became venomous, "You what! You stupid girl! Well I'm telling you now, just because you're married doesn't mean anything, it's just a bit of paper! It doesn't change the fact that he's a lying crook and that you're both up to your necks in shit! Why did you do it Ruby? Why did you steel Billy's money? I really didn't think that you were that weak, but you obviously are!"

Ruby's hopes of her and her mum getting their relationship back on track were short lived. Ruby was angered that her mum still continued to bad-mouth Shay and was hurt to now know that her own mum would believe that she would steal.

Ruby shot back at Janice, "Hold on a minute! I told you before, I don't phone you just so you can slag Shay off, I phoned to see how you were! And what's this about stealing money? I don't know what you're talking about. Why would you think I'd do that? I've never stolen a penny in my life!"

"Oh is that right! Well, Billy's shown me all of the paperwork, Ruby, and Charlie's seen it as well. Best thing you can do is come back and sort this out! Did you actually both think you'd get away with it?"

Ruby was crushed. How could a mum turn against her child like that? More to the point, why is she believing Billy over her own daughter?

"Mum, are you serious? Why are you being like this? And as for stealing, well, it's obvious that Billy's fabricated some sort of paperwork and is using it to justify his lies and despicable actions because he knows that hiring hit-men just because me and Shay want to be together is totally unwarranted and bang out of order! I tell you what, here's an accusation that IS true! Perhaps you'd better ask him about how the hit-men that he paid ended up leaving Shay's cousin and his cousin's girlfriend in hospital! If me and Shay hadn't have left when we did, the scum that he hired wouldn't have been so kind as to put us in hospital, we'd be dead! I can't believe that you believe him over me! After all we've been through, Mum. Oh and I tell you something else as well, he's many things but he aint stupid! He's doing what he always does and is telling you what he wants you to hear! Jesus Christ Mum! You know what he's like better than anyone and you still can't see what he's doing!"

"What's he doing Ruby? He hasn't done anything wrong! He's the one that's been left to clear up all the shit that you've left behind! And as for hit-men, that's a load of bollocks if ever I've heard it! Why would he do that? He's more concerned with sorting out the damage you two have caused. Well, it's quite obvious that you've made your decision, Ruby. You wanna be with that person you've apparently married, so you do that but I think it'd be best if you don't ring me anymore…. And that goes for contacting Charlie and your nan and grandad as well."

For Ruby, hearing these cruel words from her mum felt like a thousand knives being plunged into her chest. She couldn't hold back her emotion. Her tears and the burning lump in her throat choked her response, "Do you… do you really mean that, Mum? You're gonna cut me out of your life and then spend it happily with that lying, conniving, evil bastard? Well I'll tell you what, despite all of this shit that he's put me and Shay through, I wouldn't change a thing because now I have someone that I love and who really loves me. I've never had that before, not even with my own Mum evidently!... A mother's love is supposed to be unconditional and unbreakable by anyone or anything. If this is you loving me, then I'm better off without you. And as for that liar... Well, one day the truth will come out in the wash and then you and all of his other puppets will see him for what he really is."

Ruby hung up the phone and tried to control herself as she began to break down. Her hands shook as she lit another cigarette. The tears subsided and her distress turned to anger. Ruby and her mum were like best friends, they'd been through everything together; comforting each other after Billy had left his mark on them and trying to make each other laugh about the regime at home to stop one another from crying about it. How can a mother's love for her daughter be destroyed in a matter of months due to the actions of a spineless, manipulating excuse for a human being?

Ruby stubbed out her cigarette and pondered about how Shay was going react. He was already struggling with the situation. In such a short space of time they'd been locked up in a prison cell for thirteen hours unnecessarily, travelled thousands of miles to escape hit-men and Shay's cousin and his girlfriend had been violently attacked. To add to all of that, she now needed to tell him that Billy's latest scheme was to accuse them both of stealing money to justify his actions and that he'd gone so far as to fabricate paperwork. She worried that Shay might seek his own justice and that he would lose his liberty and they would lose each other.

Ruby pulled herself together and walked back down to the bottom of the garden where Shay and Bridget were still sat talking. Shay immediately saw that Ruby was upset and asked her what had happened. Ruby told Shay what had been said. He was disgusted at Janice's actions and gullibility. Like Ruby, he was in total disbelief at the fact that she'd shunned her own daughter, believed Billy over her and furthermore, how she wanted nothing more to do with her. Shay consoled Ruby and told her that one way or another that the sorry situation would be sorted out. Bridget was just as shocked, being a mother herself, she couldn't comprehend how Janice could treat Ruby that way. Ruby told Shay that she felt concerned that her brother had been manipulated in the same way that her mum had been. Janice had said about Charlie seeing the so-called paperwork and that she was not to contact him. Just the thought of Charlie turning against her hurt deeply. Ruby decided that she had to ring him and find out for sure.

Ruby wandered back towards the house and dialled Charlie's number. Eventually he answered, brusquely.

Ruby was caught slightly off guard with his curt tone and quietly said, "Charlie, it's Ruby."

"Yeah, what do you want?" Charlie said aggressively.

Instantaneously, Ruby knew that her suspicions were right. Her brother had been influenced by the tyrant and wasn't trying to hide the fact.

"What's the matter Charlie, why are you being like that?" she asked.

"Why am I being like that! Why do you think, Ruby? I've seen everything, you've been lying to me all along!"

"Seen what? Tell me what's happened, Charlie!"

"Do you know what Ruby, you just get on with it! It's alright for you two having the life of riley with all the money you nicked but I'm the one that's here having to sit everyday with my mum crying her eyes out!" he bellowed.

Ruby's initial reaction was anger. How could Charlie believe such lies and at the same time, think so little of his sister.

"You seriously think that I've stolen money? Well thanks Charlie, thanks a lot! I can't believe you're being like this! Before I left, you hated Billy more than anyone or anything on this planet and now you're talking like you're his right-hand man!"

"Yeah, that's right, I am! Look, I don't give a shit about you Ruby or that prick you're with…"

She abruptly interrupted. "Oi! Don't you dare call him a prick! He's my husband!" She shouted now fuelled with rage.

He began to shout over Ruby, "Yeah and you thought you were being clever getting married! Well you ain't clever, Ruby, you're a stupid bitch!"

Ruby couldn't listen to anymore of Charlie's abuse, so she hung up, too shocked and outraged to be upset.

Later, Ruby would contemplate her conversations with the two members of her family who she was so uniquely close with. Both her mum and brother had made it very clear that they wanted nothing more to do with her. Realisation set in that she'd lost her family. She felt indescribable, unimaginable pain because the two people she'd spent her whole entire life loving, protecting, caring for and adoring had turned their backs on her. She knew that after their acts of betrayal and treachery that there was no going back and knew that if she didn't let go and accept that fact, the bitterness and hurt would eat her up inside.

She needed something to distract herself from her torturous thoughts so she turned to the same person that she always turned to when she needed to escape… Elvis Presley.

She went into the spare bedroom where she and Shay would be sleeping and rummaged through her bag to find one of the Elvis CD's that Shay had bought her whilst they were on their travels. She lay on the bed with her headphones on and her eyes closed as her thoughts were soon banished by Elvis's extraordinary vocals. That was until, 'Walk A Mile In My Shoes' came on. Ruby quietly sang along,

> "Walk a mile in my shoes,
> Walk a mile in my shoes,
> Before you abuse, criticise and accuse,
> Walk a mile in my shoes"

Singing the lyrics, Ruby couldn't help but revert back to thoughts of Janice and Charlie. She jokingly thought to herself how it would have been very fitting to have quoted the chorus when she was on the phone them earlier.

The day passed slowly and Shay and Ruby were struggling with the jet-lag. Peter arrived at the house and joined them for dinner at four o'clock. It was his first time meeting Ruby. Peter was a gentleman and shook Ruby's hand to greet her. However, he couldn't resist in mimicking her accent, just as he did with Shay. Bacon and cabbage was the dish of the day on a regular basis at Josie and Mick's house and today was no exception.

Whilst they ate, Peter directed his conversation at Shay. "Now Shay, do yer remember that old sixties Jaguar I had back in the seventies?"

Shay continued cutting into his bacon and replied, "Yeah, yeah, I loved that motor, a bank robber's Jag! Was it red?"`

"Twas red yeah, I don't know about a bank robber's Jag, anyway, I just bought a black one yesterday. Mint condition, nineteen sixty five, she purrs so she does."

Ruby was curious. "Bank robber's motor! What's one of them?"

"Ah, a beautiful car, Ruby. A bit before your time though." Peter said.

Mick sat at the head of the table in silence listening and taking in the conversation but he couldn't resist Peter's unintentional cue and he started to sing,

"You ask me why I look so sad on this bright summers day
Or why the tears are in my eyes, and I seem so far away
Come sit yourself beside me love, and put your hand in mine
And I'll tell you of someone I loved
Long, long before your time"

Everyone looked on at Mick sat in his chair with his head

tilted back and his eyes shut as he sang. Shay and Bridget loved to hear their father sing and this particular song was one that Bridget was very fond of.

Josie hurriedly chewed her mouthful of food and then firmly brought down both hands onto the table whilst clutching her cutlery tightly before scorning Mick. "For the love of God, Mick Sullivan! Can we not have a meal without you singing? Can we not have a conversation without you bursting into song?" Then she looked at everyone else and continued, "Jesus lads, I tell ye, that man would try the patients of a saint!"

Everyone at the table was now highly amused as Mick and Josie's renowned double act got into full swing.

Later on, Mick and Josie prepared to go to the funeral mass whilst Peter and Bridget prepared to return to their home in West Cork. Bridget invited Shay and Ruby down to her and Peter's house the following day saying that she'd pick them up at twelve and that they could sleep there for a night.

Left alone in Shay's parents house for an hour enabled Ruby to get some much needed washing done. In the evening, Shay and Ruby had a very in-depth run down from Josie of who had been at the funeral and what a great turn out the man had. The report was repeated several times before Shay and Ruby eventually managed to get to bed.

Shay and Ruby entered the kitchen the following morning, Josie was singing along to a song on the radio, the table was set with a pot of tea and several rounds of toast.

"Morning kids, ye have some toast and I'll cook some sausages in a minute," Josie said.

"Morning," Shay and Ruby both said together.

Shay then continued, "No toast for me Mum, wheat plays havoc with my digestive system when I'm stressed. Morning Dad."

Mick had just entered the room and was shuffling to his usual seat at the head of the kitchen table.

"Would you prefer some Weetabix then, Son?" Josie asked.

Shay laughed. "I think there's wheat in that, Mum."

Mick coughed and suggested, "What about some shredded wheat, I find that to be a good start to the day."

"Oh Jesus Mick, he can't have that! Shur that has wheat in it, yer eejit!" scorned Josie.

Ruby couldn't look at Shay as she knew she wouldn't be able to control her laughter. So instead, she pinned her ears back to listen to the radio that was on in the background. Ruby was baffled to hear the DJ announcing numerous deaths.

Shortly after this humorous breakfast Bridget arrived to pick up Shay and Ruby. In the car Bridget and Shay sang along to 'Reason to Believe' as the Rod Stewart C.D. played. They were both massive fans.

They spent the day at Peter and Bridget's house, as arranged. The house and its surroundings were tranquil and without a doubt, extremely beautiful. Ruby was amazed at the interior design and the calming aura.

Peter was at work, projecting his natural charm and head for business in the meetings he had booked for that day. Bridget had taken the day off from her busy schedule to spend some quality time with Shay and Ruby.

That evening, they went out to dinner at Peter and Bridget's restaurant in the coastal town where Peter and Bridget lived. They returned to the relaxed atmosphere of the house at ten thirty pm and Peter retired for the night stating that he had to go to Dublin the following morning for an early meeting.

Whilst Bridget, Shay and Ruby watched a movie, Bridget's house phone rang. She answered the call and then passed the telephone to Shay. He was surprised to hear a frenzied Connor at the other end.

"Dad, Dad! I went down my local tonight to play pool with some of my mates and Billy turned up with another big lump. Dad, he's mental! I really thought he was going to beat me up! He called me all sorts, he was shouting like a lunatic and his mate threatened the landlord not to phone the police! He said that they're gonna find you and kill you, that you're a dead man walking. He kept shouting that you and Ruby had nicked his money. He said that you were a mug and that if I associated myself with you then that made me a mug as well!"

Shay felt sick to the stomach and asked, "Did he touch you, son?"

Connor took a deep breath to try and compose himself. "No, I thought he was going to. He got right in my face and had one arm pulled back. A woman in the pub shouted that she'd called the police and they left. If it weren't for her, I think he would have clumped me!"

"Right! I've had enough of this! I'm coming home to put that slag to bed! I'm not having it, I'll be back tomorrow son. Stay at home 'till I get this sorted."

Shay was incensed and paced the tranquil lounge with utter rage clearly written all over his face. He'd introduced a new aggressive vibe to the calm house, which Bridget sensed. She intervened with her calming strength.

"Now listen to me Shay, yer not going back tomorrow, you'll wait to see Danny. This is what that lunatic wants! He's done this knowing that you'll react and go back. Wise up Shay, he's trying to draw yer out! It's a means to an end… Just calm down, you're doing the situation no good by getting like this."

Ruby then added her two pennyworth. "You can't go back on your own, Shay, you could get battered."

"That mug couldn't batter fish!" retorted Shay. He continued to pace the lounge and eventually realised that Bridget and Ruby were right. He felt ashamed that he'd brought bad energy to his sister's house; that Mickey and Cassidy lay in hospital beds, that his parents had lost all of their savings due to this and now his son had been threatened. He'd lost everything and was now starting to feel that retribution of a concluding nature was the only way to put an end to it once and for all.

Bridget made tea and again told Shay to wait until they met Danny Good Looking in Cork City. Shay appeared to have calmed down a little so they all decided to call it a night and get some sleep.

Shay couldn't sleep. He turned Connor's phone call over in his mind and his anger started to build up. For the first time, Shay vented his anger towards Ruby. He shouted at her, asked indignantly about what sort of an excuse for a mother she had and how her mother could condone Billy's behaviour. The anger releasing session went on for about half an hour. Ruby was exceptionally upset but didn't say a word. She knew that anything she'd say would somehow just fuel the situation. Later, Shay would apologise to Ruby for expelling his verbal aggression in her direction.

Everybody has their limits. For Shay, berating and threatening his son was well and truly the final straw.

The following evening, Shay and Ruby returned to Mick and Josie's house where they wished the hours away for Saturday come. Both were very anxious to meet Danny and hear how he planned to resolve the situation.

To pass the time, they channel-hopped through the television and found their favourite talent show. They contently sat watching *The X Factor* and passed comments on the acts as if they were experts. One middle-aged man's song made Ruby's eyes fill with tears. The film, *Westside Story,* made her cry every time she watched it and the song was so relative to her and Shay. Shay and Ruby both intently listened to the lyrics of '*Somewhere,*' which thereafter, would become another one of 'their songs'.

It was Saturday morning. Finally, the long awaited day had come. Josie had cooked a full breakfast that was accompanied with upbeat conversation about Shay and Ruby's imminent visit to meet Danny.

Shay left the room for a cigarette. Ruby called out to him, "What time are we leaving for Cork then?"

Before he could answer, Mick started to sing,

"My home sweet home that I so fondly cherish
The dear ones there, mean everything to me
In all this world, if there should be a heaven
I'm sure its in that cottage by the Lea."

"Ah, I love that song, that was one of Nan's songs, Dad." Shay called out, and then answered Ruby's question, "Twenty minutes."

Mick lent them his car for the journey to Cork City, not without a stern reminder of how his car was not a Porsche and that he didn't want it driven like one.

NINETEEN

Danny Good Looking

Shay and Ruby arrived at The Hurlers bar, situated on the banks of the Lea river that flowed majestically through Cork City. Shay instantly spotted his uncle Danny standing at the bar drinking a coffee with the landlord who he clearly knew.

They approached the bar they heard Danny say quietly to the barman, "Coffee for t'ree at the table in the corner if you'd be so kind, please Finbar."

Danny nodded to Shay and Ruby, indicating that they were to sit down at the table in the corner. He followed not far behind them. As Ruby sat and hung her jacket on the back of her chair, she watched Danny as he walked boldly towards the table. Just as Shay had described, he was a very dapper, attractive man. It was evident how he came by the nickname 'Danny Good Looking.' Though in his early sixties he didn't look a day over fifty in his navy blue suit, crisp white shirt and red tie. Like Shay, he had broad shoulders and obviously took pride in his appearance.

They stood up and shook hands with Danny, who said "Tis nice to meet yer, Ruby, you've a good man here. Shur he's like a son to me. Jesus Shay, you've a beautiful wife bhoy. Now, let's sit down and get to business, I'm going to be very frank." He looked at Shay and said, "I take it Ruby has integrity and I can talk freely?"

"Yeah Danny, no worries, we're batting for the same team!" Said Shay.

"Huh? Batting! This is the Rebel County bhoy! We'll hurl for the same team, none of that cricket stuff!" joked Danny before he continued, "Now, this pub is safe but speak easy… yer never know who's listening like."

Shay stirred two spoons of sugar into his coffee and announced, "I gotta go back and sort that bully out, Dan. He threatened Connor the other night. He's just not gonna go away, so I'm gonna make him disappear, I have no other choice."

Danny sat leant forward with both hands on his coffee cup. His bright blue eyes framed with his dark eyebrows flashed up at Shay, "Ah, steady now bhoy, steady. I have to ask ye one more time like, everyone has it o'er there that ye had his money away, is there any truth at all in that now?" He then turned to Ruby. "Yer man is claiming that you wrote cheques."

"Nah, that's a load of rubbish. He's just saying that to try and justify his actions. We took nothing, he's the one that's taken from us if anything!" she explained.

"Danny, this is all about his obsession with Ruby and nothing more. I want my money back and want him gone!" said Shay sternly.

"Look, I had to ask ye. The money is not important bhoy, no one's worth killing o'er money. The safety of ye and the family is important. Now then, we had a meeting wit the Dempsey's last night and we have cancelled their contract. We do a lot of business wit them and they have stepped away from the contract yer man paid for. Ye won't be hearing no more from them again," Danny attempted to continue but Shay pounced.

"What about Mickey, was it them who fucked Mickey and Cassidy up?…"

Danny gave Shay a glare and sternly said, "Shay! Refrain from using bad language in front of the lady will yer! And don't interrupt me please… Now, the Dempsey's were simply carrying out their job, we've had a chat wit them and they're out of the equation now.

However, that bully, as ye rightly call him, has some smaller firms involved. Shur they're small but very dangerous like. We'll give this Billy a talking to and put a stop to all this. We won't harm him, I don't think we need to. A warning will do the job... Sorry to disappoint yer Shay." Danny grinned and then took another mouthful of coffee. He went on, "Yer man will be visited on Monday. Now, Ruby, I need some details off of you. I need his full home address, telephone numbers and details of his nightclub and usual movements like. We won't be killing him or anything like that, he has other enemies. We've heard that he upset a firm in Liverpool a few years ago and they've no time for him at all like."

Ruby was more than happy to assist and willingly told Danny Good Looking everything that he wanted to know, including the history of the verbal, mental and physical abuse that she and her mother had endured from Billy over the years.

Danny ordered a brandy for Ruby and a whiskey for himself, insisting that Shay stick to coffee as he was driving. As the landlord placed the drinks on their table, Danny stood up from the table and announced, "Ye are living in terror of a tyrant. Shur this fine country lived under tyrant rule for many a year. Now, allow me to recite a fine poem written by Pádraic Pearse, tis called The Rebel. Tis very relevant to yer own situation like."

With his untouched glass of whiskey in his right hand, Danny cleared his throat and recited proudly,

> "I am come of the seed of the people, the people that sorrow,
> That have no treasure but hope,
> No riches laid up but a memory
> Of an Ancient glory.
> My mother bore me in bondage, in bondage my mother was born,
> I am of the blood of serfs;
> The children with whom I have played, the men and women
> with whom I have eaten,

Have had masters over them, have been under the lash of masters,
And, though gentle, have served churls;
The hands that have touched mine, the dear hands whose
touch is familiar to me,
Have worn shameful manacles, have been bitten at the wrist   by
manacles,
Have grown hard with the manacles and the task-work of
strangers,
I am flesh of the flesh of these lowly, I am bone of their bone,
I that have never submitted;
I that have a soul greater than the souls of my people's masters,

I that have vision and prophecy and the gift of fiery speech,
I that have spoken with God on the top of His holy hill.
And because I am of the people, I understand the people,
I am sorrowful with their sorrow, I am hungry with their desire:
My heart has been heavy with the grief of mothers,
My eyes have been wet with the tears of children,
I have yearned with old wistful men,
And laughed or cursed with young men;
Their shame is my shame, and I have reddened for it,
Reddened for that they have served, they who should be free,
Reddened for that they have gone in want, while others have
been full,
Reddened for that they have walked in fear of lawyers and
of their jailors
With their writs of summons and their handcuffs,
Men mean and cruel!
I could have borne stripes on my body rather than this
shame of my people.
And now I speak, being full of vision;
I speak to my people, and I speak in my people's name to the
masters of my people.
I say to my people that they are holy, that they are august,

> *despite their chains,*
> *That they are greater than those that hold them, and*
> *stronger and purer,*
> *That they have but need of courage, and to call on the name   of*
> *their God,*
> *God the unforgetting, the dear God that loves the peoples*
> *For whom He died naked, suffering shame.*
> *And I say to my people's masters: Beware,*
> *Beware of the thing that is coming, beware of the risen people,*
> *Who shall take what ye would not give.*
> *Did ye think to conquer the people,*
> *Or that Law is stronger than life and than men's desire to be free?*
> *We will try it out with you, ye that have harried and held,*
> *Ye that have bullied and bribed, tyrants, hypocrites, liars!"*

Danny then sunk his whiskey and licked his lips.

Cries from the quiet bar were directed at Danny in high regard, "Good man yourself Danny bhoy! No better man!"

Ruby had sat through the entire poem in amazement. She praised Danny and said. "Oh my God that was really good, Danny. The last few lines, from where you said something about the risen people, that part is really apt."

"Ah, you've a good woman here Shay," said Danny with a smile.

Shay joked, "So tell me Danny, why do they call you Danny Good Looking?"

Ruby spoke up without any need for prompting. "Oh I can see why!"

Danny laughed. "Well, there you have it Ruby! If you can see it, that's good enough for me. Shur I'm not at all worried if this langer can't see it!" He explained that he only had a few hours left and that he was returning to London that same day.

"Now lads, I've arranged a flat for ye in Dublin. Tis secure and no one can get into it unless you buzz them in t'ru four security points. Ye'll find work in Dublin. Lay low for a while and all this will settle down, these things do in time. Here's a safe mobile to talk on, I will call ye on Monday night. Now, if ye need to speak to me, then use only this phone. Now you can drive me to the airport bhoy! I want to get home to yer auntie Kate, shur like your wife, she's my world."

Ruby sat and couldn't get over how charming, sensitive and gracious Danny was. His good manners were a rarity these days. There was a lot to take in and she struggled slightly with the Cork accent. She couldn't help but wonder to herself what Danny actually did and who were the people that he kept referring to as 'we'? His mysteriousness was undoubtedly intriguing.

En route to the airport, Danny gave Ruby the address and keys to a newly built apartment in Dublin. He told them to make their way there by coach or train the following day.

They were to be careful but reassured that all would be dealt with on Monday.

TWENTY

Dublin in Their Tears

Ruby and Shay took a train to Dublin and a taxi from the station. The taxi driver was a chatty, friendly man. He immediately struck up a conversation with Shay and Ruby, both sitting in the back of the taxi.

He looked in his rear view mirror and asked, "So are yer on yer holidays?"

"No," replied Shay. "We're moving to Dublin."

"Jaysus! Good on yer! You's from London righ?"

"Yeah. We left there last year, we've been living in Cork City. We thought we'd try Dublin instead. We couldn't get any work in Cork even though they all say in Cork that it's the real capital of Ireland," joked Shay, as he sensed that the driver was a character.

"Jaysus! Is that what they's do be saying? Huh, and tis only a small town whah. If yer blinked driving t'ru it you'd miss it!"

The playful conversation was interrupted as the taxi driver's in car phone rang, a Dublin lady spoke, "How'ya Jimmy?"

"Nancy, how's it going?" Jimmy said.

"Grand. Jaysus, the kids always go asleep easy when yer working. When yer home all yer do is fucking torment them."

Nancy was obviously Jimmy's wife.

"Jaysus Nancy! Will yer stop yer fucking swearing! I've passengers in the car righ!"

"Don't yer be shouting at me Jimmy, yer gob shite yer!"

"Nancy, call me later, for fuck sake. I've a man and his daughter in me taxi!"

As Jimmy ended the call, he looked up into his rear view mirror and said to Ruby and Shay, "Christ, sorry bout that. Twas the wife... Jaysus, always moaning about the kids whah. Shur I hope yer daughter didn't take offence."

Shay and Ruby both laughed aloud. No-one in all the months and all the miles travelled had ever picked up on an age gap.

Shay replied, "My daughter! She's my wife."

Ruby sat next to Shay finding it hard to control herself. She couldn't even look at Shay as his perplexed expression made her laugh even more.

"Jaysus! There goes me tip whah," said Jimmy who was obviously slightly embarrassed but however, proceeded to tell his funny taxi driver stories. His taxi tales were highly amusing and he'd a natural ability in comedy. Shay thought to himself how he should be a stand up comic rather than a taxi driver, he would have everyone in stitches.

They arrived at the apartment complex overlooking the Liffey River. Jimmy the jester gave Shay a card and told them that if they ever needed a taxi, they were to call him.

The apartment block was just as Danny had described. The first point of entry was through a coded gate with security cameras, which was then followed by another security gate. Thereafter, was a secure entrance to the apartment block itself. Shay and Ruby took one of the two lifts up to the sixth floor. They unlocked the double-locked front door and entered their new home.

"Wow! This place is the nuts! Getting to it is a mission, it's like Fort Knox, but it's worth it!" Ruby said as she scurried off to inspect every room, open every cupboard door and pull out every drawer. She walked contently along the solid oak floor into the contemporary kitchen and expressed her excitement at having a washing machine.

The main feature of the neutral living room was the very large, high-tech, flat screen television. The bathroom was equally as stunning and much to their delight, had a massive bath.

Ruby skipped back into the living room where Shay was sitting going through the satellite channels. She sat on his lap with one arm across the back of his shoulders and said, "Danny's really helped us, bless him. This place is great, it's never been lived in… and we've got all new furniture and kitchen stuff! I love it. Have you rang him yet?"

Shay called Danny to thank him. He then did the rounds and called Connor, his parents and Bridget whilst Ruby popped to the nearby shop for some essentials.

When Ruby returned, she started to put away the milk, bread, butter and such like whilst Shay put the kettle on.

"You wanna cuppa baby?" he asked before cheerfully expanding on his latest plan. "Ok Eyes, this is another new start! Tomorrow morning, we'll find jobs!"

"Yep, sounds like a plan, London! But tonight, we're gonna test out the new workbench!" Ruby replied cheekily.

Shay laughed as he stirred the tea and playfully said "Cor… it's all about sex with you, innit, Eyes!"

The following morning they awoke in their lovely new home and were eager to start the day. After they'd showered and dressed, they went to an internet café and registered with the many employment agencies within the locality.

Ruby's CV made an immediate impact and the mobile phone started ringing within the hour from agencies wanting to arrange interviews. She spoke with two separate agencies who had both contacted her regarding a position in an accounts department. One of the available positions was an accounts payable position at a multi-national company located in Dublin. The other was for an accounts receivable position at a local construction company. Ruby agreed to forward her application to both agencies and felt optimistic about the quick response and positive reaction that both agencies had regarding her CV and experience.

When they returned to the apartment that evening, Shay called Danny to get a run down on the planned diplomatic visit with Billy.

Danny told him that contact had been made with Billy and that a sit down had been arranged. Billy had failed to show up to the arranged meeting and was thought to be in hiding.

In his usual concise manner, Danny asked Shay, "Yer know the fellow who heads up security at the night club, he's a mate of yours is he not…? Now, what's his name and telephone number?"

"Steve Walker," Shay replied. "He was a good mate of mine but I aint spoke to him since the day I left. From what I heard, he stood in Billy's corner I think, just to get the night club contract. I've got his number written down in my book, hold on a minute I'll give it to you," he hastily searched for the book to give Danny Steve's number.

"Ok bhoy, we'll make contact with that man and I'll get back to yer," Danny said, and hung up.

Shay and Ruby went to bed that night somewhat disappointed that Billy hadn't been confronted, yet they knew that Danny wouldn't give up until he'd carried out his word.

They were awoken by the mobile phone ringing. Half asleep, Shay answered and heard the voice of his shaken father. "Hallo Shay… Jesus Shay, I was woken up with a phone call from a man saying that he and t'ree others have my address and that if I didn't give up yer whereabouts, they would come o'er to Ireland and use the heavy hand on me. The Gardaí are on their way to the house now."

Now wide awake, Shay sensed that his father was very afraid by what had happened. "Dad, I'm so sorry. I don't know why this is happening, it's madness. You shouldn't have called the Gardaí though Dad, Danny is taking care of it and …"

Mick interrupted. "Jesus Shay! Tis easy for you to say no Garda! Ye're tucked away safely in Dublin. I'm seventy nine years of age and I can't take this, you…" Mick was getting in to a state and started to have one his coughing fits.

Shay took the opportunity to interrupt and try to pacify his dad, "Ok ok, sorry Dad. You're right. I'm sorry, I don't know what to do or say…"

Mick hung up.

Shay turned to Ruby who was concerned and sat upright in the bed.

"That fucking bastard has now just threatened my dad! He's nothing but a bully! He don't show up for a diplomatic chat today because he aint got the bollocks, yet he can threaten my seventy nine year old father, my sister and my son! He pays hit men to do a job on Mickey and Cassidy and hunts us down over thousands of miles! That's it! I'm gonna go home and kill that spineless mug! I don't care if I get locked up, my family have all…"

Ruby intervened. "Shay, shut up. No one's getting killed, alright? Look, I feel responsible for all this trouble, after all, if you hadn't of got involved with me you and your family would be happy and wouldn't be suffering like this! If you want to be with me then let Danny sort it out. And stop saying your gonna kill him, he aint worth it! You're all I've got Shay. If you go to prison, who have I got… No-one! I love you Shay, more than life and I'm not gonna let that piece of shit be the reason that I lose you, we've been through too much. Before all of this bollocks, you always used to say to me that love is a stronger emotion than hate, so what are you telling me now? That you didn't mean it when you said that? I don't want you losing it all the time and I don't want this to turn you into someone you're not. I want you to be the funny, sensitive, loving bloke that you really are. No one's getting killed Shay, just leave it to Danny."

Shay listened to Ruby, he always did. He calmed down and

called his parents who said that the Garda had taken a statement and were on alert, there was no more that they could do.

The following morning Shay called Danny, who was already aware of the phone call Mick had received during the night.

Danny went onto explain that Steve had been spoken to in person last night. "That Steve wasn't very corporative, he said he didn't know where yer man was. My lads told me that security had been increased at the club. Don't worry now bhoy, we'll find him. Shur people always talk. I'll get back to yer later today."

Ruby had just made herself and Shay a cup of tea when she received a call from one of the agencies saying that she had been successful in her job application with the multi-national company. She was to start in a week. It was a highly paid, full time job with added bonuses.

Good news that day appeared to be contagious. Shay also received a call regarding an interview for the position of a contract manager for a company situated in Meath. The interview was arranged for the following week and sounded very promising.

They were equally ecstatic. Shay hugged Ruby tightly, "Once that mug's had a talking to, we'll be fine. We're living in a great apartment in a great city, you've got a job and it looks like I'll be getting mine. I love you Eyes."

After celebrating with a cup of tea, they decided to fill their empty cupboards with food and do a big shop. Having no transport, Shay called Jimmy, the comedic taxi driver. "Alright mate it's…"

Jimmy enthusiastically interrupted, "How's the going, Shay? Ye need a taxi righ?"

"Erh yeah… How'd you know it was me, Jimmy?"

Jimmy laughed. "Jaysus! Shur you're the only cockney who'd be calling me whah!"

Jimmy collected them from outside the apartment block and took them to a supermarket on the outskirts of Dublin. "Tis the place to shop, well, so the wife says, so it must be! She never gets anyt'ing wrong!" He told them that he'd wait for them, free of charge, whilst they shopped.

Shay and Ruby began to walk away from the car; Jimmy let down his window, hung over the side of the car and shouted, "Come here, get us a Kit Kat, I'm on me break whah!"

They were as quick as they could be in the supermarket and returned to the taxi with a trolley full of food. Jimmy was speaking on his hands free kit so he nodded at Shay to put the shopping bags in the boot.

As Shay and Ruby got into the back of the taxi, it became apparent that Jimmy was talking with his wife, Nancy, again.

"Jaysus Nan! I got the tickets for free righ! I just wanna…"

"Don't be calling me Nan, yer gob shite yer! I'll bleedin brain yer so I will," snapped Nancy.

Shay and Ruby grinned at each other as the pleading Jimmy grovelled, "Sorry Nancy, sorry. Jaysus, meself and Declan just wanna see Ireland beat Cyprus, tis a world cup qualifier! He won't bother his ars going if I'm not going. Have you not any patriotism in yer?"

"If you and Declan go to that match I'll beat the head off yer, then I'll leave yer, yer bowsey!" She hung up.

Shay leant forward and gave Jimmy his Kit Kat and a drink.

"T'anks a million, Shay. I really wanted to go to the match but herself is not at all happy, the kids are playing her up I'd say. Do yer like football, Shay?"

"I love it, Jimmy. Followed Chelsea home and away for years," Shay said proudly.

"Jaysus, Chelsea! Shur I'm a Liverpool fan. Hey do yer wanna see Ireland play Cyprus tonight at Croker? Tis a fine stadium."

"Yeah I'd love to! It was always my intention to take my son to see Ireland play at Landsdowne Road. How much are the tickets?" Shay asked.

"Ah, you can have them. I got them for nothing meself. Christ almighty… women whah."

Jimmy dropped them off and reminded them to make sure that they called him if they needed a taxi.

They began to unpack the shopping and the mobile rang, it was Danny. Shay answered it.

"Shay bhoy, the meeting took place. Jesus, yer man was like a raging bull to begin wit! My lads let him tell his side of t'ings for twenty minutes or so and then one of them did the talking and he was told to listen."

"What was said? Did he listen?"

"I can't go into detail Shay, best you don't know. Once my lads introduced themselves he sat up and listened. Tis guaranteed though that he won't bother any of the family ever again. He basically denied everyt'ing but shur we know for a fact that all the trouble is down to him like. Now, that should be an end to it bhoy. I would say that ye should make a go of it in Dublin and not to come back to England for a while, that Billy is a bit of a langer altogether, he could rear his ugly head again. He has plenty money that's for sure!"

"So is that it for definite?"

"Not'ing is ever definite bhoy but he'd be very foolish to misbehave again. Oh yeah, yer man tried to convince my lads that ye stole his money. Everyone t'inks ye have, shur why wouldn't they? With ye being gone, it looks that way."

Shay thanked his uncle and told Ruby the great news.

"Onwards and upwards now, Eyes! Jaysus, whah, brutal!" Mimicked Shay in a very poor Dublin accent.

In high spirits, Shay and Ruby got ready to attend Croke Park to watch Ireland v Cyprus. They left their apartment and unsure of where to go, like two sheep they followed the crowd of fans.

At the stadium, they climbed the many steps to their allocated seats that were positioned high in the notable arena. Shay, who had visited stadiums around the world, was impressed with Croke Park and excited for the match to commence.

Ireland got off to a flying start. Just five minutes after kick off, there was a goal from Robbie Keane that transpired to be the only strike of the match.

Good enough performance but a disappointing atmosphere, thought Shay. He'd expected the noise from the supporters to be a lot louder.

In high spirits, they went to a Chinese restaurant after the game and enjoyed a lovely meal. They held hands on the walk home and were both relieved that everything was starting to work out. They discussed Billy and laughed at how he'd tried to avoid the meeting with Danny's men and how the men had allowed Billy to rant and rave for twenty minutes before they told him what's what. They both found particular satisfaction in the fact that Danny had cancelled the Dempsey contract behind Billy's back, which was undeniably a show of power. Although, they were still saddened by the injuries and fear that were inflicted upon Mickey and Cassidy and felt responsible.

The following morning was chilly but sunny. Shay and Ruby sat on the balcony having a coffee and a cigarette as they admired the views of Dublin City and watched people busily walking going about their business.

Shay spotted a man in his thirties standing with his back to the Liffey River, taking photos of the apartment block, he mentioned it to Ruby. "Ere, look at that geezer over there. I'd have been proper paranoid about him a couple of days ago."

Ruby laughed and replied, "Cor yeah, can you imagine? We'd be thinking he was taking photos of us! He's probably taking photos of the apartments for estate agents, most of these are still empty."

The photographer moved briskly across the main road and ran down the narrow side road of the complex, which prompted

Shay to comment, "That's weird…" He then sat up prominently in his chair.

They watched as the large camera lens slowly appear on the top of the advertising hoarding and Shay jumped to his feet. "He's taking pictures of us! Fuck! I'm telling you Ruby, he's photographing us!"

"Don't be a plum! He's not, he's probably getting every elevation in."

"Oh right! So why would he hide behind the shuttering then? This aint right Ruby." Shay was clearly disturbed by the presence of the unknown photographer.

The camera lens then disappeared, and so did the photographer. Shay ran into the lounge and went straight to the intercom camera, which clearly displayed images of the main entrance. He studied the screen and saw nothing to be out of place.

"We'll probably carry that paranoia with us for a little while yet, just calm down," Ruby said.

They went out for the day on foot. Ruby bought herself a suit for her new job that was commencing in a few days.

That evening, as she sat on the balcony having her 'after dinner cigarette', she abruptly called Shay out to the balcony. "Shay! Quick! Come out here!"

Shay ran through the living room and out to the balcony. Ruby continued, "That black BMW has been circling here for ages. Bit weird don't you think?"

Shay lent on the balcony and looked down. He saw a man in a black suit and white shirt sitting in the car staring up at him and Ruby. Suddenly, the BMW sped off in the direction of the main entrance elevation.

"That aint right…" Shay was suspicious.

They ran to the intercom camera that was positioned by the lounge doorway. Shay engaged the main entrance camera, which to their horror, showed the same BMW speeding past into the heart of the cul-de-sac that was unfortunately out of view from the camera lens. "Right, let's wait a minute, that car or that bloke will have to come back as it's a dead end," Shay said hesitantly. "I tell you what, you stay watching this and I'll watch the lift through the spy hole on the front door."

Ten minutes had passed with Shay calling out to Ruby every other minute asking, "Have you seen him yet?"

"Nope, not seen a thing," she said.

After another five minutes of intense observation and Shay complaining that his eye was hurting from straining to view the lift through the keyhole, he exclaimed, "Fuck this, we're going mental. We're starting to imagine things!"

Shay laughed and as he walked from the hallway to the lounge, he heard Ruby scream. "Fuck! He's here! He's got a fucking bat in his hand!" She jumped away from the intercom and ran frantically into the centre of the lounge. She held her face as she stood trembling with fear. Initially too shocked to cry, she let out a high pitch wail.

Startled by her hysteria, Shay ran into the living room. With all colour drained from his face, he shouted, "Call the Gards!" He engaged the camera and plainly saw an average built man in a black suit and white shirt. Scowling, he lent in and slowly waved a baseball bat at the camera lens.

With her hands shaking Ruby dialled 999. "Quick, quick! There's a bloke with a baseball bat trying to get into our apartment! You've got to come now! Please! Hurry up!"

As Ruby sat on the settee violently shaking and crying, Shay ran to the kitchen and took out the biggest carving knife from the knife block. He then pulled the small fire extinguisher from its holder in the hallway.

Ruby darted back over to the camera. "Shit! I can't see him!"

Shay went to take a look for himself but was stopped in his tracks by the sound of sirens. They looked at one another and ran to the window of the balcony. They could see that the Gards were getting close. Two patrol cars and an unmarked car arrived within minutes.

The buzzer rang. Cautiously, Shay answered and could see a man and a woman standing at the gate. He allowed the two CID officers to enter the into the apartment block. As they made their way up to the room in the lift, the buzzer went again. Another male CID officer held his identification up to the lens and Shay let the third officer in.

Ruby sat in the living room frozen with fear and Shay waited by the front door to let the officers in. The female officer seemed to be in charge.

Shay explained their situation but was unable to tell them everything due to Danny's involvement. She told Shay and Ruby that she would contact DCI Turner in England to get the history of their situation and asked for a description of the car and man.

Ruby tried to compose herself. With fright, she sat white knuckled, clenching a sodden tissue. Through her tears she described that the car was a black BMW with a private English number plate. She'd mentally noted WWD 22 as the registration number.

The male officer, who was last to arrive at their apartment, asked if Ruby was one hundred percent sure of the registration, to which Ruby replied that she was certain.
In his early fifties, he looked like the real deal; almost like a movie hard man cop. He was very empathetic and explained that if anything out of the ordinary was to happen, they were to call 999 immediately. Shay and Ruby were without a doubt, utterly petrified. In his efforts to pacify them, he assured them that anyone trying to get in would have an extremely difficult job.

Shay escorted the officers to the front door and the tough cop remarked, "It's highly unlikely, but if someone manages to get to yer front door, use a weapon on them. But after yer use it, be sure to shout out a warning so that all the neighbours hear yer. That way you'll be covered. Hit them over the head with something but don't use a knife!"

Shay thanked them all for the prompt response and went to comfort Ruby.

They held each other tight as they sat on the settee. Shay was the first to break the silence. "Have you any doubts about what you saw, baby?"

"No, none whatsoever. He was waving a goddam bat at the camera! Why? Do you doubt me?"

"No of course I don't, Eyes, but I doubt myself lately. What you saw is exactly what I saw, I just had to double check."

Ruby continued to monitor the camera whilst Shay called Danny and told him what had happened.

"Jesus Shay! Why did ye call the Garda? Ye should have left them out of it. Jesus bhoy, ye should have called me," Danny grumbled.

Shay apologised and explained that in the heat of the moment and blinded by fear that they needed to act quickly.

Danny sighed. "I know, I know but we don't want them getting busy like. Anyhow, let me have a t'ink… Ye are better off sleeping in shifts tonight. Shur ye can't sleep at the same time, one of ye needs to keep a watchful eye like. Be sure to call me if anymore happens. Yer know how to protect yerself Shay, do that and don't call the Garda again. Now, I'll have to make some more enquiries. Jesus, that fecker was warned. He's a stupid man. He clearly doesn't know who he's dealing wit! I got to go Shay, we'll speak later. God bless."

Shay told Ruby that Danny wasn't happy that they'd called the Garda but that he was going to be making more enquiries.

They spent the entire evening going back and forth from the intercom camera to the balcony, where they would scrutinise the traffic and have a smoke in the process.

They discussed the man with the BMW and wondered why he had acted alone. Was the stranger just letting them know that he'd found them? Would he and others return in the night?

Ruby asked Shay, "Do you think that bloke does the finding and that others then come back to do the job?"

"Nah, I think the geezer with the camera yesterday done the finding. I knew he was photographing us. I can't work out what that bloke was doing tonight though… perhaps it was scare tactics? He's got to have known he couldn't get in. I tell you what though, Eyes, going outside the flat makes us sitting ducks. Let's just sit tight 'till Danny gets back to us. Go on, you go to bed, baby, I'll stay up for the night."

"No! I'll stay in the lounge with you. If I do sleep, I'll sleep here on the couch… we could take it in turns to sleep." The night passed slowly, each minute feeling like an hour.

Eventually, the morning arrived, Shay spoke with his parents, Connor and Bridget and assured them all that he and Ruby were safe. The fear, pressure and uncertainty was starting to take its toll on Mick and Josie. Given their advanced age, it was undeniably having a major effect on their nerves and health.

Ruby prepared coffee, which they shared with the usual nicotine intake on the balcony. The mobile phone rang from the lounge. Shay went inside to answer it and spoke with Danny.

Danny explained that Billy had evidently not taken heed of the warning giving to him. Furthermore, contacts of Danny's felt uneasy now that Shay and Ruby had involved the Garda. He told Shay to sit tight whilst he found out who had visited them.

Ruby obsessively checked the intercom camera every five minutes and at eleven o'clock noticed a Shogun jeep parked opposite the entrance gate. Shay then looked and saw four large men sitting inside the vehicle. "'Ere, Eyes, there are four big lumps in that motor outside but at the moment they're just sitting there… it's probably nothing to do with us."

Shay continued to vigilantly watch the Shogun with the motionless men sitting inside it. Ruby took the opportunity to go onto the balcony for a cigarette. Only minutes after of her being out on the balcony, she screamed, "Shay he's back! Look! He's stopped at the traffic lights! It's the same bloke in the same motor!"

Shay ran to the balcony and instantly recognised the black BMW. He hastily wrote down the registration number, WWD 22. As the BMW slowly proceeded to move on the green light, Shay shot across to the intercom camera like a bolt of lightening. Breathing heavily from the sudden injection of fright and adrenalin, he studied the camera and saw the black BMW speed out of sight down the cul-de-sac, just as he did the day before.

The four large men unfolded themselves from out of the Shogun and stood waiting on the pavement.

"Oh my God! I'm calling the Garda!"

"No wait!" Shay insisted whilst still fixated on the camera.

"Fuck that! I'm not waiting!" She dialled 999.

Much to his horror, Shay noticed that the man who had visited the previous night was walking towards the four men who stood by the Shogun, this time minus his baseball bat. "Fuck Ruby! Get the Garda here now!" Shay was now starting to break out in a cold sweat.

Ruby stood on the balcony as she phoned the Gardaí.

"They're coming! They're back! Hurry up!" she shrieked.

Within minutes, they heard the welcome sound of sirens getting closer. Shay observed that the man from the BMW was pointing in the direction of their gate and was having a discussion with the four cumbersome men from the Shogun. With the high pitched noise of the sirens getting louder as they got nearer, the four men swiftly got back into the Shogun and sped off; leaving the man from last night sprinting back down towards the cul-de-sac. In a matter of seconds, his BMW sped back out of the cul-de-sac.

Shay and Ruby stood by their front door, anxiously waiting for the Garda to buzz. The buzzer never sounded. They'd seen squad cars outside of the apartment but no one had come to see them. Shay impatiently called the CID 'hard man' who visited the previous night. He advised Shay that he was aware of the call and that uniform officers had attended and informed CID that when they arrived no one was there. He asked if the registration given by Ruby the night before was correct. Shay confirmed that the registration was correct as he'd now seen it for himself. The officer added that between British and Irish Police, it had been concluded that the BMW had been fitted with false number plates. He kindly reminded Shay to call if anything out of the ordinary occurred.

Shay called Danny and told him of the latest event. Danny listened intently and told Shay that he'd call him back in a few minutes.

Danny rang back promptly. "Now, listen up bhoy, in twenty minutes ye are to go down to the basement car park, the lift takes you straight to it. They'll be a bread van down there, one of our lads will put ye in the back of the van and take ye to a car in North Dublin. Ye're to drive to Rosslare and get the ferry to Pembroke tonight, then head for London. Shur ye'll be in London for seven o'clock tomorrow morning, head to Shepherds Bush, I'll meet ye there and we'll talk. This shite has to end. Now, only pack a little bag between ye and I'll see ye tomorrow."

Slightly dumbfounded, Shay told Ruby of the precise itinerary that Danny had given him. She was lost for words, feeling scared and confused. In less than twenty four hours, their new start in life had been taking away from them before they'd even had a chance to live it.

They apprehensively made their way down to the basement car park where a man in his fifties stood waiting with the side door of the van already open. "Go'wan now, jump in there, and not a sound out of ye."

They obeyed the stranger's instructions and jumped into the van. The door was rapidly slid shut.

They sat in darkness and Ruby whispered, "Who IS Danny connected to?"

"Quiet back there!" shouted the surly driver.

Thankfully, the uncomfortable, bumpy journey was short and came to an abrupt end.

The driver opened the side door and handed Shay keys to a Ford Mondeo. "Now, head straight to Rosslare Harbour, no one will be looking for ye at that port but they may be watching Dublin Port. Ye lay low 'till the night ferry arrives. Ye can buy a ticket at the harbour. Oh… and here's some float money to get ye across the pond. Tis a low key car… keep low key yerselves righ. Good luck."

With that, the man jumped back into the bread van and drove off.

Extremely bewildered and in a state of shock, Ruby turned to Shay and attempted to speak, "What the…"

Shay interrupted her. "C'mon, Ruby, no time to talk, we'll talk in the motor, alright."

TWENTY ONE

London's Calling

Shay drove as Ruby lit them each a cigarette and asked, curious, "London, where's that Ross... whatever it's called?"

Shay exhaled the long drag from his cigarette. "Rosslare. It's in County Wexford, Eyes. We're doing as Danny says and we're gonna get the night ferry to Pembroke in Wales and then drive through the night to Shepherds Bush in West London; don't ask me anymore than that. But I'll tell you this, I've had enough of this fucking nonsense, we should never have left London."

They drove warily through Dublin and eventually got onto the N11 and made their way down to Rosslare.

Once they arrived, Shay paid for the car and two passengers. The ferry didn't sail until nine pm and would arrive in Pembroke at one am. They'd had no sleep and with another sleepless night ahead of them, they decided to get some shuteye in the car until seven pm. They awoke feeling just as tired as they did before their nap. Shay booked a two berth cabin and were they both asleep before the vessel had even sailed.

At twelve twenty am the alarm on their mobile phone woke them up and they both took showers. When the ship had docked they returned to the car and waited to disembark.

Back on the road, Shay drove at high speed through the dark Welsh countryside.

Once on the M4 motorway and conscious of getting back to London in good time, he continued to drive speedily.

They stopped at a service station in the Swindon area where they stayed a while as they had arrived sooner than they'd anticipated and more importantly, Shay didn't want to be sitting idle at Shepherds Bush Green for too long. They felt strangely excited about the return to London but were also very apprehensive.

It was still dark when they arrived in Shepherds Bush. They parked at Shepherds Bush Green and sat waiting for half an hour. In the darkness, a black taxi flashed its head lights from behind them. Shay saw the driver in his wing mirror, it was Danny and he waved as he drove by.

Shay followed the taxi as Ruby commented, "Oh, I didn't know Danny was a taxi driver!"

Shay laughed. "He's not, it's just a front. He's being inconspicuous, Eyes."

"Oh, sorry, I'm tired," yawned Ruby.

Danny drove up Goldhawk Road and took a left half way up. He pulled in after another hundred metres and they pulled up behind him. By this time, Danny had already left the taxi and ran up the asphalt steps to the communal front door of a large house that had been converted into flats. Ruby quickly followed, as did Shay whilst carrying their one bag.

Danny unlocked the front door of the ground floor flat and held his index finger to his lips demonstrating that silence was a necessity.

Once safely inside the flat Danny shook their hands. "Ok, tis not the Ritz but it's clean and it's safe. I want ye to get some sleep like. Later on, you and I have an appointment Shay, and you have a hairdresser coming round to see yer, Ruby."

Ruby was baffled. "Ay? A hairdresser, why's that?

"Ah, a change of hair colour will do yer good! Shur dark hair would be better under the circumstances, oh and a pair of designer glasses with clear lenses. I don't want ye spotted, no one knows ye're in London. Tis the last place anyone would look for ye like. Shay bhoy, take this hat and these glasses. I'll come back this afternoon and pick yer up, we'll have a chat. Now then, no going out... the fridge and cupboards are full, smoke in the lounge if ye have to and keep the curtains shut."

They thanked Danny as he left. Physically and mentally exhausted, they went to bed, after having set their alarm to wake them at midday.

When they awoke, Shay made coffee for them both and Ruby sat in the mid-sized lounge in one of the dark blue armchairs; with her knees curled up to her chest and sleepy eyed she surveyed the high corniced ceiling and huge fireplace.

As she gratefully took her mug of coffee she asked, "So London, what's the plan then? What's Danny got in mind?"

"Dunno babe, we'll see this afternoon. Now I'm home in London I feel a bit better. Now all I wanna do is put an end to this shit and clear our names," replied Shay.

Ruby showered, got dressed and then prepared a chicken salad for them both. As ate they discussed how far they had travelled; they guessed that they must have travelled at least thirty thousand miles since the day they left their homes.

As Ruby washed up in the large, clinical looking kitchen, Shay put on his glasses and hat and slyly entered the kitchen.

Ruby turned and laughed and said sarcastically, "Oh yeah! That's a blinding disguise! You look like Shay Sullivan with a hat and a pair of glasses on!"

"Ere you go, put your glasses on." Shay handed them to her. She put the glasses on and balanced them on the tip of her nose.

"Cor! You look like a sexy librarian! We should've got you a pair of them ages ago!" he laughed.

The caged couple spent a couple of hours flicking through the television channels.

At four pm they heard a gentle knock on the front door followed by the sound of a key being turned. Ruby panicked initially, but Shay knew it was Danny.

They heard Danny say, "Don't panic lads, tis only me and Siobhán." Danny walked into the lounge with Siobhán following behind. "How are ye? Did ye get some rest? This is Siobhán, she's a good friend and a hairdresser, she'll look after yer Ruby dar'lin."

Siobhán smiled and said, "Alright mate? Alright Ruby? So you up for a colour change then Ruby? C'mon, let's get started." The self-assured Siobhán took Ruby by the hand and led her into the kitchen.

Shay sat in the lounge with Danny and heard Ruby and Siobhán laughing from within the kitchen.

He turned to Danny to ask, "So what's happening then, Danny?"

"Put on that hat and them glasses bhoy, we've got an appointment," said Danny softly.

As always, Shay respectfully did as his uncle Danny asked. Before leaving the flat, Shay went into the kitchen that now resembled a hair salon, to tell the girls that they he and Danny were going out for a while. The two girls were laughing and joking and were unaffected by Shay's news of his and Danny's departure.

Shay followed Danny out to a Mercedes that was parked directly outside. As Danny pulled away and accelerated, he turned to Shay. "I tell yer, bhoy, that Billy Gower won't give up the hunt! We'll have to deal with him like. Jesus, we can't have our entire family being under threat. Trouble is, now the Garda in Ireland are aware and they're in contact with the Police in England, my lot won't get involved."

"I'll do it then, I wanna do him anyway, Dan."

"Huh, I'm sure yer do, bhoy, but it has to be done right. We'll do it together. Will Ruby talk though, Shay?"

"Nah, Ruby won't say a word. Let's have it right Dan, we can't keep running can we?"

Now at Hanger Lane, Shay wondered where they were going. Danny explained, "We're gonna head up the M40 to a remote warehouse we have out there in the sticks. This has to be done right. Yer not gonna be boxing in a ring or fighting Tottenham fans down Fulham Broadway like yer used do, like an eejit. Have you ever used a firearm, Shay?"

"No, you know I haven't Dan," Shay replied nervously.

Nonchalantly, Danny explained, "Well, yer gonna get some practice this evening. We've a guest being collected and we'll have a talk with him in the warehouse."

"Who? Billy? We gonna do him tonight?" Shay asked enthusiastically.

"No, that Steve, the fucker who betrayed yer. He'll talk tonight, that's for sure. How long have yer known that langer?"

Shay began to feel slightly apprehensive and his hands were clammy. "Twenty two years, we were good pals."

"Well, I can tell yer for a fact that once the Dempsey's contract was withdrawn, Steve put a naughty crew together to find ye, on behalf of yer man. Twas his people who found ye in Dublin like. We don't know how they did, but we'll find out tonight. Steve can assist us now, we'll acquire his services this evening. I'm sure he will be more than happy to help us out after a few negotiations," Danny explained.

Shay was livid at his uncle's revelation. "Fucking Judas!"

"Ah, shur I told yer all that lot were no good years ago bhoy. They have no loyalty and no souls. Anyt'ing for a few pound, shur they'd sell their own mothers!" said Danny indignantly.

Ultimately, they arrived at what seemed to be a disused warehouse in the middle of nowhere.

Danny unlocked a gate and then opened an electric shutter by pointing a fob at it. It was a single shutter with a solid hardwood door behind it. The industrial doors and all of the windows were shuttered and remained so.

The warehouse was in darkness and felt cold. Their footsteps echoed as they walked further into the vacant warehouse. Danny flicked on all the light switches to illuminate the premises. As the fluorescent tubes warmed up they made a purring noise, exacerbated by the large, empty space inside the warehouse.

Danny turned and locked the door behind them before walking over to a strong room, which he unlocked using three different keys. Shay waited just outside the strong room whilst Danny went it. He suddenly threw out a boiler suit. Shay wasn't expecting to catch a boiler suit and he bent down to pick it up from the dusty concrete floor, to find that the boiler suit was brand new and still in its original packaging. This boiler suit turned out to be one of many that were stored in the small dark room. Danny then proceeded to throw out a pair of gloves and a balaclava.

He called back to Shay, "What size boots do yer take, Shay?"

"Er, eleven," he said, slightly confused.

A new box containing a pair of new black safety boots landed on the floor at Shay's feet.

Danny made his way out of the little grotto and said, "Now bhoy, get into costume and I'll do the same! We'll let you have a practice with the gun and then wait 'till our guest of honour arrives. I've four lads collecting him as we speak. When he's here, no names are to be mentioned. He'll know you, but only you. He'll have no idea of mine and the lads identity."

Shay dressed in his dark boiler suit and boots. He watched Danny lace up his boots and thought to himself about how composed and calculated Danny was.

Danny looked up. "C'mon on now bhoy! Put the gloves on and cover your head, tis a full dress rehearsal!"

Shay obeyed and looked on as Danny did the same.

Bewildered, he felt as though he was caught up in a massive whirlwind. He had no idea of what events lay ahead of him but that didn't stop his imagination running wild.

Danny re-entered the strong room, opened up a safe and removed two chrome trimmed hand guns and methodically explained, "Now, these are loaded, just as they will be on the day. When yer hold it, do not hold your finger over the trigger, tis sensitive like and the slightest touch will set it off. Treat your gun like a woman, bhoy, be gentle wit it and only caress the trigger when you mean business like. Then, all yer do on the day is aim and fire. When we have Billy you'll do just that, tis not like the movies wit a parting speech, we just get the business done, we clean up and we leave. Now, come o'er here and we'll get yer used to the power of that beast in yer hand!"

Shay was nervous as he'd never held a gun before. He wasn't scared or frightened as he trusted his uncle immeasurably. There was mutual respect, loyalty and conviction between them both. He would willingly put his life in Danny's hands without hesitation and knew he would never do him a wrong.

Prepared for the drill, Danny walked gun in hand with Shay over to a solid chamber that was filled with water and had a steel funnel protruding from the dark, murky water. Danny stood, with his feet slightly parted and with both hands on the gun that was secluded by the funnel from the water. He fired a single shot down the funnel into the water. The loud bang startled Shay who jumped.

Danny turned to him and in a blasé tone said, "Now, that's what I want yer to get used to. I don't want yer jumping around like a toad when yer hear the bang! I need yer to be calm like, panic leads to conviction as we say. Now then, remember she's ready to fire, so only caress the trigger when yer in place. I want yer to let two rounds off, so caress the trigger gently twice."

Shay stood with his legs spread apart and fired two quick

shots into the water. It felt good, he liked the powerful feeling and vigorous sensation.

Danny slapped Shay firmly on the back. "Not a flinch!" Cried Danny, "Ah, yer a natural bhoy and why wouldn't yer be! Yer a Sullivan!" Danny carefully removed the firearm from Shay and continued, "C'mon now, we'll make a cuppa tay whilst we wait on the arrival of yer friend."

Back at the main floor of the warehouse, as the two men sat in the company of a boiling kettle, they heard the noise of a diesel engine pull up outside. Firmly placing both hands on the table to lever himself up from the chair Danny said, "Ah here's the lads. C'mon then, let us meet and greet our guest!" and proceeded to pull down his balaclava.

The door clunked as it was unlocked and a man wearing jeans, a black jacket, boots and a balaclava nodded in Danny and Shay's direction. Danny simply nodded back and not a word was uttered. Then another man dressed identically entered, closely followed by the distinctive bulky figure of Steve who had a black hood over his face whilst being escorted by two additional men in balaclavas.

They led a disorientated and frightened Steve to a solid chair that was bolted to the concrete floor. As two of the clones tied Steve to the chair, Danny asked, "Any trouble?"

"Nah, piece of piss, like taking an apple from a tree," said the largest man of the four with a strong London accent.

Walking with large strides, Danny approached Steve and pulled off his hood. Steve gasped and frantically looked around in sheer panic. His eyes bulged at the sight of the six men in balaclavas surrounding him like a pack of wolves.

"What the fuck have I done! What's this all about?" Yelled Steve.

Danny bent down towards Steve, almost whispering, he spoke very softly, "Now now, stay calm Steve. We won't hurt yer if you comply wit what we say." With that, Danny nodded at the man who had led the procession into the building.

The man roared, "Right! We know Billy Gower paid you to carry out a hit on your mate Shay! How'd you find them in Dublin?"

Steve's yelling turned to more of a loud whine. The veins in his neck clearly bulged as he strained in his reply, "Fuck me! Is this what this is all about? I was paid to find him and teach him a lesson…"

Shay couldn't control himself. He pounced and unleashed a powerful right hook onto Steve's nose, catching him square on and he shouted with venom, "You fucking Judas slag!"

Steve squirmed with pain in the chair as he took the full impact. Restrained in the fixed chair, he sat with his eyes watering and his nose bleeding profusely.

"Stop that!" Shouted Danny, "For fuck sake! Leave it to my man!"

Shay continued to be disobedient and removed his balaclava. He stared hard into Steve's eyes with complete acrimony.

Danny's man continued his interrogation, "Are you hard of hearing, mate, or what? I said… How'd you find 'em in Dublin?!"

Steve stammered in response, "Erm… erh… I… I… I've had a bloke watching Shay's parents house. He tracked them to Dublin, then lost them, but found them again. He took photos of them and e-mailed them to me, then I sent some people over to do a job…"

Shay's disgust and fury could not be contained and he erupted.

"You fucking cunt! How many years we known…"

His verbal attack was interrupted by Danny, who shouted,

"Shay! I won't tell yer again! Stop losing the head and calm yerself bhoy!"

Shay wiped the spit from his mouth and obediently stepped back.

The interrogator continued. "Now, this is what's gonna happen, you're gonna help us put an end to this, like a good boy. You're running security at Billy's club, we want the keys and codes from ya and then you will disable the CCTV for us…"

Steve began to plead whilst frantically wriggling in the chair.

"No, no! Please! I don't want anymore part in this! I wanna…" But was stopped in his tracks at the sight of the interrogator, who lit a blow torch and beckoned one of the other men to assist. The crutch of his jeans darkened as they became wet with urine. He screamed and whined as the other man undid the buttons of his jeans, revealing his genitals.

The interrogator swiftly moved in and held the blow torch close to Steve's testicles, near enough for his pubic hair to singe.

"Now, d'ya feel the heat, mate? Well in ten seconds, I'm gonna torch the bollocks off ya!" The interrogator began to count aloud down from ten, moving the blow torch just that little bit closer as every second passed.

Shackled, with beads of sweat rolling down his face and his finger nails clawing at the arms of the chair, he screamed. "Alright! Alright! Whatever you want I'll do it! Just get that fucking thing away from me!"

Danny waved his hand for the interrogator to back off and gently said, "We don't want to harm yer, Steve. We want to remove the root of the problem and to do that, we need yer to cooperate and give us what we want." He then turned and put a hand on Shay's shoulder before continuing, "This man's family are important to him, as I'm sure your's is just as important to you. Now then, all yer have to do is give us the keys, codes and disable the CCTV when we tell yer. Then all yer need to do is keep yer silence and you'll be grand. Shur we wouldn't want yer wife or kids coming to any harm now would we…."

Danny's concise words seemed to have imposed more fear in Steve than the blow torch.

He sat bound in the chair and trembled as the interrogator asked conceitedly, "Have we got your attention now, big boy?"

"Yeah, yeah, I'll do whatever you want! Please, don't hurt me or my family, please!" begged Steve.

He gave them the four digit code 1905 needed for the office entrance of the club and explained that if they parked in the rear car park that an iron staircase would lead them to the main office, with Billy's office being the last office down the corridor on the right. He said that he'd disable the security system once the club closed in the early hours of Sunday morning. He informed them that Billy always left the club at ten pm on a Saturday night but religiously returned on a Sunday morning at about eleven am to deal with the takings, which were kept in the safe inside his office. Steve finally added that Billy was always alone on a Sunday morning at work.

The four men removed Steve from the chair and at gun point told him that they would drop him off just the same way that they had collected him.

Just before they placed the black hood back over Steve's head, Steve looked at Shay and said feebly, "Sorry Shay, it was business mate. Nothing personal."

Danny was unimpressed at Steve's half-hearted apology. "Get that fucker out of my sight!" Steve was swiftly bundled back into the van and taken away.

Unfazed by what he'd just witnessed, Shay turned to Danny and asked, "How can we be sure he won't talk, Dan?"

Danny laughed as he put an arm around Shay. "He won't be talking now. Shur the lads will be showing him photos of his wife and kids that were taken earlier today, that'll keep him quiet for a while like. Anyhow, after Monday he won't be able to talk at all if yer get my drift. C'mon bhoy, let's head back. I wanna talk to Ruby the brunette."

They returned to Shepherds Bush. Back inside the flat, Ruby and Siobhán sat in the lounge sharing a bottle of wine. Shay and Danny admired Ruby's hair.

"Do you like it, London?" asked Ruby, "It's alright innit, Siobhán's done a great job. We've had a right laugh."

After a series of compliments, Danny handed his car keys to

Siobhán. "Siobhán dar'lin, you take my car, I'll have someone collect me later. I need some time alone with Ruby and Shay. Shur yer did a fine job dar'lin, God bless yer, yer a star." He walked Siobhán to the door and bid her a safe journey home.

Now alone, Danny sat Shay and Ruby down in the lounge. He primarily directed the conversation at Ruby and explained in detail where he and Shay had been and what had happened. Then he began to enlighten them both with a new itinerary; they would drive to Scotland on Sunday afternoon and stay in a safe house, then within six months they'd be able to live wherever they chose.

Ruby was shocked and struggled to absorb everything that she'd just been told. She outwardly expressed her concern over an arrest being made and her fear of losing Shay. Danny assured her that this would not be the case. He admitted that the police would want to talk to Shay but that Billy had many enemies, especially the firm from Liverpool.

Danny was soon collected by an acquaintance. He left Shay and Ruby knowing that they had much to discuss.

Shay and Ruby lay in bed, contemplating the imminent future. Ruby was fretful about everything that was going on. Like a thunderbolt, she was hit with the harsh reality that her husband was now personally involved in Billy's demise. She couldn't help but pessimistically think that she was going to lose Shay, such thoughts were unbearable.

Shay recognised Ruby's despair and confidently explained how highly organised Danny was.

She felt more at ease and reassured. As she snuggled into Shay's chest, twiddling with his hairs, she looked up at him, and said, "Y'know I could've told you the entry code and the safe code, it's 5872."

As he gently stoked her back, he replied, "Not anymore baby, it's been changed to 1905. What a mug, picking that as a code!

That's the year Chelsea was founded, I should've guessed that myself really."

They fell asleep in each others arms and remained so until the next morning.

TWENTY TWO

Taking The Rubbish Out

It was Sunday morning. Ruby clung to Shay and begged him not to go, whilst Danny sat outside waiting in his car.

"Ruby, I've gotta do this! I didn't want it to come to this but we'll never be free if I don't do it, we can't live the rest of our lives looking over our shoulders!" The last thing Shay wanted to do was upset her but he knew it was for the best.

"Alright, alright. Go then, but please be careful. I can't be without you, Shay. I love you so much," she sobbed.

He kissed her passionately and left, closing the door behind him.

Danny drove the forty minute drive back to the warehouse, he explained that they would collect a British Telecom van, the clothing and the guns. They were both calm and focussed. Danny also explained that he'd arranged for someone to meet them in Harrow afterwards. There, they would remove the clothing and swap vehicles. The guns, clothing and British Telecom van would be disposed of, never to be found again. Danny would then take Shay back to Ruby at the flat. He and Ruby were then to leave immediately for Scotland in the Ford Mondeo. They would remain in a safe house for six months.

Inside the warehouse, they put on their cover clothing and made hats out of their balaclavas, just as they'd rehearsed. Danny retrieved both guns from the safe before he and Shay got into the British Telecom van and made the short journey to Middlesex, with Danny doing the driving.

Danny approached the club car park with caution. Sure enough, as he parked, they saw Billy's Audi 4x4 with its private number plates parked at the bottom of the iron staircase.

Danny undid his seatbelt and removed the guns from the glove box. He looked hard at Shay. "Right, no messing now bhoy. In and out, no talking, yer shoot him twice and if the jobs not done I'll give him a double tap to the head. We'll remove the casings and be on our way."

"Let's do it, let's put that mug to bed for good." Shay was focussed but very nervous.

The two moved swiftly and silently up the iron staircase. Danny entered the code 1905 and turned the handle after he heard the lock disengage. They entered the corridor and moved briskly but silently down the corridor and entered Billy's office located on the right hand side.

"Oh fuck!" exclaimed Shay.

There was Billy, laying in a pool of blood on the floor, clearly deceased.

"Shay, c'mon, let's get out of here bhoy," Danny said, unruffled by their findings.

Shay ran down the staircase as quick as he could whilst Danny closed the doors and calmly walked back to the van.

Driving away from the club, Danny was completely at ease as if nothing had happened.

Shaken, Shay sat breathing heavily. With quivering hands, he tried to light a cigarette.

Being anti-smoking, Danny said, "Wait 'till we're in Harrow bhoy, then have a smoke."

"What the fuck was all that about?" Shay asked, still trembling.

"Shur I told yer he had enemies like. He ripped off the crowd in Liverpool in a dirty drug deal. They must have got to him before us. It changes nothing though, the police will still want to talk yer like, so we carry out the plan as arranged."

Shay sat in total disarray, struggling to comprehend what had happened as Danny drove them to Harrow whistling a tune.

They pulled into a garage in Harrow where a man stood by the open door. As they slowly pulled into the garage, the man closed the doors behind them.

Danny and Shay got out of the van and removed their clothing and threw it and the guns into the back of the van.

The man spoke. "Alright Dan, you alright, Shay?… You look shaken mate."

Shay instantly recognised it to be the voice of the interrogator who he'd met at the warehouse.

"Nah, I'm alright," replied Shay.

"Any problems, Dan?" asked the interrogator.

Danny laughed and replied, "Twas the easiest job I ever done! Shur someone had beat us to it like, he was dead when we got there."

"What a touch ay! Must have been that scouse firm, that mob in Liverpool had him on their list for a while. Right, take the Volvo out there Dan, this lot will be scrapped in ten minutes. 'Ere Shay, good luck in Scotland, mate. If you ever want work, with luck like that you'd be more than welcome on the firm mate!" Said the chatty interrogator.

Shay shook his hand and thanked him.

"No problem Shay, anything for your uncle Danny. He's a top bloke. Oh by the way, I said hello to Steve for you this morning… He's disappeared by all accounts, don't think he'll be seen again, know what I mean." The interrogator grinned and Shay and Danny got into the Volvo.

Danny drove steadily through the traffic as Shay smoked his long awaited cigarette.

"Them t'ings will be the death of yer, Shay! For the love of God! Would yer give up that dirty habit!" exclaimed Danny as he dramatically began to let down the windows to make a point.

They arrived back at the flat in Shepherds Bush and saw Ruby and her dark hair up at the window with her spectacles on.

Danny turned to Shay. "Look after that young girl now, bhoy, she's a good woman. God knows ye have been to hell, but ye're back now, so live long and live happy. C'mon, let's get ye out of here."

Danny and Shay entered the flat. Ruby ran to Shay and hugged him with all her might, "Thank God you're both safe! I've been pulling my hair out here!"

Shay took off Ruby's glasses, kissed her and said, "It's over now, Ruby. It's finished. C'mon, liven up, we gotta go, I'll explain it all to you in the car, where's the bags?"

"They're already in the boot of the car, we're all set to go," she said.

Shay hugged his uncle Danny tightly and thanked him.

Danny got very emotional. "I'll come up to Scotland to see ye, when the times right like. Go'wan now Shay! Off wit yer! And look after Ruby or you'll have me to deal wit!"

Shay made his way out of the flat as Ruby hugged Danny and expressed her gratitude for all that he'd done for them both.

Danny was still emotional. "Look after that man of yours for me, I love him like a son. Yer good for him Ruby, I'm glad he's got yer. Now go'wan, ye need to get on the road. I'll see yer soon."

As Ruby went to leave she turned back to Danny and quietly said, "Danny, could you do one more thing for us?"

"Anyt'ing dar'lin but be quick, ye have to get going like."

Ruby pointed at the built in lounge unit. "I've left Billy's gun in that drawer. Would you mind getting rid of it for me, please?"

Danny's face beamed and he laughed. "Jesus! I've seen it all now! I knew Shay had found a good woman in yer. Leave it to me, go'wan now."

Ruby smiled. "I couldn't risk losing him, Danny." She adjusted her glasses and proceeded to walk out of the front door. "See you in Scotland, Danny Good Looking," and she blew him a kiss and got into the car.

TWENTY THREE

Taking Care of Business

R uby watched from the window as Shay and Danny drove away from the flat.

Once out of sight, Ruby left the flat and drove the Ford Mondeo to Middlesex and parked in a road near Billy's nightclub.

Time was pressing, she knew Billy's routine better then anyone and was aware of his methodical timing. He would always leave the house at eleven o'clock every Sunday morning, without fail, to be at the club for ten past eleven. In the past, Billy often took Ruby with him on a Sunday morning and he would boast whilst the two of them counted the Saturday night takings. He'd try to impress Ruby in the process; however, Ruby was far from impressed, as his bad moods would outweigh his good moods. She also knew that not all of the money in the safe was acquired through the club. She didn't know where eighty percent of the money came from, but assumed it was from large drug deals.

Ruby calmly made her way up the iron staircase knowing that Billy's car was not there.

She entered the code 1905 and stepped into the corridor, closing the door behind her. She made her way to Billy's office and entered the code 1905, again, the lock disengaged. She immediately went to the safe and entered 1905, the lock rejected the code. Ruby thought and then tried the old code 5872, the safe unlocked. Ruby removed the .38 calibre revolver that Billy had previously shown her how to use, in another failed attempt to impress her.

She placed her glasses and the gun on the desk whilst she bent down to take the leather holdall from beneath Billy's desk. The holdall was always kept there and she filled it with the cash from the safe. As she started to zip up the holdall she heard the main entrance door unlocking. With gun in hand, she sat herself down in the large leather chair at the desk. As she sat composed in the chair, she heard Billy's aggressive tone getting louder as he approached his office.

He was obviously talking on his mobile phone. "Where the fuck is that Steve? I've paid him to take care of them pair of cunts! He was meant to call me this morning and I ain't heard from him!"

She heard his heavy footsteps come to a stop in the corridor and he continued to shout, "Well find out what's happened to him you prick! When I ask you to do something, you do it! That's what I fucking pay you for!"

Billy opened his office door. He stopped in his tracks at the sight of Ruby sitting back in his chair at his desk holding his gun. Wide eyed, Billy stood motionless. With the gun pointing at him, Ruby flicked her wrist, indicating that he was to sit in the visitors chair. Billy obediently moved away from the door and sat down in the chair.

Billy sat back. He laughed nervously before asking, "How the fuck did you get in here? What you gonna do? Shoot me?"

"Ten outta ten, Billy."

"Don't be so fucking stupid! You aint got it in ya! You won't get away with it, you know this place is camered up!" Billy had clearly began to perspire.

"Yeah you're right, I do know the system here, don't I, thanks to you. And I know I'm gonna get away with it 'cos Steve disabled the security system last night. Think about it, Steve's disappeared and the money from the safe has been taken. The theft of your cash was his motive," explained Ruby calmly.

"I could take that fucking gun off you right now, you stupid slag!" Barked Billy.

"Go on then bully boy, make your move. Hurry up though ay 'cos I've gotta be going. My husband needs his money back."

Billy sat silently and looked into Ruby's eyes and saw how cold they were.

With the gun still pointed in Billy's direction, Ruby casually leant forward on the desk and spoke calmly. "Do you believe in God, Billy? Well, I once heard a saying that goes… God takes those too good to stay and leaves behind those too bad to take away. Guess what Billy? That's why I'm here, so now might be a good time to say a prayer when you think about it. Oh… Here's another question for you, do you know what retribution means?… No?… Okay, I'll tell you… Retribution is the act of taking revenge by harming someone in retaliation for something harmful that they've done. You've been very harmful throughout the years haven't you, Billy. You've terrorised and bullied my mother, my brother, my friends, and of course me; all of which has gone unchallenged for years. You've hired people to kill my husband. My husband's family have been living in fear and trepidation. You've threatened a man of seventy nine, my husband's son and my sister-in-law. You had relations in California hospitalised and you've taken my family from me. The list is endless, Billy, but time is ticking and I've gotta be somewhere. I only came here for my own retribution. Your days of harming the people that I love are over."

Billy jumped up from his chair and shouted, "Go on then you…" *Bang!!*

The bullet Ruby fired hit Billy's big chest at close range and he fell to the carpeted floor.

Ruby calmly put on her glasses, picked up the leather holdall

248

and stood up from the chair. She walked from behind the desk and stood over Billy who lay groaning and clenching at his bleeding wound.

Pointing the gun, Ruby smugly said, "I've booked you a one-way ticket somewhere hot and full of likeminded scum. Rot in hell, Billy…" *Bang! !*

The fatal bullet was fired at his head and put an end to his pitiful existence.

Collected and now contented, Ruby left the office and exited the club. She casually strolled back to the car and placed the leather holdall containing the money and Billy's gun into the boot, drove back to Shepherds Bush and prepared for the return of Shay and Danny Good Looking.